ARMOR OF ALETHEIA

SACRED ARMOR TRILOGY—BOOK ONE

ENDORSEMENTS

In *Armor of Alethia*, Ralene Burke has crafted a fast-paced novel filled with surprises that young readers of fantasy and adventure are sure to enjoy. Filled with unique characters, this first installment of the series will be quickly devoured.

—**Patrick W. Carr**, Author of *The Staff and the Sword* trilogy

Burke's *Armor of Aletheia* is a novel that feels at once familiar and new. Fantasy fans will feel right at home in this sprawling adventure, and admirers of Lewis's *Narnia* will appreciate the allegorical accents woven through the text. This novel of political intrigue, romance, faith, and friendship is rife with memorable characters, a twisting plot, and high stakes.

—**Aaron D. Gansky**, author of the *Hand of Adonai Series* and *Heart Song*.

Magic, romance, danger, Aletheia has it all. This fantasy by Burke follows the traditional fare the likes of J.R.R. Tolkien and Terry Brooks. Fantasy fans, you don't want to miss out in this one!

—**Morgan L. Busse**, award-winning author of the *Follower of the Word* and *The Soul Chronicles*.

ARMOR OF ALETHEIA

SACRED ARMOR TRILOGY—BOOK ONE

Ralene Burke

ELK LAKE PUBLISHING INC
Plymouth, Massachusetts

Cover and Interior Design: Derinda Babcock

Editor(s): Linda Rondeau, Deb Haggerty

Author Represented by The Seymour Agency

PUBLISHED BY: Elk Lake Publishing, Inc., 35 Dogwood Dr., Plymouth, MA 02360, 2018

Library Cataloging Data

Names: Burke, Ralene (Ralene Burke)

Armor of Aletheia: Sacred Armor Trilogy—Book One / Ralene Burke

268 p. 23cm × 15cm (9in × 6 in.)

Description: A world in danger, a betrayed queen, a reluctant hero …

The death of her king changes Karina's life forever. Fleeing the royal house, she must leave her life behind to seek out the Armor of the Creator—to save the very people who now hunt her.

Identifiers: ISBN-13: 978-1-948888-24-0 (trade) | 978-1-948888-25-7 (POD) | 978-1-948888-26-4 (e-book)

Key Words: speculative fiction, fantasy, young adult, quest, self-confidence, courage, self-discovery

LCCN: 2018950364 Fiction

DEDICATION

For my amazing children: Alana, Kyra, and Connor. May you always heed the Creator's call, no matter where it takes you. Embrace it with your whole heart and enjoy the wild ride!

CHAPTER ONE

"By all that is created!" Karina Dubrev bit back the rest of the curse, plopped in a chair, and hunched over her throbbing finger. Several strands of dark hair fell across her hand, and she pushed the lock back before it could slide across the wound.

"Watch your words, Karina." Her mentor, Jace, pierced her with a disapproving look.

She chose not to respond. Instead, she reached over to the table and dipped her hand in a shallow container. The offensive green concoction smelled of honey and the aptly named Scorch flower—sweet and nauseating at the same time. She smeared on the ointment and wrapped her finger with a clean cloth, then stood to smooth the wrinkles from the dingy apron covering her deep-blue dress.

"Please keep an eye on the tincture in the pot, Karina. We cannot let it burn." Jace's gentle warning was no less authoritative—like a stern master who would not be denied. She tried to pay attention, but she wanted to do something more active, like picking herbs or mixing ointments, not watching a black pot boil.

The single window adjacent to the fireplace let in the last light of day. Sinking below the mountains, the sun cast halos around the towering peaks. How much time had passed since she had started helping Jace restock medicines? Her gut clenched. She stole a glimpse at the elderly man hovering over a table loaded with the various bowls and utensils used in their healing craft. Did her master realize what time it was?

"Karina!" A familiar, shrill voice shouted from the open door.

She closed her eyes, breathing deeply. Obviously, too much time had passed.

"Karina, I do not know who you think you are that you don't have to attend the evening meal with the rest of the royal household."

Karina dared to exhale, then turned.

Queen Anaya of Aletheia stood in the doorway, hands on her hips, her porcelain face puckered, her blond curls piled atop her head. The purple jewels in her crown matched her purple and silver gown. She quirked an eyebrow and waited.

Karina balled her fists. When pain ripped through her burned finger, she winced. "My apologies, Your Majesty. I was helping Jace restock the shelves—"

"You may well be the royal healer's apprentice ..." She sniffed. "... but you are also the king's ward. He expects you to join us for meals, especially when we are hosting Aletheia's nobility. Honestly, at seventeen years of age, you should understand this."

Karina bowed her head. "Of course, Your Majesty."

The queen was silent for a moment, and, with an exasperated look, pointed down the hallway. "Now!"

"Oh." Karina turned toward Jace. "My apologies, sir. I must take my leave for now, but I will return."

Jace offered a sympathetic smile that etched well-worn lines in his face—much like her father's smile. "Do not worry, Karina. I am almost done. You may return tomorrow to help me distribute the medicines."

She nodded and shuffled after Queen Anaya who silently led Karina through the labyrinth of the royal house to the dining hall.

The room was already bustling with activity. Nobles and other guests crowded together at long wooden tables on the sides of the room, imbibing the finest wines and gorging on pre-meal delicacies as they gossiped and laughed. On the far end, King Pistis sat alone at a smaller table perpendicular to the others, an empty chair on each side of him. He glanced up from his food trencher. A huge smile stretched across his face as he rose from his ornate chair and extended his hand toward Queen Anaya. "Ah, my beautiful wife and lovely daughter have joined us." His voice boomed above the din.

The room quieted, and everyone stood. The nobles' bright clothing stood out against the white stone walls. Above the crowd, equally colorful tapestries hung between the windows. The room felt alive, and Karina let the atmosphere seep in to energize her soul. She gazed at her favorite decoration—the family crest—a gold sun with two silver stars—displayed on alternating purple- or cream-colored banners suspended from the ceiling. A symbol of Aletheia's history.

With head held high, Queen Anaya strode up the aisle between the tables. At least, the queen would not chastise her in this public place. Karina followed behind, smiling and nodding to the nobles she knew. She and the queen circled the head table in opposite directions, curtsied to the king, and waited. King Pistis kissed Queen Anaya's hand—her placid expression like a snake watching its prey.

The king released his wife's hand, then turned to Karina, gifting her with his customary bright grin. He pulled her hand to his lips, but paused, his eyes widening when he noticed the bandage on her finger.

Her cheeks heated.

"Please, do not worry, Your Majesty. The burn is not serious,"

"Ah, good." His grin returned. He kissed her hand quickly before facing the crowd.

The king's auburn hair stuck out beneath his gold crown that bore a large purple amethyst at the center and white stones on either side. A tall man, his presence filled the entire room—more from an inner grandeur than because of his height—a characteristic Karina wished she possessed as well.

"Greetings to all present tonight. It is my pleasure to host this evening's feast in honor of the new year now upon us. The Creator has blessed Aletheia mightily in these last years, and I pray he continues to do so." He raised his goblet. "To Aletheia—may it continue to prosper."

Lifting their glasses, the people repeated, "To Aletheia."

"And to the Creator—may he reign forever."

"To the Creator!"

King Pistis took a long sip, and the nobles followed suit.

Smiling, Karina took a sip of her watered-down wine from her golden goblet, observing the crowd's love for a noble king. Her smile widened even more.

King Pistis sat and gestured for everyone else to do so.

Servants set platters of food in the middle of the tables. The cooks had outdone themselves tonight. Savory aromas of duck and lamb mixed with the sweetness of baked bread and the pleasant scent of a melody of fruit. She sighed as her body relaxed at last.

King Pistis winked as he leaned over the arm of his chair. "What were you and Jace doing this afternoon?"

She bit her lip to hide her smirk. "We were restocking. I apologize for being tardy to the celebration."

He shook his head and chuckled. "It amazes me how you two become so lost in the healing arts. I remember when I was Jace's student. Every day, he'd swat the back of my head several times to keep me awake."

Karina imagined a younger version of the king bouncing around the healer's workroom and grinned. As an older man, he still could not sit still for council meetings. "I can see that."

Queen Anaya straightened in her smaller, but no less ornate, chair. She glared disapprovingly at both Karina and the king. "Karina needs to accept her position as your ward—leave behind the fancies of youth." She sliced the duck on her plate while she spoke. "Her duties should include more household management, less healing."

Karina wrinkled her nose. And lose the chance to be out among the people of the royal city, helping and healing?

The king patted his wife's arm before she yanked it from his reach. "Dear Anaya, I would no more pull Karina away from the study of healing than I would wish myself to take her place. The Creator has blessed us all with different gifts, and we should put those gifts to good use."

The queen glared but said nothing more on the matter.

The next day, Karina suppressed the urge to skip from her bedchambers to the healer's workroom. How she looked forward to delivery days, for the chance to visit with the people of Calliope. Her heart fluttered. Although Jace was the royal healer, he often made extra medicines and ointments to distribute around the capital city at various shops and homes.

Her dark-blue skirt swished as she hurried down the hall. She knocked at the plain wooden door, then scurried inside without waiting for permission to enter.

"Karina, my dear. I would tell you to come in, but I see you are in already." Jace finished piling crates, then waved at a guard who stood in the corner. "Please take these to the cart."

Karina placed an empty crate on the worktable and helped Jace fill the box with the remaining jars. They worked quickly and silently with a comradery Karina treasured.

When they had finished, she grabbed her cloak from the peg by the door. "Where are we headed first? North or south district? Or do we want to be completely different and work east to west?"

Jace chuckled as he slid into the chair by the fireplace. He motioned for the guard, who had just returned, to take the last box. "Actually, Karina, I am not going with you today."

She paused, letting her hands fall to her side. She couldn't recall a time when he had missed the monthly distributions. "Are you ill?"

He shook his head. "I received news this morning of the passing of my sister. I must travel to Soter's capital for her sendoff ceremony."

Karina took a step back. He was leaving? Now? "Could you not wait until after the deliveries?"

"Karina!" He furrowed his brow beneath a mop of gray hair.

She shook away her selfish thoughts. Jace had suffered a terrible loss. During many evenings of drying and crushing herbs, he had regaled her with tales of the childhood adventures he and his sister experienced. "Of course, of course. You must leave immediately. Are you in need of anything for the trip?"

"The king has provided me with his horse and carriage, so I should be able to make the trip more quickly."

"I am very sorry for your loss, sir."

Jace pushed himself up again. "It is well, my dear. My sister was much older than me and lived a full life. If the Creator thought it was time for her to join him in the Lighted Realm, I am sure she was happy to go."

How wonderful to have lived such a full life as to be ready when the Creator called. So far, all she had managed to do was study the craft of healing.

"You best be on your way. If you tarry much longer, it will be nightfall before you return to the royal house."

She groaned. "All I need is to give the queen more reason to hate me."

Jace's eyes softened with sympathy. "She doesn't hate you, Karina."

She bit back a retort. *If he only knew …*

No use dwelling on things she couldn't change. Instead, she gripped his withered hands and offered him the Blessing of Three Kisses—one on each cheek for joy and love, and one on the forehead for wisdom. "May the Creator's strength go with you."

He patted her hand. "And with you, dear child."

The cart stopped in the south district of Calliope amid a mass of chaos. Karina accepted the guard's assistance as she stepped to the street. She pulled her cloak closer against the winter's chill. All around her, the town teemed with life. People hurried from the storefronts to the colorful booths along the road. Merchants shouted above the crowd, enticing shoppers to explore their wares. The smell of baked pastries and smoked meats wafted to where Karina stood. She took a deep breath and grinned. Market day.

"Would you mind grabbing one of these crates?" she asked the guard who had helped her down. To the one who still sat atop the cart, she nodded her thanks. "We should only be a few minutes."

Karina led the first guard around the corner of a grand storefront and down one of the wider alleys. Several dirt-streaked children, dressed in little more than long-sleeved tunics, scurried past them, then disappeared into the flurry of the market street.

About halfway down the alley, a dilapidated door stood open. Shouts came from inside as three more children rushed out.

Karina stepped between the children and the guard with the box. "Be careful!"

"Sorry, Princess," the children shouted in unison without even stopping.

Ana appeared in the doorway. "They get wilder every day."

"That's the fun of childhood." Karina smiled as she hugged her friend.

Wisps of brown hair stuck out from a loose bun at the nape of Ana's neck. The apron covering her faded red dress was smudged, as were her hands. She swiped the floor a few times with a straw broom and leaned against it. "They sure keep me on my toes."

Karina bit her lip to keep from frowning. The orphanage needed more financial support. She would have to talk to King Pistis about finding a new location. For now, she motioned for the guard to step forward. "I have brought more supplies for the orphanage. King Pistis gave me money for clothes this month too. I hear the children's merchant will be coming through next week. I'm sure he will have some clothes."

"Thank you, Karina. And please express my gratitude to the king."

A little girl peeked out from behind Ana. "Good morning, Princess."

"Good morning, Mia." Karina knelt, tilting her head to the side. "I brought a surprise for you." She pulled a little bag from the top of the crate and handed it to the pig-tailed girl.

Mia snatched the bag, dug her hand in, and pulled out a stick of hard candy. She squealed as she threw her arms around Karina. "Thank you, Princess!"

Karina's spirit lightened to see the girl's joy.

Ana chuckled as Mia scampered back into the house. "She'll make all the boys jealous."

"Serves them—"

"Stop! Thieves!" A series of shouts came from the market street.

Wielding daggers, two disheveled men dashed into the alley but stopped when they saw Karina and Ana.

Ana gasped, but Karina grabbed her arm as a warning to be silent.

Karina's guard pulled his sword and stepped toward the thieves. The men ran back into the street and were pursued by more guards.

Karina frowned. Crime had never been a significant issue in Calliope until recent months. Now the prison mines were overcrowded with criminals. She glanced at Ana, whose face had paled. "I do not know whether to hope you take in a few more girls so Mia has someone to play with or to be glad there haven't been more orphans in the city."

Ana picked up the broom and resumed sweeping. "Actually, I've taken in three new wee ones in the last two weeks. With so many families making their way to Aletheia, I'm sure I'll see even more. Not sure where we'll put them."

"New families? Where are they coming from?"

Ana raised an eyebrow. "People are leaving Tzedek in droves. They say the king is crazed, dealing in stuff folks ought not to be dealing in."

Karina bit her lower lip. She had yet to hear such rumors. Did the king know? He had to, right? She shook her head and pasted on a bright smile. "Well, I have a present for you too."

"Oh, no, Karina. I am fine."

"Nonsense. Your cloak is threadbare." She pulled a long, rust-colored cloak from the crate. "You need this. No arguments."

Ana's eyes misted. "Thank you," she whispered as she accepted the cloak. "I'd best get back in there before one of the boys tries to steal Mia's candy." Ana motioned for the guard to follow her inside to drop off the box.

In the meantime, Karina made her way back to the main road. Sumptuous smells invaded her senses again, and her stomach rumbled. But more deliveries still needed to be made.

She arrived back at the royal house well before the dinner bell. Plenty of time for a hot bath.

No sooner had she entered the main hall than a servant, dressed in a gray tunic and black pants, found her. He bowed his head. "Princess, the queen would like to see you in the study."

Of course she would. Karina nodded, and the servant backed away.

She followed the maze of halls to the queen's study on the second floor. The nearer Karina drew, the slower she trudged. Being in the queen's company never seemed to end well despite Karina's best efforts. She had no idea what she had done to alienate the queen, but the queen had despised Karina for as long as the girl had been in the castle.

Karina sighed. *Just get it over with.* As she approached the double doors—opened a crack—voices seeped through from the other side.

"I do not think you really know her." Queen Anaya's tone was insistent.

Karina peeked through the doors into the darkened room. Gone were the pastels and open windows. The queen had paneled the room with dark wood imported from somewhere beyond the Barrens and replaced the bright curtains with heavy green drapes. Now, besides the fireplace, the only light came from the candelabras.

The queen sat in a tall chair behind her desk while King Pistis paced in front of the great stone fireplace.

"You are being ridiculous, Anaya. She is doing no harm here."

"People become confused by her presence. Is she your daughter? Is she truly a princess? How do we address her?"

"I do not think those things matter."

The queen waved. "Of course not, sweetheart. To us, they don't. But I am talking about the people."

"I am not going to turn my back on her. She may not be my daughter by birth, but my heart no longer knows the difference." He clasped his hands behind his back as he straightened. A sign Karina knew meant he would not tolerate argument.

Karina's own heart pounded beneath her chest. She could not believe what she was hearing. Were they really having such a discussion? Why would the queen not want her around? Karina's breath caught. Did the queen know her secret? How would she have found out?

Queen Anaya stood, circled the desk, and gently rested her hand on the king's shoulder. "I'm not suggesting you throw her out, my lord. I am merely suggesting she remain a healer's apprentice as when she first came to the royal house."

King Pistis shook his head. "Absolutely not."

"We need to make a strong stand. Rumors are rife concerning our household. Our enemies will knock on our borders if they suspect strife."

"Enemies?" The king shrugged off her hand. "What enemies? The Three Kingdoms have been at peace for many years."

"You-know-who still lingers in Tzedek. You've heard the stories from the people who have escaped."

Karina sucked in a quiet breath. Was that what Ana had been talking about?

King Pistis nodded.

"You know I am right about this."

"Anaya, your words may be wise, but I will not deny Karina her rightful place."

"Why will you not desist?"

"Because Karina is family now." The king moved out of Karina's view, but she could still hear him. "The matter is closed. Any further talk of it will incur my—"

The door opened, and Karina stumbled back against the opposite wall of the hallway.

"Karina?" The color drained from King Pistis's face as he glanced up and down the hall. "How long have you been standing there?"

She narrowed her eyes and quickly looked away. "Long enough."

The queen peered over the king's shoulder. "See? Trouble!"

Karina wanted to snarl at the woman. Could she not say one nice thing?

"Silence." The king's pallor changed from white to crimson as he turned toward his wife. "You shame me with your fearful resentment. Karina is our daughter, and I expect you to treat her as such. Is that clear?"

Queen Anaya pressed her lips into a thin line as she nodded. Without another word, she disappeared inside the room.

The king slammed the door behind him, then helped Karina to a stand. "I am sorry you had to hear that, my daughter."

She shifted her weight, not certain what she should say.

"Come now, let us go to the kitchen. I am sure we can find heated cider to warm our insides."

Karina shook her head. "If you would please excuse me, I'd like to return to my bed chambers for the night."

"Karina, please, do not worry about—"

She placed her hand on the king's arm and forced a smile. "It's not that, my lord. I have been in town all day for deliveries, and I am very tired."

The king patted her hand. "Of course. Sleep well, my child."

Sickened by what she had overheard, Karina sought the safety of her bed chambers. But was it really hers or a temporary room for a guest?

CHAPTER TWO

The winds shifted. Cold breezes whipped Karina's dark hair like rapids rushing through a canyon. She shivered as she snuggled deeper into her wool cloak. The brisk chill invigorated her body. Never did her world seem as clear as when she stood atop the wall surrounding Calliope.

After the argument she'd witnessed between King Pistis and the queen two nights before, Karina needed this retreat—this reminder. She leaned against the battlement. Aletheia's majestic landscape sparkled in late winter's blanket of ice and snow that stretched all the way to Shadowed Forest in the east.

She turned to the mountains poised like solemn sentinels watching over the capital city. Mount Jyal pushed up to the outer wall on the north side. The sun hovered behind a line of menacing clouds shrouding the distant peaks of the Western Mountains, and the clouds billowed faster than normal.

Karina crossed the wall, squinting at the unusual sight. What would make the clouds move like that?

The northern winds clashed with a frigid gale from the west. They swirled and fought—a celestial battle that transformed Karina's moment of peace to turmoil. Her cloak swirled behind her, offering no protection against the sudden burst of bitter cold.

The black clouds morphed into a massive hand that traversed the mountains as quickly as a streak of lightning. She lifted her arm to block the wind, so she could see. What was going on? What was that thing? As the giant, mysterious hand neared the castle wall, it shriveled in size to that of a man and reached across the battlements.

Karina screamed, then ducked to avoid the hand. Too late.

Its ice-cold nails pierced her skin, forcing her to look upward.

But she didn't want to look, didn't want to know, didn't want to be here now. She closed her eyes. Why were the guards not rushing to her rescue? The unrelenting pain made her heart race. With effort, Karina glanced toward the west.

Terrifying, red-eyed creatures danced in the clouds. With each gust, they changed shape—dragons, lupens, and goblins. An all-consuming darkness, wrapped within a blanket of deathly cold, engulfed her.

No! Karina squeezed her eyes shut, and tears stung her cheeks. What were those things? And where was help? She wrenched her head from the hand's grip. With a shout, she lurched back until she slammed into the battlement, then shrank against the wall. She gripped the rough stone with aching fingers. Her mouth went dry. Her chest hurt, and tremors rattled her body as she gasped for air. "Creator! Help me."

"Karina!"

The winds died.

She opened her eyes. The frightening fiends had disappeared, but dark clouds still hovered in the distance.

"Karina!" a masculine voice called from the nearest turret.

She steadied herself against the cold stone.

Sam ambled onto the wall. He hiked up his dirty pants and wiped at a smudge on his cheek. His mop of light brown hair flopped with each step.

Her first instinct was to confess everything to her closest friend, but she doubted he would believe her. She wasn't sure she believed what she had seen. She faked a smile and hid her trembling hands behind her back. "Wh-what brings you up here at this late hour?"

Even now, the shadows stretched before them as the sun sank behind the ominous clouds.

He held out his hand to help her up. "The king is ill. Her Majesty sent me to fetch you."

The blood drained from Karina's face as she stood. She had just spoken with him this morning, and he had been well, talking about their plans for a horseback ride through the mountain pass tomorrow. "How bad is he?"

Sam glanced at his worn shoes. "I don't know. Her Majesty's maid came into the stables, looking for you. Said the queen was screaming like a madwoman."

Karina's stomach tightened, and a different chill ran up her spine. She shrugged off the feeling as well as the earlier terror—her only thought the welfare of the king.

"Let's go." She pushed past Sam as she ran into the tower. She flexed her hands. This couldn't be good—the king had never so much as sneezed that Karina could remember. Why now?

Because Jace was gone. Her shoulders slumped. Why did her mentor have to leave her alone? Surely his sister's family would have understood if he had not attended her sendoff ceremony. She chastised herself for her insensitivity.

She and Sam made their way to the inner bailey, where the usual bustle of daily life had ceased.

"Do you need me?" Sam asked, his voice uneasy.

She shook her head.

"I'll be in the stables."

Without looking back, Karina dismissed him with a wave.

She approached the main entrance to the royal house, and a set of black-armored guards pulled open the heavy doors. Once across the entry hall, she climbed the grand staircase, veered to the right past displays of tapestries and portraits and up another set of stairs.

On the third floor, numerous staff and guests lingered in a sitting area, conversing quietly. Some sat while others paced, sneaking quick looks down the long hall.

Karina gripped the railing—their forlorn faces churned her stomach. Was she too late? She rushed down the hall.

Loud voices filtered through the ornately carved door to the royal chambers—Queen Anaya's shrill voice and the deeper pitch of the Captain of the Guard. Though their words were muffled, their tones sounded urgent.

Karina knocked softly at first, but when the arguing continued she rapped harder. Her foot tapped in time with her heartbeat. She willed her breath to slow and her head to clear. Today she was not the beloved ward. She was the royal healer.

The door eased open. Captain DeMarco raked a hand through his dark-brown hair, his face pale, and his eyes dimmed by apparent worry. He ushered her in with a solemn nod, his normally cheerful smile absent.

Queen Anaya stared at Karina from the other side of the large bed. Red splotches set off her teary, sapphire eyes, and her lip curled before she turned away with a swish of her purple skirts.

What had she done this time? The queen never seemed happy to see Karina, not even now, though she was the only available healer.

Across from the massive bed, a fire crackled in the stone fireplace, filling the room with a faint sweet smell. Someone had dropped the red curtains to hide the fading light outside the line of windows. The king reclined against a pile of brightly colored pillows, his square chin resting against his chest. His auburn hair, flecked with gray, stuck out contrary to his usual unruffled style. Could he just be sleeping?

Panic seized her. More than anything, she wanted to curl up at his side and listen to his stories.

Karina fisted her hands, her fingernails pinching her palms. She needed to relax. She had to be the healer today. No one else could do her job for her. But what if something happened to the king? She swallowed the lump in her throat and side-stepped the tall captain to enter the room. "What happened?"

The queen sniffed. "He was in a meeting with the council. They said he started moaning—then fell unconscious. The guards brought him to his chambers where he awoke shortly after."

Captain DeMarco gestured toward a bowl on the table by the bed. "He is weak and does not seem to be responding to the basic remedies I have tried."

Karina tasted the medicine. Sweet with the spicy twinge of tamar root. "Where did you learn these skills?"

He shifted, his black chainmail clinking with his movement. "I thought it prudent to be knowledgeable in basic healing in order to better serve my fellow soldiers on the battlefield."

"Very wise, Captain." She glanced toward the king.

King Pistis rested between crimson sheets, his eyes closed. The strong man Karina knew, whose presence demanded attention from everyone in a room, yet who stooped to embrace a broken-hearted orphan, now seemed as helpless as an infant.

She wrung her hands as she stepped away from the bed.

The queen quirked a perfect eyebrow. "What troubles you, child?"

"I wish Jace were here."

Captain DeMarco placed his hand on Karina's shoulder. "You can do this."

She stared at King Pistis. Jace had complimented her healing abilities many times in the past two seasons, but her skills paled in comparison to his. Still … She nodded with renewed confidence. "I *can* do this."

The queen rounded the bed. "Of course, you can," she said, her lips taut. "You are an excellent healer, an honor to your craft."

The words rang hollow. Did the woman ever have a sincere word to say? Karina unclenched her jaw. "Thank you, Your Majesty." She sat by the king's bed and placed her hand atop his. "King Pistis?"

His light-green eyes fluttered open, and a smile lit his face as he turned toward her. "Karina, my dear, I am so pleased to see you."

Her heart melted at his handsome smile. She leaned over and kissed his cheek. "What happened?"

"I felt a pain in my chest. The next thing I knew, I was here in this bed." He raised his head slightly, turning to the queen. "That confounded woman will not let me out of bed."

"Where you should be!" Karina chuckled as she glanced up at Anaya. "I see he's being his usual difficult self."

The queen rolled her eyes, but the corners of her lips twitched.

Karina evaluated the king's condition. His heart rate was elevated. Sweat soaked his bed clothes, but his forehead was cool to the touch. His symptoms pointed to a heart condition, which was difficult to observe. She shuffled to the table and poured water from a cold pitcher into a goblet. "Your Majesty, drink this while I retrieve my medicine bag."

"No!" Queen Anaya smoothed her skirt. "Why don't you let Captain DeMarco get the bag and whatever herbs you might need?"

Karina furrowed her brow. "Fine. But I also need someone to bring water and fresh linens."

The queen nodded. "I can assign those tasks to servants."

Karina gave Captain DeMarco a list of needed supplies and then advised the queen as to additional tasks.

When they were alone, except for a guard by the door, Karina gave the water to King Pistis.

He gulped the water, placed the cup on the side table, and eased back between the sheets. "Karina," he mumbled. "Though you are my ward, I have always considered you a daughter—a real princess. I ... ask for ..."

His eyes closed, and he fell asleep again.

Tears stung the corners of Karina's eyes. He didn't need to say such things.

Captain DeMarco returned with the requested herbs and then excused himself to attend to other duties. A servant entered with a tray of warm cider and citrus puffs. The buttery smell filled the room, but Karina could not bring herself to touch her favorite pastries.

She spread the supplies on the table to make a tonic of aloe and sable. If the problem were his heart, she would need to clear the air passages and slow his heart rate—the tonic would do both. Her hands shook as she ground the leaves.

The king's pallor grayed even more in the next half hour. He did not respond when she tried to wake him, murmuring something about traitors and lupens.

Traitors. Karina gulped.

She spooned a few drops of the tonic into his mouth and set the bowl on the side table. Leaning forward again, she gently stroked his stubbly cheek.

The king eyes fluttered open. He cleared his throat. "I know who you are."

Her stomach tightened. She opened her mouth to speak, but nothing came out.

The king pulled her closer. "Do not fear, Karina," he whispered.

Do not fear? His last five words could turn her world upside down. Blood pounded at her temples. Voices in her head taunted her, telling her this would be her last night in her home.

The king stared at the gold canopy draping the bed posts. "I have known for quite a while. You resemble your mother in so many ways." He chuckled. "But you definitely inherited my brother's stubborn streak."

She looked away at the mention of her birth father.

"Still, I love you. You may have been the daughter of a traitor, but you are now a princess. One whose grace and compassion are renowned throughout the kingdom. We have been blessed—I have been blessed—to have you in our household. I never thought my heart would heal after—" He winced and gasped for breath.

"Your Majesty!" Karina listened to the king's shallow breaths and moved the bowl to his mouth. "Come on, please."

He pushed it away. "Karina, remember," he rasped.

She shook her head. "No, please. Don't try to talk. Drink this." She held the bowl up again, but he refused.

"Remember, it is by the Creator's grace that any of us are here. You have a purpose—to take my place as I have no other heir."

She backed away. What was he talking about? Heir? She was not fit to rule a kingdom. That was meant for the royal line. Her breath caught. She remembered how the queen had rocked yet another stillborn child. A tear slid down Karina's cheek. She shook her head in persistent denial.

Her uncle patted her hand as his eyes closed. "I have told Anaya and Captain DeMarco everything. These guards also were witness to this." His breath rattled. "You must know, though, there are rumors from Tzedek. Faramos …" His words slurred, and he quieted.

"Your Majesty?" she whispered. "Uncle?" His breath was a mere feather on her cheek. For the first time since her parents died, she let the tears flow. She could not lose this man who had been a father to her. He was all she had.

His chest ceased to move.

"Uncle? No, please, no." She buried her face in his chest, breathing in his scent. Her flood of tears dampened his robe. Why? Why now? Depths of sorrow wrenched her very soul. Finally, spent from grief, she rested her forehead against his.

"What have you done?"

Karina spun toward the wail.

Queen Anaya, one hand on the iron knob, leaned against the door as if too weak to stand on her own. The look of pure hatred in Queen Anaya's eyes—her aunt's eyes—sent shivers down Karina's spine.

Queen Anaya grasped her husband's hand, her tears staining the crimson sheets. "Karina, please let me be. I want to be alone with my husband for a few minutes."

With a quick nod, she grabbed her cloak and left the room.

Suddenly, the royal house, with all its bed chambers, staff quarters, and ballrooms, seemed stifling. Karina needed fresh air. She raced down the stairs, out through the inner bailey, and skirted the central fountain as she dodged soldiers with pikes and servants with baskets.

Sam rounded the stable corner, leading her horse behind him. "Hey, I was just going to take Lady Belle out for some ex—"

She snatched the reins from his hand, swung up onto Lady Belle, and urged her into a gallop.

Sam hollered something after her, but she ignored him.

"Open the gate!" she shouted at the wall guards who speedily obeyed.

Karina urged Lady Belle through the sliver of an opening, then raced toward Mount Jyal, her refuge—and the Creator, her strength.

An hour later, the red-orange sun made its appearance as she tied Lady Belle to the limb of a fallen log. The damp morning air clung to her skin, chilling her to the bone. Calliope and the plains stretched before her—all the way to Shadowed Forest. She gasped in awe at the beauty. Miles of snow. Such magnificence. Even with all the open space, grief still crushed her heart.

She fell to her knees on a flat rock near the edge of a precipice as she shouted to the Creator. "How could you take him from me?"

This time tears refused to fall. She remembered her last conversation with the king.

I cannot believe he knew. He knew! Creator, I do not understand. He never said a word. He hated my father. How could he love me if he knew who I was?

None of the secrets mattered now—the only father she had ever known and loved was gone. As the coarse wind blew through the mountains, she heard the faint jingle of his laugh, like when he found her covered in red juice as she played in the berry patch.

She waited—waited to discover his death was just a dream. But it wasn't.

She gazed at the capital below as she considered the magnitude of the king's last words. Her—Queen of Aletheia? The idea was laughable. She was only seventeen, and she had never been trained in matters of state. She was a healer's apprentice. Ask her about herbs and healings, and she could quote the text from memory. But govern a country? She was the child of a cleric-turned-traitor, not honorable nobility.

She huddled beneath her azure cloak. The fresh air and magnificent views offered little solace. She longed for a warm embrace, a sense of peace.

Creator, I feel so lost. I fear what is to come. What is your will for me?

She dried her eyes with her cloak then surveyed the far mountains and the approaching dark clouds. The clouds towered over the mountains now. She recalled the evil hand she had seen only yesterday. What had the king said about the neighboring kingdom of Tzedek?

She brushed the dirt from her hands. Someone needed to be informed of this coming evil.

Out of nowhere, a billowing light burst before her, growing in intensity until its brightness forced her to cover her eyes. When she shuffled back, her foot slipped. Rocks crumbled beneath her, pitching her toward the cliff.

CHAPTER THREE

The edge of the precipice loomed a mere two steps away.

Karina scrambled. More rocks broke loose.

One step.

Too late, she flung herself forward and landed hard on the cold stone. Her body skidded over the edge. "Help!"

A strong hand snaked around her arm.

Her breath caught as her feet dangled over the sheer drop. She wanted to scream but couldn't. She looked up into a man's stone-gray eyes. His warm smile eased her fear. A heartbeat later, he pulled her up and placed her gently on solid ground.

Karina fell to her knees. "Thank you, Creator." She touched the cold ground. She had almost died. Right here. She turned to thank her rescuer.

The man stood a body's length from her. He wore an odd wrap, whiter than the snow around them. His blond hair and pale skin stood out against the dark mountain behind him. His glowing skin burned her eyes.

She shielded her face as she stood. "Wh-who are you?"

"I am Garon, servant of the Creator." He bowed, revealing the ethereal wings tucked behind him.

She swallowed hard. She had heard stories of servants. Few had seen them, and even fewer had ever conversed with one.

He smiled. "I bring you encouragement on this sorrowful day."

She trembled in his overwhelming presence. What was she supposed to say to a servant?

He softly stroked her cheek. "Dry your tears, dear princess. The Creator has heard your prayers. You have been greatly blessed. Your faith, compassion, and integrity are that of a prophetess." He reached into the pouch at his side, then placed two fingers on her forehead. "I, Garon, servant of the Creator, anoint you as prophetess, for the Mighty One has chosen you." He stepped back again.

Karina shivered. A prophetess? Not likely. What about—

"You will take your uncle's throne but not now." He gestured toward the darkness spreading over the Western Mountains. "As you have seen, there is a great evil pressing upon this world. The Creator is sending you to destroy it."

"Me?" she scoffed. "I am merely a healer. How could I ever stop such a thing?"

The servant clasped his hands together. "Your quest is to seek out the Armor of the Creator. Six sacred relics divided among the three kingdoms."

The three kingdoms? She remembered traveling through each kingdom with the orphan caravan. Aletheia was home, of course, and Soter was nice enough. But Tzedek—the minute the caravan crossed into that kingdom, Karina had been ill with unease.

And for what now? Armor? She could barely wield a sword, much less fight in a battle. "I—I could never accomplish such a monumental task."

"Nevertheless, the Mighty One has chosen you. Do you refuse His call?"

She bowed, feeling contrite at the servant's rebuke. "Of course not. I beg your pardon."

"It is not mine to give," he said simply. "However, the Creator will send others to join you in this quest. As a prophetess, you will lead them."

"What will I do with this armor?"

"Each piece possesses certain gifts. You and your comrades will use the armor against the warlock who released the darkness and against the evil itself." He placed his hand on her arm. "Have no fear, Prophetess. You will not be alone."

Karina scanned the valley below. People wandered about their daily lives in Calliope, oblivious to the coming evil. She turned to the mysterious clouds in the west. Could she refuse this quest? Her family needed her, and the kingdom needed a ruler.

If she refused, would the Creator find another or let his people fall to ruin? Surely not. Still, could she chance the Creator's wrath? She thought of the king—her uncle. He always put his people first, above himself. She blew out a long breath. "Where do I start?"

"Return to the royal house and ask the queen for the location of Aletheia's sacred temple. There you must complete the elders' challenge before you receive the armor. Be careful, because the challenges are not as easy as they may appear. You will need to look deep within to find the virtue needed." Garon smiled, his eyes shining. "And when you are scared, remember the Creator is always with you."

Karina looked back to ask another question, but the servant had vanished. With a sigh of determination, she made a vow. *I am yours, as always, and desire to follow where you lead. Please give me the strength and wisdom to do so.*

She lingered a moment longer, her heart pulled by conflicting emotions. Just when she managed to find resolve, the long moan of the royal horn echoed throughout the kingdom. The king's death had just become public knowledge.

Karina mounted Lady Belle and rushed down the mountainside. How could she explain this quest to the queen? Was she prepared for a quest like this? What if she failed the Creator? She could hardly fathom the thought.

Since returning to the royal house eight years ago, she rarely left the safety of Calliope's walls. Visions of the mercenaries who killed her parents and the bandits who burned the orphan caravan still plagued her dreams. She remembered living in the woods alone, scrimping to survive, a cold and lonely life.

Karina slowly picked her way along the trail. By the time she reached the royal house, she had convinced herself the Creator had been mistaken. When she had prayed for direction, she meant as Queen of Aletheia. *Mighty Creator, I fear I misunderstood your servant's calling. Isn't my place here? Perhaps I could send a squad of knights to the temple to retrieve the armor. There is so much to do to prepare for the sendoff ceremony and to assure the people of Aletheia the royal line will uphold the integrity of King Pistis's reign.*

A palpable sorrow had settled over the kingdom as the royal house mourned the loss of its king.

Karina found Anaya in the parlor off the great hall. She sat in a dark blue settee with her back to the door, staring into the fireplace. Her handmaid stood off to the side, but otherwise the queen was alone.

Karina took a hesitant step into the room. "Your Majesty?"

Anaya dabbed a white cloth under her nose and turned to Karina, her black gown rustling with the movement.

Overwhelmed with emotion, Karina crossed the room and greeted her only remaining family member with the Blessing of Three Kisses.

"Where have you been?" the queen barked.

Karina cringed. "I was seeking the Creator's guidance on Mount Jyal." This did not seem the right time to discuss her encounter with his servant. She sat next to her aunt.

Anaya rolled her eyes. "What is with you and that silly, cold mountain?"

It's warmer there than in here. Karina gazed at the flames licking the logs in the hearth. They sat in silence for what seemed like hours.

Finally, Karina faced the queen. "When I was with the king last night, he mentioned he knew who I was."

Anaya glared. "So he informed me moments before you arrived."

Once more hatred flared behind her aunt's blue eyes. To continue would only serve to intensify her animosity. Yet, this discussion was necessary. "He also said I was the rightful heir to the throne, though I assumed you would rule in his stead—not me."

Anaya chuckled in disdain. "You are so naïve, Karina. Since I am merely queen through marriage, I have no rightful claim to the throne under our laws. I am merely relegated to a pithy noble title—*Lady* Anaya."

"So why did the king keep this secret from me? Why didn't he prepare me for this day?"

"Just like a widowed queen, the king's ward cannot inherit the throne. Since there was no heir, the kingdom would pass to the Captain of the Guard. I saw no need to train you in the affairs of state." She glanced once more at the fireplace. "Do not ask me what was going on in my husband's head where you are concerned."

Karina tugged her skirt. "What should we do now? Will you help me?"

"I am not sure I trust you."

Anaya's words stung. "What—what do you mean?"

"It seems to me you have been deceiving us for many years, like your father did."

"I know, but—"

"For all I know, you planned this all along."

Karina stood. "Planned what?"

Anaya's glare bore through Karina like a bull's horn.

How should she respond to so painful an accusation? Her cheeks flamed. Did her aunt truly believe Karina capable of killing anyone, much less the compassionate man who had welcomed her as his own daughter? She shook her head. Ridiculous. "I assure you, I did not *plan* anything."

Anaya turned her back to Karina, an obvious dismissal.

Karina pressed her lips together. Anaya's mind was made up, regardless of any argument Karina could present.

Defeated, she retreated to her chambers. Mauri, her handmaid, hung freshly laundered dresses in the oversized wardrobe. Karina slammed the door and plopped onto the four-poster bed and crossed her arms. "She is so infuriating."

"Who, m'lady?" Mauri's blond curls bounced as she put clothes away.

"Mauri, I've told you not to call me that. You are my friend."

Mauri's pale cheeks reddened.

Karina groaned. "Queen Anaya thinks I murdered the king."

Mauri dropped the petticoat she'd been folding, then quickly retrieved it. "Why would she think such a thing?"

The sun shown in, but the air remained chilly.

Karina rose from the bed and paced along the burgundy carpet, stopping to glance out the window at Mount Jyal. Not even its grandeur could calm her spirit. "Yes, I lied about who I was but only to protect myself. They never would have allowed me to stay in the royal house if they'd known the truth."

Mauri shrugged her shoulders. "I'm not sure I understand. What did you lie about?"

Before Karina could answer, a loud knock prompted Mauri to open the door.

Captain DeMarco bowed. "Your Majesty, I have searched for you everywhere."

Your Majesty? Karina looked for the queen but quickly realized the captain was referring to her. A knot tightened in Karina's stomach. Ready or not—she was the queen now.

She exchanged glances with Mauri. "My apologies, Captain. I—uh—needed some air."

"I understand." His face showed signs of grief not unlike her own. He straightened. "I am sorry to bother you, but we must make arrangements for the sendoff ceremony."

"The sendoff?" Her knees buckled under the weight of responsibility.

"There is much to discuss. We only have a couple of days."

"Discuss? What do you mean?"

Captain DeMarco offered a sympathetic smile. "Your Majesty, as queen, you must make the arrangements."

Of course. Would she ever feel comfortable in this new role? She sighed. If King Pistis had faith in her … "What needs to be done first?"

Through the remainder of the day and into the next, Karina's stomach ached like never before. Amid all the chaos of sendoff ceremony arrangements, she refused any food Mauri brought her. Karina had dismissed the ache as grief. But with each passing hour, the pain intensified.

Her aunt, preoccupied with the planning, seemed indifferent to Karina's suffering, her few glances toward her niece filled with loathing.

They sat alone in the dining room. The crackling fire to Karina's right did little to dispel the chill. Before the king's death, he would have sat at the head of the table, while Karina and the queen sat on either side. Surprisingly, Karina now occupied the king's chair while Anaya, dressed in informal black, sat at the opposite end with six chairs between them, three on each side.

The firelight from the iron sconces danced around the stone room. Colorful tapestries of mountains and oceans hung on the walls. What was once a room full of mirth now exhibited all the cheer of a dungeon cell.

Karina placed her fork on the plate. "The sendoff ceremony is tomorrow morning. Is everything prepared? Do you need me to help with anything else?"

"I think you have helped enough."

Anaya's icy tone grated on Karina's resolve. She tired of these passive attacks on her character—attacks she'd endured since returning to Aletheia as a child. What had she done to this woman? She moved down the table to sit next to her aunt, who wrinkled her petite nose. "Tell me, why do you hate me?"

Anaya dabbed her lips. Leaning in, she matched Karina's glare. "Because you are your father's daughter."

The words stung. She could not even think of a response. The depth of hatred in that answer seeped into her bones and left her feeling cold and alone. She would not be able to win over Anaya tonight. Sorrowful, Karina rose without a word and returned to her bedchambers.

Anaya's words churned through Karina's mind throughout the night. The light of the full moon splayed across her burgundy coverlet. She understood her family's hatred for her father. He had done the unspeakable. His thoughtless mistake had left the kingdom vulnerable, even though he thought his actions were justified. Every time she closed her eyes, she saw her uncle's corpse on the throne with her father's corpse in the regent chair behind the king. So much death.

When the morning trumpets blared, Karina rolled out of bed with a groan. Little sleep led to a troublesome headache. She rubbed her temples as she gazed out her window at the bustling activity in the square below.

Mauri rushed in, tying a white apron over her black dress. "My apologies, m'la—Karina—but everything is quite out of the normal today."

"Do not worry, Mauri. I needed the extra rest."

"I understand. A lot has happened, and you have not had time to deal with any of it. Today, we celebrate your uncle's life and lay his body to rest. Let that be your focus."

Mauri was right, of course.

She scowled as she handed her mistress a courtier's dress the color of midnight. "How can you stand to wear a frock like this?"

Karina smirked. "I've never been fond of these poufy, formal dresses. They're too restricting. Perhaps I should show up in the light blue sateen?"

Mauri giggled. "If you wanted to get a rise out of Lady Anaya …"

Karina gritted her teeth. For propriety's sake, she donned the somber dress. Mauri twisted Karina's hair into complicated knots and painted her eyelids with traditional dark kohl.

Karina rested her chin in her hands.

Mauri patted her back. "Is something else wrong?"

Karina shook her head. "I have a nervous feeling in my stomach, like I'm forgetting to do something."

"Like what?" Mauri wrestled with the bed sheets.

Images of Karina's encounter with the Creator's servant flitted across Karina's mind. She did not want to revisit that scene—not today. "I'm not sure," she said with a smile. "Is it time to go to the sanctuary?"

With her hands on her hips, Mauri looked around and nodded. "It is."

Karina stood under a chapel archway. Sunlight filtered in from the stained-glass windows, a gift from the Temple of Aletheia when King Pistis had turned the massive ballroom into a sanctuary for the Creator. Now, people from all over Aletheia had come to pay their respects to a much-beloved king. They chatted quietly as they filled the pews.

Two tapestries hung behind the raised dais at the front of the room. On the left was the family crest and on the right was the crest of the Creator. Below the tapestries, King Pistis's body lay on a marble table. From here, his face looked calm, serene—but too pale against the purple burial robe designed for the royal family. Except for her parents …

Karina shook her head. This was a time to celebrate King Pistis's life, not mourn past mistakes.

The cleric wore the traditional garments for a sendoff ceremony—a white robe and a white sash decorated with gold suns. In his right hand, he held the Word of the Creator. With his free hand, the cleric beckoned her.

She searched the room for Anaya. Earlier, Karina had seen her aunt from across the hall, but she had made a point of avoiding Karina.

She could barely breathe. Must she mourn her uncle under the scrutiny of prying eyes? The people of Aletheia meant well, but she desired to process her grief alone. She straightened, determined to represent the royal family with dignity. She marched down the aisle, stood by her chair, and waited for Anaya. Dressed in a black gown with matching train and lace veil, her aunt made her way through the crowd. She and Karina sat on the right side of the dais, facing King Pistis's body.

Karina felt numb. She'd shed many tears over the past few days and welcomed dry eyes. Besides, royalty must appear to be in control—emotions, a sign of weakness.

The cleric gestured toward Karina and Anaya. "Your Majesty, Lady Anaya, and people of Aletheia, today is a day of great loss as well as a day of great celebration. Today we lay to rest the body of King Pistis—a great man, loved by all."

Karina's mind wandered as the cleric continued. She scanned the sea of people. Most had their eyes riveted on the cleric, but a few strayed their gazes to the stained glass or to people who stood nearby. At the center of the rows, she spotted Mauri sitting next to Jace.

Jace! His familiar blue eyes and graying beard were a welcomed sight. He nodded to her, a sympathetic smile softening his features. After all, his sister had just crossed to the Lighted Realm as well. Karina acknowledged him with a slight nod.

As the cleric droned on, Karina stared at her hands. Her thoughts bounced between her father and her uncle. How many times had she cried herself to sleep because she missed her parents? Even after all these years, she still mourned their loss. Would grief never end?

She had to be courageous—to be what her uncle would expect from his successor. Strong. Decisive. But gentle. Gentle, she could do. Strong and decisive?

When the service ended, Anaya leaned toward Karina, whispering through clenched teeth. "I know you killed the king. Make no mistake, I will die before I see you on my husband's throne."

Karina stared at her. Anaya's hatred, like the evil she had sensed near the Western Mountains, squeezed Karina's heart until she felt certain she'd faint.

Anaya hurried down the aisle and disappeared through the open doors. The rest of the crowd followed.

Karina stood, unsure of what to do next. She prayed for guidance but received no definitive direction. If anything, her despair deepened.

Jace approached the dais and offered his hand. She fell into the warm embrace of her mentor. He smelled of sable and flowers. She didn't want to let go, but eventually he pulled away.

"My dear Karina, I apologize I was not here sooner. The king's death is a great loss to us all."

She nodded, biting back tears.

"I hear you have been keeping a secret." He raised an eyebrow.

Her cheeks heated. "I am sorry I never told you. I thought it was … safer that way, for both of us."

He pulled her arm around his. "Don't worry. I already knew."

"What?"

He chuckled. "The day I picked you up on the trail eight years ago, I thought you looked familiar. But there was one morning during our training when you made a comment that reminded me of your father. In that moment, all the pieces fell into place."

"Why—why didn't you say anything?"

"It was your secret to tell when you were ready." He tipped his head toward her. "I had hoped it would have been a little sooner."

She had no defense for her misjudgment. Instead, she let Jace lead her from the sanctuary. Mauri followed them as they made their way to the banquet hall for the celebration of life meal.

Karina paused at the open doors. People hurried back and forth, anxious for the feast. Servants weaved between tables with pitchers and trays. Musicians sat on one end of the room, their instruments loud enough to be heard over the crowd—first with somber melodies, then with celebratory beats in honor of a noble king.

She motioned toward the door. "Would you mind if we sat in the parlor for a bit?"

Jace furrowed his brow. "Lady Anaya will wonder where you've gone off to."

"At the moment, I do not much care what she thinks."

"Very well."

Karina motioned for Mauri to follow them as they entered the quiet parlor. The fire's glow seemed restful, not quite as lively as it had been a few days ago. Karina sat on the settee, then beckoned Mauri to sit next to her. "I want you to hear this too, Mauri."

Jace leaned back in the armchair, a patchwork of dark blue and pewter designs. "I must say, my dear, you have me intrigued. What troubles you, child?"

How could she explain something she could not believe herself? "I think I made a mistake."

Jace offered a reassuring smile. "I am sure we can fix it."

"Tell us," Mauri said.

"I have failed the Creator."

Jace harrumphed. "Nonsense."

"No, I have." Karina's voice cracked as she told them about the mountaintop encounter with the Creator's servant—how she'd been chosen for a quest—and her quiet rebellion. She trembled as she posed the question. "What should I do?"

Jace stroked his beard. "I think the answer is obvious."

Karina waited.

"My dear Karina, the Creator has given you an important quest. All this despair, all this fear, is because you are not listening. You are choosing a path contrary to the one he has given you."

She hung her head. Jace was right. She had known the answer all along. The Creator would watch over Calliope and the rest of Aletheia in her absence. Excuses … that was all she had.

Jace stood. "Preparations must be made. You and Mauri return to your room and pack."

"What about tonight's Lighted Realm Ball? The—the coronation tomorrow?"

"Those are not important. Enough time has been wasted. You must go—now." He waved at a passing guard. "I will inform Lady Anaya of your intentions. I am sure she will want to give you money and a squad for your journey, if for no other reason than to be rid of you for now."

CHAPTER FOUR

Karina pulled on her white leather jerkin and oiled pants and shoved her feet into the heavy boots required for traveling in the mountains. Her dark hair hung in a fat braid down her back. A quick look in the reflecting glass revealed dark circles under her blue eyes.

Not too long ago, those eyes had sparkled with joy from serving others, finding purpose as a healer in the royal house. All that was gone. Somehow, she had acquired the responsibility of managing a kingdom and protecting it as well. Her shoulders wilted under the weight.

Mauri held up Karina's brown knapsack and another bag. Her brow furrowed. "Are you sure you do not wish me to come along on this journey?"

Karina tucked a stray hair behind her ear. "No, Mauri. I need you to stay here to help with the farewell banquet and attend to whatever Lady Anaya needs." She clasped her friend's hands. "Besides, I would not willingly put you in harm's way."

Mauri threw her arms around Karina's neck, an outburst of affection not typical for the proper handmaid she loved. Karina embraced her friend in kind, not knowing if this would be their last time together. Surely not. Karina pulled away and lifted her cloak from the chair. "Shall we?"

Mauri followed Karina out the door where they nearly toppled over Jace.

White-faced and out of breath, he herded the girls back into the room, shutting the door behind them. "Karina, my dear, trouble surely follows you."

"What do you mean?"

He held up his hand while he caught his breath. "Anaya is sending guards to fetch you."

"What?" Karina sank onto the vanity chair. "Why?"

"She insists you poisoned the king."

Not that again. "Maybe I need to stay here and see this through. It won't go well for me if it looks like I'm running away."

"We need to get you out of here. Your quest for the Creator is more important than whatever lie Anaya has thought up to quell her grief. I will defend your reputation in your stead."

Mauri wrung her hands. "How do we get her out of here?"

Jace moved toward the door. "I will take care of the guards. Mauri, you take Karina down the back stairs and out through the kitchen. You'll find a bag by the door. Once outside, head straight for the stables."

"Yes, sir." Mauri gathered up Karina's belongings.

Someone rapped at the door.

They froze, looking at each other.

Another knock.

"What do we do?" Karina mouthed to Jace.

"Your Majesty, it is Captain DeMarco. I mean you no harm."

Jace sighed as he opened the door. "Get in here!" Pulling the captain inside, he searched the hallway behind him before shutting the door again.

Captain DeMarco readjusted his ebony breastplate and smoothed his somewhat wild hair. After he surveyed the room, he gave a quick nod. "I told Queen—er—Lady Anaya I would seek out Karina myself. That will give you a short amount of time to escape."

He turned to Karina. "Your Majesty, over the years I have observed your close relationship to the king. I cannot believe you would have harmed him. I pledge my loyalty to you, as I did your uncle. I understand you will be going on a quest given to you by the Creator himself."

She nodded.

"Then I will do my best to make sure you succeed. I have instructed four of my most trusted knights to meet you outside the castle walls. They are aware Anaya is on the warpath, but that you are not guilty of killing the king." He took Karina's outstretched hand in his own.

"And I trust you will look after Calliope—and all of Aletheia—in my stead," she said.

"Of course. Then you wish me to be your regent?"

"Yes. You have always been loyal to the king's family. He trusted you above anyone else—you were his regent. I know you will do what is right in the eyes of the Creator."

Captain DeMarco knelt and gently kissed her outstretched hand. "Thank you, Your Majesty."

Karina ruffled at the term but remained composed as the captain stepped away.

Jace held out a bag of coins. "This is all I have."

Karina suddenly felt exhausted and very sad. "I cannot take your money, Jace."

"You must. You will not get far without money for supplies. Anaya refused to give you any, but I did retrieve this from the king's chambers." He reached into the pocket of his dusty blue robe and pulled out a signet ring—a large stone the color of the sun with an A etched in silver. "This should help if you run into any money trouble."

Captain DeMarco held up his hand. "While I do suggest you take the signet ring, Your Majesty, Jace's money is not necessary. The lieutenant I'm sending with you has plenty. You will not want for anything."

"Thank you, Captain." Jace smiled as he handed the ring to Karina. "It is time we say goodbye." He offered the Blessing of Three Kisses. "Be safe and trust the Creator always."

She resisted the urge to cling to him as she did when they first met so long ago.

Captain DeMarco bowed. "Send word if you ever need anything. Hopefully, by the time you return, we will have cleared your name."

Not likely.

"We'll watch the front stairs. You take the back." Jace took one last look, then the men left.

Mauri snatched the ring, placed it on a long chain, and hung the chain around Karina's neck. "Tuck that in. We need to leave now."

Mauri peeked out to make sure the hallway was empty. They hurried down the back stairs, then through a short hall to the kitchen. The savory smells of meat and vegetables made Karina's empty stomach growl. She had not eaten much since dinner two nights past, and who knew when she would have time to eat a proper meal again.

The cook and her servants bustled about the kitchen, looking up long enough to bow their heads as Karina passed through.

As Jace instructed, Mauri grabbed the burlap sack near the door.

The kitchen was not far from the stables, but Karina and Mauri kept to the shadowed walls, stepping into direct sunlight only when necessary. A swoosh of air followed them into the stables.

Sam jumped up from the tack box in the corner. "What are you doing here?"

Mauri dropped the bags to lift Karina's saddle from its peg. "We need to get Karina out of here."

"What?" His eyes widened and then narrowed at Karina. "Why?"

"Because Anaya thinks I killed King Pistis."

He chuckled. "That woman is impossible. Crazy, even."

Karina crossed her arms. "There is no humor in this, Sam."

"She's serious." Mauri wiped her hands on her apron. "Can you help me with this saddle? We have to hurry."

Sam looked from Karina to Mauri, then hurried around the corner.

Karina slumped against the nearest stall. Her head swam with myriad thoughts. Why did Anaya persist with her accusations? Where was Aletheia's sacred temple? Had the Creator completely deserted the land because of Karina's resistance to the Creator's call?

Sam returned with Lady Belle behind him. He lifted the saddle with ease. "Where are you going?"

Karina stroked Lady Belle's honey-colored hide. "The Temple of Aletheia."

"Why?"

Karina picked up the bags as Sam secured the saddle and finished preparing the horse. "I wish I had time to explain, but I must get out of here. Mauri will fill you in."

He shook his head. "I'm going with you."

"No. I need you to stay here."

"Not going to happen."

"Look." Karina glared as she jabbed his chest. "I am not going to put anyone else's life in danger. I want you here. And here you will stay. On my orders!"

Sam muttered something unintelligible as he shrank back. Would he listen this time?

As she mounted Lady Belle, he stepped forward. "Karina, wait." He reached into his pockets and then placed an object in her hand. "Here—in remembrance."

"Thank you, Sam." She opened her hand to find a pounded piece of pewter in the shape of the sun with a thin, black rope threaded through a hole at the top. "Did you make this?"

His sheepish grin never failed to bring her joy, even in times like this.

She examined her gift, admiring each detail, her eyes stinging with tears she refused to let fall. Her life was being turned on end once again, stability pulled from under her feet. She was leaving her best friends. *Oh, Creator, protect them!* She inhaled deeply and then pulled the necklace over her head. "It's perfect."

Shouts came from beyond the stable doors.

"Hurry!" Mauri waved her arms. "Go out the east gate." She threw open the stable doors. "Go!"

Karina pressed her horse into a gallop, fleeing the cover of the stables.

A squad of men in chainmail swarmed into the square between the royal house and the stable. How could so many turn on her at the mere word of the former queen? Yet others remained as loyal to Karina as Captain DeMarco did.

She urged Lady Belle to move faster. They raced through the streets in a serpentine fashion. The horse's mane rippled in the wind like waves in the ocean.

The postern gate loomed ahead. Closed.

Karina groaned. What should she do now? She eased Lady Belle into a trot as Karina answered her own question. She squared her shoulders and lifted her chin. She must convey authority.

"Good day, Your Majesty," shouted a guard who stood near the gray-stone wall. "Escaping the crowds?"

She nodded, not trusting her voice at the moment.

"I wouldn't want to be amidst all those people either." He motioned for the men to open the gate.

Lady Belle pranced beneath her, as if she sensed Karina's fear.

A shout came from behind them.

She pulled Lady Belle around in time to see mounted guards racing toward her.

The heavy gates creaked as they swung open. Karina breathed a sigh of relief and snapped the reins.

If not for her fear, she would be amused at the wall guard's apparent confusion at the melee. His grimace was a reminder of the time she and Sam switched the king's watered wine for soured berry juice. The memory induced a pang of grief, but she subdued the emotion. She must be done with mourning.

The guard 's expression hardened as he bellowed. "Close the gate!"

The gates paused before they began to swing inward. Karina urged Lady Belle forward. "Faster, Lady Belle," she whispered. The doors were almost closed. Maybe they could squeeze through …

And then she was out the gate.

She raced into the protection of the boulders and barren trees beside the walls. Soft snow deadened the pounding of Lady Belle's hooves. She located Captain Demarco's men a short distance from the main gate. Could she trust them?

Behind her, guards spilled into the woods. She must make a quick decision. Captain DeMarco said they would protect her. She took a deep breath. Hopefully, he had not steered her wrong, or this would be a very short quest.

Not wanting to reveal her hiding place to anyone else, she called to them from the partial cover of the trees.

They turned and trotted toward her. The lieutenant removed his helmet and ran the back of his hand of his dark-skinned forehead. "Your Majesty, what's going on in there?"

Karina breathed a sigh of relief. Henry—another dear friend. He would not betray her. "Anaya thinks I killed the king."

"Captain DeMarco filled us in on the conflict. Why would she think you capable of something that horrendous?"

Karina hesitated, not certain how to answer Henry. "She believes I wanted the throne all along, though I did not know the kingdom would fall to me. Nothing I have done has convinced Anaya otherwise—I think she's overcome with grief and looking to place blame somewhere."

Henry shook his head. "Anyone who knows you knows you are incapable of such an act—especially against King Pistis." He paused before continuing. "So, Captain DeMarco said something about a quest?"

"Yes." She looked back toward the walls as guards gathered at the top. "I'll explain on the way. We are headed to the Temple of Aletheia."

Henry raised an eyebrow. "In Shadowed Forest?"

"You know where it is?"

"I've never been there, but I've heard rumors of its location, yes."

"Lead the way." She steered her horse around.

They rode hard across the Ice Plains. Snow crunched beneath the horses' hooves. A blanket of white stretched in all directions, the peaceful scene a stark contrast to Karina's raging thoughts. She struggled to keep her emotions under control. So much had happened in so little time.

The sun had descended behind the mountains. She longed for a chance to close her eyes, but Henry insisted they keep going until they reached the cover of Shadowed Forest. The Ice Plains were best passed in broad daylight when they could see the enemy coming.

Enemy? Was she already calling Anaya the enemy? What was her world coming to? She glanced back once more, still afraid the former queen would send soldiers after them, and at the same time praying the kingdom accepted Captain DeMarco as regent.

Once under the cover of the majestic trees, Henry called over his shoulder. "Halt!"

In front of them, a path extended into the woods before disappearing beneath the cathedral of limbs and pine needles. Branches grew over the path, shielding the ground from what little light the half-moon offered. Dead leaves mingled with the remnants of snow. The earthy smell soothed her spirit, even as Karina's heart still raced.

"Although the path is wide enough to ride in pairs, we will travel in a single line." Henry pointed to two of the knights. "Braun and Ewels, behind Her Majesty. Lars, you're behind me."

Karina cringed. Most of her friends did not address her so formally—her preference since being officially named the king's ward. Henry, or rather, Lieutenant Mason, as he preferred to be addressed—had insisted Karina be called by her proper title, even though he was only a couple years her senior, and they had played together as children before he joined the Royal Guard.

Braun and Ewels were both taller than the other two knights. Braun's sandy brown hair hung over his ears, and his gray eyes flitted back and forth as if he were constantly searching for something. Ewels was more carefree. Although Karina did not know him well, she had seen him in the royal house many times, often with a smile that was never far from laughter. His blue eyes reflected the sparkling snow beyond the tree line.

Karina had never met Lars, but she understood he had only been a knight for a few months. This was his first assignment beyond the capital city walls. His young face had yet to harden, and his blue-green eyes, hidden beneath a shock of red hair, had not yet lost their youthful gleam. He was the shortest, but his chin jutted out with rebellion, the urge to prove himself.

Henry chewed his lower lip as if he wanted to speak but did not dare.

"Out with it, Henry—I mean, Lieutenant Mason," Karina said.

"I'm not one for fanciful thinking, but the rumor is the ghost of an old witch roams these woods. I know several people from both Aletheia and Soter have disappeared amongst these trees. It's best we be as quiet as possible."

"Thank you, Lieutenant." Karina did not believe these stories either but that did not mean something—or someone— did not dwell within the woods to protect the sacred temple. Henry had said the temple was on the far side of Shadowed Forest, near the ocean. They had at least another day's journey, if not more, depending on weather and terrain.

The squad set out on the path as darkness closed in on them. She surveyed the trees on both sides. Some were short and spindly, the branches reaching out like ancient fingers. Others shot up straight to the sky, their canopies empty this time of year.

As they rode on, Karina felt certain they were being watched. The moon rose to its pinnacle in the sky, spreading its light through the barren branches. Shadows danced across the ground as thin limbs waved in the chilly evening wind.

At one point, two of the knights rode off. When they returned, they reported the royal guards had turned back to Calliope.

They approached the side of a large hill and found a small clearing. Henry held up his hand. "We will camp here tonight." He looked at each knight. "I'll stay here with the queen and unload. The rest of you search for firewood and fresh water. Stay within a horn's call."

The men scattered in different directions before Karina had dismounted. How wonderful to finally stretch. Had she ever been so sore before? Even her bones ached. She reached to unclasp her leather riding sack.

Henry stepped to her side. "Here, Your Majesty, allow me."

"I have it." She loosened the belt.

"No, really, I insist." He gently pushed her hands away and undid the belt.

"Henry!"

Her shrillness surprised even her. He stopped.

She inhaled slowly. "My apologies. Henry, you know I am quite capable."

He nodded. "You are. But you are also a queen, even without an official coronation. You must learn to allow others to assist you."

"Why do we stand on formalities out here in the middle of nowhere? You and I are friends. I would never want you to feel like things have changed so much you cannot call me Karina."

He smiled. "They *have* changed, Your Majesty. I can no more call you by your given name than I could your mother—er—aunt."

At the mention of Anaya, Karina wrinkled her nose. She backed down—for now—and found a decrepit log to sit on. "She will no longer claim me as her daughter or her niece."

"Beg your pardon, Your Majesty, but we should not discuss such matters." Henry dropped the sack beside her.

She cried as she threw her hands upward in protest. "If I cannot talk to you, who am I to talk to? Mauri and Sam are not here, and I do not have any other friends." She stared pointedly at Henry.

He frowned as a sad shadow passed over his face. "Your Majesty, I understand your frustration. I don't think you realize the implications informality can have on a kingdom, especially when others in places of power consider friendliness with servants as a weakness."

Of course, she had not considered how much her life would change. Why would she? She had been only a *pretend* princess for half her life. Not like she was privy to affairs of royalty. She huffed as she prepared a pit for the fire, using a large stick to loosen the dirt while Henry unloaded their supplies. At least he was smart enough to hold his tongue as he worked.

The other men returned with wood and water aplenty. The sack Mauri had picked up in the kitchen contained various vegetables, meats, and breads. Once the fire was lit, one of the guardsmen concocted a hearty stew. They enjoyed a delightful meal with the knights trading exaggerated stories of their adventures, despite an occasional disapproving glare from Henry.

Before the night turned late, Henry stood and stretched. "We have an early morning tomorrow. Let's seek our dreams and prepare for what is to come. Four watches tonight, two hours each. Ewels, you take first, then down the line. I'll take the final shift." He turned to Karina. "Your Majesty, I bid you good dreams."

She nodded, and the men prepared the camp for the night. The wind howled through the trees along the hillside. Far off, a lupen called to its mate, who answered moments later.

Karina stared at the sky.

"No worries, Your Majesty," Henry whispered. "The lupens don't often venture into these woods. Take your ease and dream well."

She climbed onto the makeshift bed and nestled underneath the wool blankets.

The first knight took up his position beside the fire. The other men laid with their heads propped up on large rocks, except for Henry, who used his knapsack as a pillow.

Surrounded by trees, Karina felt trapped. She could not see past the tree line, and who knew what lay beyond? Her muscles ached as if she'd been battered and bruised. A cold draft seeped into her bed as she settled in. She pulled the blankets to her chin for more warmth. What she wouldn't give for a mug of aromatic callow tea and a grand fireplace with a cozy chair in which to read an old manuscript. She smiled at the thought. After hours of tossing and turning, she finally drifted into a fitful sleep.

A twig cracked.

Karina jolted upright. Typical sounds—the hum of bugs, the crackle of the fire—filled the night. In the low firelight, everyone seemed asleep except for Ewels, who sat close to the flames, whittling a chunk of wood. Apparently, he had not heard anything. She rose, using her blanket as a cloak.

Apparently noticing Karina's movements, Ewels placed the wood on the stone beside him. He brushed off stray bits and stood. "Is there something I can help you with, Your Majesty?"

"Did you hear that?"

He shook his head. "Hear what?"

"That sound. I thought I heard a twig snap."

He chuckled. "Was probably an animal. They won't come too close to the fire. Scares 'em."

She chewed on her lip. Intuition urged otherwise.

When she didn't move, he smirked, his eyes dancing in the firelight. "If you'd like, I can do a perimeter sweep, make sure there's nothing out there."

She let out a huge sigh. "Would you? Please?"

"I'll be right back." He picked up his shield and soon disappeared into the forest.

Karina edged closer to the fire and stoked the flames, welcoming its warmth.

Why have you come?

Karina jumped at the voice in her head. She glanced at the sleeping men, but they seemed undisturbed. Did the voice speak only to her?

Why have you come? the disembodied voice asked again.

She glanced toward the forest. Nothing but inky darkness. Not even the moonlight pierced the canopy beyond their clearing. She scanned the trees surrounding their camp. Only a common field hawk perched on a low branch. Why would a hawk be roaming at night?

Who are you?

"I am Karina," she whispered, careful not to wake the sleeping men who would think her insane.

Why have you come to Shadowed Forest? The voice was distinctly feminine but did not seem angry, merely curious, possibly defensive.

"I am seeking the sacred temple in these woods."

For what reason?

Karina squared her shoulders. She did not have to answer to a faceless entity. "Who are you?"

I am Rashka, Guardian of Shadowed Forest. Again, I ask. For what reason do you seek the temple?

She could only imagine what the entity would think of her quest, but what else could she say? "The Creator sent me."

The Creator charged the guardian to protect the temple from those who would destroy it.

"No! I do not wish that." She put a hand over her mouth as Henry shifted positions. She had to calm down, speak quieter. How could she convince this being that she intended no harm? "There is an evil coming. Garon, the Creator's servant, told me to retrieve the Armor of the Creator."

A bright light shimmered from where the hawk sat on the tree branch. As quickly as the light had appeared, it vanished. Beneath the branch where the hawk had perched stood an elven woman with eyes like gold and hair blacker than midnight. Her skin was pale, but smooth and perfect. She held a large bow with an empty quiver strapped to her back. She stepped toward Karina.

Karina stumbled back, hitting a fallen log.

Rashka smirked. "You? The Creator chose you?"

She scowled. "You know nothing of me."

Even more amused, Rashka raised an eyebrow. "Oh, but I do, Karina. You are the daughter of the traitor, heir of Aletheia."

"How do you know these things?"

"The woods speak in whispers. I hear most everything."

Before Karina could respond, a yell sounded from behind Rashka, and Ewels charged at her from the trees. The other men leapt from their resting places, swords in hand.

"No, wait!" Karina called out. "Stop!"

Either the men did not hear her, or they chose to ignore her pleas. They swept toward Rashka, poised to attack.

Unabashed, Rashka jumped, then disappeared in a flash of light. The hawk returned, soared up into the sky and circled the campsite.

I will let the Temple Trium know of your arrival. They will want to prepare.

Karina's throat tightened. Prepare? That did not sound promising at all.

CHAPTER FIVE

Tristan hunched over his table in the corner of the Burok Inn, facing the door. The hazy atmosphere reeked of smoke and liquor, both equally repulsive. From beneath his hooded cloak, he watched the jovial crowd—ignorant of life around them—though a few nearby imbibers tossed an occasional wary glance his way.

The plump barmaid, a new hire, stopped by his table once more. "You sure I can't get you anything? Ham said you usually order a mug of callow tea." An overly wide grin shoved her lips into her chubby cheeks.

He offered his own tight smile as he shook his head. Business first. Waiting in River Branch was quickly trying his nerves. Faramos had said he didn't have much time, emphasizing how essential this task was.

The barmaid traipsed over to the next table, leaving him in peace.

"Hey, let go of me!"

From the other side of the room, another barmaid struggled against a man twice her size. Her blond hair loosened from its leather tie as she pulled away.

"Just one kiss," the man slurred.

Ham slammed a mug on the bar. "Leave her be. This is a respectable establishment!"

The ogre-like man glared. Ham was neither weak nor small, but he was still no match for the instigator, who towered at least six inches over him.

The drunk pointed at the barmaid. "I'll pay you well for time with her."

The woman shrieked and kicked the man in the shin.

"Feisty." He grinned, gripping her arm.

Tristan glowered. *Disrespectful, arrogant pig.* His may not be a savory job, but at least he had a few boundaries.

The man tore at the barmaid's puffy sleeve. "Oops. Let me help you with that."

Tristan retrieved a dagger from his sleeve and sent it flying. It caught the offender's hand before he could further assault the poor woman. Howling in pain, the brute fell into a table, then crashed to the floor. He lay on top of the heap, moaning.

Tristan smirked. *Serves him right.*

The man's comrades lifted him from the floor. "We're sorry," one of them mumbled as they helped him out of the tavern.

Ham rushed to the woman's side, exchanged a few words, and pointed to the door. With a quick smile, she grabbed a cloak from beside the door and left with another man. Perhaps someone she knew who had promised to keep her safe.

The innkeeper kicked at the fallen table as he surveyed the damage. The rest of the crowd went back to their drinks, but Ham turned and stared at Tristan, who held his gaze but didn't move. Ham gave a barely discernible nod.

The door banged open again. A stout man with a scruffy beard rushed inside. His soiled hat covered a mop of dirty brown hair. He nodded to the tavern keeper, then made his way to the corner table where Tristan sat.

Tristan gazed up at the man. "I trust you have news for me."

"I do. Drinks first?" The man sat.

Tristan shook his head. "First the news."

The man scowled. "Very well. The rumors are true. King Pistis died four mornings past. However, the Captain of the Guard is not the one to take the throne."

"Of course not. His brother's offspring has first right."

The man sat back in his chair, brow furrowed. "How did you know?"

"I have my ways."

"Turns out the offspring had been living in the royal house the whole time. Queen Anaya accused her of killing the king, and the girl took off."

Tristan raised an eyebrow and leaned forward as his informant continued.

"She left yesterday evening, traveling off the main road toward Soter. I'm not sure where she's going. Most of the information I obtained is hearsay."

Tristan stood. If *Queen* Karina were on a religious quest, as Faramos had suggested, most likely she was headed to the sacred temple on the other side of Shadowed Forest. If he left now, he would catch up to them before they reached the temple.

He flipped a coin to the man. "Well done. If I need more information, I will find you."

She looked harmless.

Tristan remembered the twig of a girl he'd met in his youth—he, a mere boy of seven; she, an innocent girl of four. This woman barely resembled the ramshackle creature who strutted into the throne room, her dress covered in dirt and her hair poking out of a tangled braid. Very nice.

The sun had already descended, sapping the warmth of the day. Clouds drifted in from the north. Tristan peered over the edge of the overhang to watch the busyness below.

Aletheia's new queen wandered about the small camp beneath the outcropping. She didn't look like she could squish a bug, much less topple anyone's master plan. He contemplated his mission. Faramos wanted this girl alive. He had paid Tristan for her capture, not for questions.

Before settling down, the young queen rolled out a leather skin blanket on a large, flat stone close to the fire. She unloosed her braid of smooth dark hair. When one of the knights called her name, she lifted her head and smiled. She chatted while she helped with the evening meal. The men seemed to enjoy her company, which Tristan found hard to imagine. Royals were all the same—conceited, rude, only interested in money or power … or both.

A light snow fell as two of the knights finished tying a makeshift tent over the camp. Soon the night would be full dark, and the travelers would seek their dreams. Lucky them.

Tristan pulled back from the edge, found a smoother path, and made his way to the camp, remaining out of sight. Karina was asleep. Three of the knights rested on the other side of the fire. The fourth had apparently been assigned first watch and leaned against a boulder at the opposite end of the camp.

Best to wait a couple of hours. Tristan retreated behind a large pile of rocks.

In the emptiness of the night, the sounds of scurrying nocturnal animals brought him some comfort. Not that he needed comfort. He preferred the night, the peace. He closed his eyes and rested.

When the half-moon hid behind the veil of passing clouds, Tristan rose. He tucked his light brown hair under a hood and readjusted his black jerkin. He pulled several daggers from his belt, a precaution as he ambled toward the camp. He preferred not to kill innocent bystanders—in fact, he preferred not to kill at all. He'd seen enough death to last him three lifetimes. In his line of work, though, avoiding the kill wasn't always possible.

To his surprise, the guard had managed to stay awake. Courageous. That was fine. Tristan would still obtain his objective. He circled the camp, his breaths shallow and quiet. A massive boulder towered over the guard, who stood less than a five-man span from the huge rock. Tristan rested against the outcropping, scanning the area.

Now.

He placed the knives back into his belt. With a running start, he leapt onto the boulder and then quietly climbed to the top. The knight stood below Tristan, rubbing his hands together. He needed a distraction. He pulled one of the daggers from his sleeve and tossed the knife to his right.

Startled at the clink of metal on rock, the guard drew his sword and took several hesitant steps toward the noise.

"What was that?" one of the other knights shouted.

The guard waved his comrade away.

Without a sound, Tristan dropped on top of the guard and squeezed his throat with practiced precision. The guard sank to the cold ground.

"Intruder!" the other knight shouted as he charged at Tristan.

The two other men rolled from their beds, weapons ready.

Tristan easily sidestepped the first knight. He shoved his booted foot into the man's back. The knight stumbled and smacked into a tree, then slouched to the ground in a heap.

Karina scrambled out from beneath the pile of wool blankets, her eyes wide with fright.

"No need to fear, Your Highness. I assure you I intend you no harm."

"Get away from her!" the knight with dark skin ordered. He lunged toward Tristan's middle. Dodging the man's thrust, Tristan landed a punch to his nose. He stumbled. The young knight with red hair stepped in, swinging wildly.

Tristan managed to stay ahead of the blade. He weighed his options. *Use the terrain, Tristan.* He grabbed a tree branch with both hands. Swinging forward, he planted his feet on the knight's chest. The poor lad fell backward against the dark-skinned knight, and they both toppled to the ground, moaning. Tristan delivered a swift punch to each of their temples. That would put them out for a while.

He smacked the dirt from his hands, then turned toward the queen—who had disappeared.

He swore, retrieved his dagger, then circled the camp. He found a set of small footprints leading from the camp to the trees. He followed their serpentine trail. A familiar lavender scent wafted toward him—Karina's scent. He picked up his pace.

Ahead, twigs snapped in the snow—the sounds of fleeing royalty, most likely. He could easily outrun her. He pushed through the trees and underbrush.

A shout echoed through the woods. What had she done? He emerged from a cluster of trees to find Karina had fallen to her knees.

She glanced up at him, fear in her eyes. "Who are you?"

"Not someone to trifle with." He took a step toward her.

"What do you want? Are you going to kill me?"

He shook his head. "If I were going to, you'd have never seen me coming. No, I'm supposed to bring you in alive."

Her pretty features scrunched together "You—you're a bounty hunter?"

"Yes'm. Now, we have a four-day journey ahead. I much prefer to do this the easy way. I have two horses camped around the bend."

She shuffled backward.

"I would advise against resistance."

She glanced over her shoulder.

Don't do it. He stared her down. When she didn't move, he held out his hand and stepped forward.

She bolted.

He cursed, then sprinted after her.

She tore through the trees. But with no aim or direction, her flight posed little challenge. A mere arm span distanced them. Her ragged breath revealed her waning strength. With a grunt, he grabbed her around the waist.

Karina toppled forward … her body went limp. A trickle of blood stained the white snow.

He groaned. The stubborn woman had hit her head on a stone. Now he'd have to carry her back. Why didn't she listen? He lifted her over his shoulder. Too bad he didn't have any rope on him, or he could have tied her up, then run for the horses. A much easier option.

Karina rubbed her sore temple. Had someone knocked her upside the head with the hilt of a broadsword? Her eyes begged to remain closed. For some reason, she did not feel the stir of the wind nor could she hear creatures scurrying around in the underbrush.

She groaned as she turned to her side, forcing her eyes open. Across from her, a gentle fire flickered in the hearth of an old fireplace. Shadows danced in cadence with the bouncing flames. She lay upon a straw mat and was covered with a wool blanket. On the wall to her left was a simple wooden table and two chairs. To her right, a battered door let in the whine of the early morning wind. Through a tiny window next to the door, she could make out the first wisps of dawn rising over the mountain range.

The thuds of heavy footsteps came from outside.

Karina sat up as events came rushing back to her. The man in the woods. Running. Falling. That explained her pain.

The door slammed against the wall, and the mysterious man entered, carrying an armful of firewood. He wasn't a large man, but the contour of his chest and arms showed through his fitted shirt. What he lacked in size, he made up for in agility as evidenced from his attack.

She hitched a breath. *Give me courage, Creator.* She peered at the fortifications. Escape would not be easy—if at all possible.

The man dropped the wood against the far wall and turned toward her. Not a hint of light or laughter shone from his emerald eyes—in fact, his presence felt cold, empty. She almost pitied him.

"Finally awake?" He rifled through a knapsack on the table, then tossed her a chunk of bread and a wheel of cheese. "I suppose I might have given you too much of the sleeping drought when you started to come to during the ride here. You might have a headache for a while."

She stared at him. Who was he? What did he want?

He grunted, taking a bite of bread. "Eat and get some rest. We leave in a couple of hours." He finished his meal and then plopped down with his back against the far wall and closed his eyes.

Once more she looked over at the door.

"There's nothing around here for miles."

She startled, then glanced back at the man. He hadn't moved.

"If you run, you'll freeze before you find shelter." He opened his eyes, his gaze hard, almost cruel. "Besides, I have the eyes and ears of a lupen. You'd never make it past the tree line."

Karina looked down at the food in her lap. Might as well eat, though she had no appetite. What was to become of her? Surely this was not what the Creator had planned. She took a few bites. Overcome with drowsiness, she lay down on the mat. Perhaps the sleeping draught had not worn off entirely.

CHAPTER SIX

When Karina awakened, the sun appeared to be at mid-day. The man trampled about the room throwing things into a large knapsack.

"Where are you taking me?"

He glanced up from the table. With a flick of his head, he brushed away a lock of hair that had fallen over his eyes. "Not sure you want to know."

She contemplated the worst possibility. "Please. I mean, if I cannot escape, then I would like to prepare myself for what lies ahead."

"Faramos."

She gasped. Her uncle had mentioned Faramos' name before he died. "The warlock? What does he want with me?"

The man grunted. "I haven't a clue." He placed the remnants of their food into the bag. "Something about you toppling his plans."

"Me?"

"Let's go." He swung the knapsack over his shoulder, ambled toward the door, then paused to glance back. He tugged the hilt of the short sword at his waist. "Are we doing this the easy way today? I'd hate to see you mar that pretty face more than you already have."

More? She ran her hand over her forehead and found a small cut near her hairline, tender to the touch and caked with dry blood.

"Did you happen to grab my bag when you kidnapped me?"

"Perhaps if you hadn't run, I might have." He strutted out the door before she could debate the matter.

Of all the rude, incompetent men! She huffed as she snatched her cloak from the chair and then opened the door to search for the man. From around the corner, she heard the nicker of a horse. If he was tending to the horses …

She glanced in the other direction. Was there time to make it to the tree line? She dashed toward the woods.

"Hey!"

She would not let the man's shout deter her. She would escape. The Creator did not choose the wrong person for this quest.

Strong footsteps thudded behind her. She ran as fast as she could, but she was not used to this sort of exercise. Her sides ached, each breath a burning struggle. She dashed into the trees, shoving aside twigs and dodging bushes. No stopping. Not until she was free. The man's hard body slammed into hers, and they both tumbled to the ground, rolling to a stop beside a copse of trees. Dazed, Karina could not even move.

"Cofounded woman!" The man's face was red with rage, though he was hardly out of breath.

Karina swallowed, unable to speak.

Her silence only seemed to fuel the man's anger. He grabbed her wrist, yanked her to her feet, and dragged her out of the woods in spite of her struggling.

In front of the dilapidated cottage, a large stallion, the color of midnight, stomped at the ground. Beside the magnificent beast, a brown horse with gentle eyes nudged Karina's hand as they approached.

She must escape. Perhaps if she lulled the man into complacency—made him think she'd given up—when he let down his guard, she would make a run for the temple. Then they would see who would have the last laugh.

With little more than a grunt, the man lifted Karina onto a makeshift saddle. She studied his face, the hard contours and the weathered skin. What kind of man was he that he would steal a woman in the dead of night?

"Might I know your name?" Karina rendered a thin smile. "I mean, if we are to be traveling together."

He eyed her through squinted slits. "Tristan." With seemingly practiced grace, he mounted, then grabbed the reins of her steed. "No more trouble today."

The gruff whisper of his voice held enough warning to elicit a small nod from her.

They traveled in silence for most of the afternoon, except for Tristan's barked orders when they stopped for a late afternoon meal. The sun sank low on the horizon, casting the woods into premature darkness. They emerged from the tree line to find a well-traveled road. Karina glanced both ways but saw no one else. "Where are we?"

Tristan nodded to his left. "Soter's that way." He pointed to his right. "And the other way leads back to Calliope."

She remembered now. She gazed at the towering mountains in the distance. The royal house in Calliope rested at the base of the mountains beyond the Ice Plains. A sigh escaped her lips. She stole a glance at Tristan, who seemed to ignore her.

He led them to the left, toward Soter. "When we get to River Branch, we'll refill supplies. I'd prefer to spend the night at an inn rather than on the trail." He brandished his dagger as a warning. "You will not say a word to anyone. At all. Pretend to be a mute if you must." He leaned toward her. "If you do not do as I say, the rest of the trip will be most unpleasant. Faramos said I had to bring you in alive, but he was not specific as to your condition otherwise. Do I make myself clear?"

She returned his glare. "Crystal clear."

An hour later, they entered the mud-ridden streets of River Branch, a village Karina knew bordered Aletheia. She estimated the bridge to Soter to be only half an hour beyond the southern edge.

Karina took in the sights and sounds of the hustling town. Men with stick carriers layered with animal furs maneuvered their way through the streets. Women with gourds mounted on their heads scurried from the well. Everyone averted their gaze. Not a friendly place—though not surprising for an outpost village where strangers stopped for no longer than a night. As instructed, Karina remained quiet but made note of every building, every potential hiding place.

Tristan led them to one of the larger buildings. Its white-washed, wooden slats were new compared to the rest of the town.

"Is this—"

A sharp glare from Tristan silenced her. This man was unyielding.

She sighed. She must be patient. The Creator would provide a means of escape … in his time.

Tristan helped her dismount, then gripped her waist as he leaned in next to her ear. She inhaled the sweet smell of sweat and some sort of foreign soap. He pulled back to look her in the eye. "Do not forget my warning, Your Majesty."

She held her head high and refused to acknowledge his threat.

They entered the well-kept inn during the evening meal. A few men dotted the tables, laughing as they sloshed mugs of ale. A barmaid approached with an attentive smile. "Tristan! Back so soon?"

He returned her smile. "Yes, I am, Cara. We need a room for the night."

The barmaid wrinkled her nose, studying Karina as one assesses a romantic rival, then blew stray strands of black hair from her eyes. "Not a problem. I think there's a couple available. Ham's behind the bar." She peered at Karina once more. "Looks like you could use a good night's rest."

"That she does," Tristan wrapped his arm around Karina's shoulder. "It's been a long trip, and we still have far to travel. Is there a stable hand to care for our horses?"

"I'll send my boy."

Tristan nodded. "Thank you, Cara."

Maybe this villain had a civil side after all.

Cara giggled as she headed toward a different table, not the least bit shy as she tossed another glance over her shoulder.

The man Tristan called Ham scratched his oversized belly as he led them up the stairs. "Will you be needing one room or two?"

"One," Tristan replied with a wide grin.

Karina bit back a protest. A respectable woman did not share a room with a man who was not her husband.

Ham stopped at a room halfway down the hall. "Here you go. Food?"

"Yes, please. Could you have two plates and ale brought up?"

Ham laughed. "Sure thing." He nudged Tristan's shoulder with a brotherly tease. "By the way, thanks again for your help the other night. Some men don't know when they've had enough to drink."

"I know what you mean." Tristan stepped aside to let Ham amble back down the hall.

Karina scanned the quaint quarters. Simple decorations and minimal lighting. A small dresser sat in one corner opposite a table with two chairs. In the middle, a bed covered with a ragged, blue blanket stuck out from a wall. She sighed as she sank onto the rather large bed—the only bed. She gasped.

Tristan snickered as he closed the door behind him. "Do not worry for your honor, Your Majesty." He threw a pillow and extra blanket on the floor. "I'll sleep here."

Praise the Creator for small favors. "When will we go out for supplies?"

Tristan unlaced his boots. "First thing in the morning. For tonight, we eat, and then we'll sleep."

Karina woke with the dawn, mesmerized by the pink rays filtering through the smoky glass. The night had passed uneventfully. Although sleep had come slowly, she had slept soundly enough to ignore the soft snoring coming from Tristan's spot on the floor.

She stared at the door. Would he hear her if she slipped out of the room? She could enlist Ham's help or maybe the barmaid. Friends of Tristan's or not, surely, they would not betray her once they realized who she was. After all, they were still in Aletheia.

As she eased out of bed, the wooden bed frame creaked. She froze, not daring to breathe, expecting Tristan to leap into action.

He snorted, then turned on his side.

Ears of a lupen? Karina smirked.

Her shoes and cloak were by the table, but she did not dare venture that close to Tristan. No point in waking the dragon until she found reinforcements. Instead, she tiptoed across the room and gently pulled the door open. The wood scraped across the floor, the hinges whining in protest. Her breath caught in her throat. She eyed Tristan and sighed with relief at his soft snore. With renewed courage, she stepped into the hall and shuffled to the top of the stairs.

The clanking of mugs below meant someone must be up and about—perhaps Ham, preparing the morning meal. She grasped the railing and stepped toward the clatter.

Rough hands snaked around her mouth and waist, then yanked her backward. She struggled to regain her footing.

Tristan dragged her into the room, pushed the door shut with his foot, then shoved her up against the wall, pinning her wrists beneath his vise-like hand. His eyes filled with rage as he waved his dagger under her chin.

Would he really slit her throat and lose his bounty? Inside, every muscle quivered, begging to be released from the rising panic. But she pressed her lips together, meeting his glare with one of her own. She refused to give him the satisfaction of frightening her into submission.

With the vehemence of a crazed man, he roared and threw her onto the bed. His face flushed with hot anger.

Karina scrambled back against the headboard and wrapped her knees close to her chest. Her heart raced with the uncertainty of Tristan's next move. Was he going to yell at her? Beat her? Tie her up, throw her over one of the horses, and ride hard and fast to Faramos's fortress? She asked the Creator to protect her from this madman—this heartless bounty hunter with no thought of anyone but himself.

Tristan snatched a rope from his bag and fastened her arms to the headboard.

"What are you doing?" she yelled as he cinched the rope tighter. His icy eyes held not a trace of compassion. What had she done? "Tristan, please. You don't understand. The Creator—"

His eyes bulged. "Don't speak to me of the Creator."

Karina forced slow breaths as she sat back. So many questions she'd like to ask, but this was not the time. She pulled at the rope. "Tristan, please, I will not—"

He tied a rag over her mouth. "I'm going to get our supplies. Since I cannot trust you, you get to stay here." He slung his bag over his shoulder. At the door, he bowed. "Your Majesty."

Karina struggled against the ropes until her wrists bled. "This is useless!" She kicked the bed like a child in a full-blown tantrum. What did the Creator expect from her?

Some said the followers of the Creator were bathed in light. Yet, how could this be true? Being a follower did not guarantee a life of ease. She remembered the darkness that chilled her bones in the days after her parents' slaughter—a horrific act she'd been forced to watch.

Now that King Pistis was dead, and Anaya had accused her of murder, Karina was orphaned once more. What good was she? How could the Creator possibly deem her worthy? With all her heart, she longed to speak to him—to the Creator—not just in prayer but face-to-face. The servant told her she would stop an imminent evil. Instead, an ancient evil was about to stop her.

A nugget of peace wiggled its way into her doubt. The servant also had said the Creator would never leave her. Surely, he knew her plight. Maybe these current struggles, as well as Tristan himself, were a part of the Creator's plan. She shook her head. Ludicrous. Tristan was not only an unbeliever, he wasn't even a good man.

She remembered her aunt's accusations, distrust borne from Karina's status through her father's lineage. Should she judge Tristan, a man she knew nothing about?

What was a glimmer of peace now filled her. Only the Creator knew where her captor fit within the master plan. Like it or not, she would have to trust the Creator did indeed have a plan for her, as well as Tristan.

Hours passed. Where was Tristan? Karina's stomach gurgled. She had yet to break her fast, and the morning sun had just begun to rise. She wrestled the ropes one more time. They cut deeper into her wrists, the pain so unbearable her eyes welled with tears.

Heavy footsteps pounded down the hall. The door opened.

Karina shrunk back against the headboard. What would Tristan do now?

He stormed into the room, threw a plate onto the table, and stomped toward the bed. Karina braced herself. He untied her and, with barely a glance at her wrists, pulled her up and then forced her to sit at the table. "Eat. We leave in five minutes."

"But—"

His glare warned her to be silent.

She turned to the spread before her—a chunk of bread, two eggs, and a square of cheese. She wanted to ask for a glass of milk to wash down the dry meal, but Tristan's mood had not lightened a bit. She choked down the food.

"Get up. We're leaving." He ushered her outside and helped her mount the smaller horse. He mounted his stallion and took the reins to her horse. His constant glare assured her any attempts at escape would not end well for her.

Tristan led them away from town. Most likely, he would follow the river through the Barrens, the desert at the base of the Aletheian mountain ranges. From there, they would probably cross the river into Tzedek, ending up at Faramos's fortress.

The tales of Faramos's dark magic had spread through the three kingdoms. Some said he had even killed his father, the former king of Tzedek. The Barrens isolated Faramos's fortress, so the Aletheians had not feared him. However, rumors of border skirmishes between Soter and Faramos's army had reached Aletheia. Without a formal call for help, they dared not interfere. Magic was not to be tampered with and avoided when possible.

As they neared the river, Tristan turned onto a barely discernible trail. They had not traveled much further when tortured cries broke the silence. Tristan slowed the horses.

A man yelled, "Melinda, you have to bend your knees and push!"

"I'm trying, I'm trying," a softer, feminine voice whined.

Through the trees, Karina spotted a small buckboard wagon. Beside it, a young woman wrung her hands. Where was the man? The wagon was cockeyed—the front wheel at a strange angle. From beneath the wheel, the man screamed in pain.

Karina glanced at Tristan.

He sniffed as he guided the horses away from the trouble.

"Mama, what's going to happen to Papa?"

Karina peered over her shoulder. The woman handed a small, red fruit to a petite girl with fair hair and a younger boy. "Tristan, they need help."

"Be quiet," he growled, yanking the reins.

"The man is injured and stuck. His wife and children cannot get him out alone. Few travel this path. We might be the only ones who pass by."

"That is their problem. We do not need to make it ours."

The man cried out in pain once again.

"We cannot just let them suffer. What about the children?"

Tristan remained rigid as he circled the wagon and continued away from the travelers. Would he listen to one more attempt at reason? "I know you are a mighty bounty hunter, but these are innocent people who need a hand."

He shook his head as he plodded forward.

How could he be so insensitive? Seeing no other choice, Karina threw herself off the horse and landed on her hip. She groaned as she rolled to her back.

Tristan cursed as he dismounted and ran toward Karina.

She pushed herself to her feet. Walking backward, she held up her hand. "I will scream if you do not agree to help them."

"And what if I do?"

She gazed toward the canopy. What could she offer him? She had no money—not even her uncle's signet ring. She sighed. "I promise I will not be any more trouble."

"Really?" He raised an eyebrow.

"I will stay with you until we reach Faramos's fortress. I will not try to escape."

He shook his head.

"I give you my word as Queen of Aletheia, I will give you no more trouble."

Tristan growled, and his eyes narrowed. "I don't know that your word is any good, but, since you are so determined, I'll help them anyway." He grabbed the horses' reins and stalked past her toward the family.

Thank you, Creator. She hurried after Tristan.

They entered the clearing together.

"What happened here?" Tristan asked as he tied their horses to a nearby tree.

The man glanced over his shoulder, his face red and sweaty. "Oh, praise the Creator! I thought we'd never see anyone on this trail. I was trying to fix the axle when the wagon rolled forward, trapping me under it."

The woman and children stood behind the wagon. Mother and daughter were dressed in similar gray dresses, a simple pattern, with their hair knotted at the back of their heads.

Karina smiled at the woman. "Are you all doing well?"

"Yes, m'lady. Thank you."

Tristan squatted beside the man, then glanced toward the woman. "Ma'am?"

She smiled. "Melinda, please."

Tristan gritted his teeth. "Melinda … could you come over here?" He motioned to Karina. "You too."

When they approached, he pointed to the wagon box. "Melinda, I want you to help me pick this corner up. Your Ma—Karina, you hold the wagon wheel. When we lift, the wheel will likely fall off. Just roll it out of the way."

She nodded.

"On the count of three." Tristan and Melinda grabbed the bottom of the wagon box. Karina held the wheel. "One … two … three." Tristan grunted as they strained to lift the wagon a hand's span. The wounded man moaned as the wheel fell away, and Karina rolled it off into the high grasses.

"Karina, pull him out." Tristan wheezed. "Hurry."

She rushed back and grabbed the man under the arms. She heaved several times, then finally managed to drag him free of the wagon.

"Papa!" The children flung their arms around their father's neck while Tristan and Melinda eased the wagon down.

Tristan ran a hand over his reddened face. "Well, folks—"

Karina shot him a look and shook her head. She turned back to the man and his family who knelt beside him. "I am a trained healer. Let me look at your leg." She gestured to Tristan. "And I'm sure my companion would have no trouble fixing that wheel for you."

"Yes, of course," Tristan muttered through clenched teeth.

CHAPTER SEVEN

"Where are you and your family coming from?" Karina asked as she cleaned the man's wound.

He winced with pain and his leg jerked. "Tzedek. We left our village on the northern edge."

"Why?"

Melinda looked back from her spot beside Tristan. "Faramos's evil is spreading throughout the villages. Those not loyal to his cause are murdered." Tears welled in her eyes. "Whole villages have been wiped out."

Tristan paused, mallet in mid-air, then resumed repairs to the wagon wheel without a word.

Karina fought against the rising panic, wanting to be brave for this family. She wondered what evil awaited her when she reached Faramos's territory.

"I couldn't let that happen to my family." The man wiped his sweaty brow. "When we heard the army was heading toward our village, we fled in the opposite direction. Of course, the only way north is through the Barrens."

"You're not far from a village. River Branch is just through these woods. I'm sure you can find rest there, possibly even a home." Karina tore a shirt Melinda had given her into strips. "At the least, you will need to seek a healer who can stitch your wound. I have nothing to sew with here."

The man glanced from Karina to Tristan. "I thank you for the help you provided—both of you."

Tristan's jaw twitched, but he managed a nod of acknowledgement.

"Where are you two headed?" Melinda asked.

Tristan brushed his hands on his pants as he stood. His glare warned Karina to let him answer. "To Braumin—a small fishing community in the southwest corner of Aletheia."

The man pushed up on his elbows. "Never heard of it."

Tristan and Karina helped the man into the back of the wagon, and the children scrambled up beside their father while Melinda hiked up her skirts and climbed atop the driver's bench. "You two be careful out there."

Tristan held out the reins to the brown horse. "Ready?"

Was that a trick of light, or did he briefly hesitate? She narrowed her eyes. Whatever flash of concern had been there was gone now, so she merely nodded. What had she been thinking, promising Tristan she would not try to escape? What horrors lay before her now? She took the reins. At the least, she could now command her own horse.

They continued for hours. The sun rose to its pinnacle, then began its descent in the west. Its light warmed her, a shield against the worrisome cold threatening her soul.

By late afternoon, the sky darkened with menacing thunderheads. An early spring storm was imminent, and they had yet to reach the Barrens.

"Tristan, shouldn't we be looking for shelter?" she called ahead to the same back she had been staring at since helping the family in the wagon.

"What do you think I'm doing?" he shouted without turning around.

Gale-force winds whipped the tops of the trees. Within minutes, the first drop of rain fell on Karina's nose. Too soon, the innocent drops turned to icy daggers, and Karina bowed her head to keep the sideways torrents from slashing her face. Her clothes were soaked through. Her teeth chattered, and her hands trembled. Unable to find shelter, they trudged on through the storm's worst temper.

They left the cover of the trees, and the Barrens stretched before them, dark and foreboding in the downpour.

"I think we need to get away from the river," she shouted to Tristan.

He slowed his horse and turned. "What?"

She pointed toward the rising waters to their left. "The river! We need to get away before it floods."

Tristan nodded, a lock of dark hair falling across his eyes. "There's a cave ahead. I've camped there before."

Lightning streaked across the sky, then a loud crack boomed behind them.

Karina's horse reared. She gripped the saddle horn.

Tristan grabbed for the reins, but her horse took off, ripping the leather strips from his grasp. "Karina!"

The world rushed by in a blur of darkness, made even more indiscernible by the heavy rain. To her left, the river overflowed its banks, and a stream of raging water rushed toward her. All she could do was hold on and pray for the Creator's help.

Above the raging storm, a clear voice whispered in her ear. *Open your eyes.*

She bit her lip and peeked out her right eye. Raindrops fell in sheets amid the darkness. She had to control this horse. Lady Belle always understood what Karina needed her to do. Not this stubborn mare.

She squinted. Through the torrent she could see an expanse spreading before her, unlike the firmness of the woods behind them. She strained to see a waterfall cascading from above into … into what? She could not tell for the water disappeared.

A cliff.

Her breath caught. The horse was going too fast, and she could not reach the reins.

"Whoa!" she commanded, but the horse ran even faster. "Stop!" She dug her heels into her flanks and pulled her mane.

Nothing.

Creator, help!

In a few seconds more, the horse would tumble over the ledge along with its rider. Karina could barely breathe, the blood rushing through her veins her only defense against the urge to faint. She knew what she had to do.

With one last cry to the Creator, she leapt from the horse. Her body slammed into the ground, then rolled several feet away from the drop. Her arm snapped underneath her. And all the air whooshed from her lungs as she came to rest in a pool of mud.

The foolish horse plummeted over the edge, her high-pitched screams fading into horrifying silence.

Instinctively, Karina curled into a ball, dazed, struggling to breathe. Rain splattered across her face. White-hot pain radiated down her right arm, so severe she could not even scream.

The rain eased to a steady drizzle as she succumbed to the enveloping darkness.

Warmth drew Karina from a surprisingly restful sleep. But from the moment she opened her eyes, agony became her companion. She noticed her arm was wrapped in a sling. She scanned her surroundings. How did she come to be in a cave? When she tried to sit, fiery pain seared through her arm, and she fell back down.

"I wouldn't try to move." Tristan sat several feet away, poking at a fire.

The cave offered some comfort, as well as a wide mouth that allowed a view of the Barrens. From somewhere behind her, water splashed on the rocks. Otherwise, all was quiet. A bright moon cast an eerie glow, washing the sparse tufts of grass in muted grays.

She felt warm, tucked under two wool blankets. Had Tristan deprived himself in order to help her? She gazed up at him. "What happened?"

"I was hoping you could tell me. I can't even find the mare you were riding."

She shivered as she remembered the horse's terrifying end. "I think—I think she went over the cliff."

Tristan raised an eyebrow. "Obviously, you jumped before that happened."

She stared at the dancing shadows on the cave's sand-colored walls and sniffed. "I tried to stop her, but she would not listen to my commands."

"That crazy horse was always a few apples short of a barrel." Tristan scooped stew from a pot on the fire. "Found you about a five-man's span from the edge, half-dead. Eat something."

She tried to raise her arm, the pain unbearable. "I broke it, didn't I?"

"Yes, but a clean break. I've splinted it—should heal just fine."

If I live that long. Still, his knowledge of field medicine surprised her.

Tristan gently helped her sit up, though the smallest jarring of her shoulder caused minutes of tortuous pain. At last, she leaned up against the cool stone, sweat trickling down her temples.

Tristan set a bowl and large spoon beside her. "There are herbs in the stew to ease your pain."

She fed herself with her good arm, amazed at the tasty rabbit and vegetables, and licked her lips. "So, a doctor and a cook? You are full of surprises."

Tristan grunted as he filled his own bowl.

"Where did you learn to cook?"

He shrugged. "It was either learn the ways of medicine and cooking or risk dying on the job."

Self-taught? "What of your family? Surely you must have family somewhere."

He glowered. "No."

Given his curt response, Karina decided to abort her attempt at conversation. She finished her stew in silence. With something warm in her belly, she soon surrendered to sleep.

When she finally roused, the sun shone, yet the cave remained cloaked in shadows. Her arm still ached but with much less intensity. A wave of dizziness swept over her as she pushed herself to her feet. She steadied herself against the cool stone. Where was Tristan?

The sound of birds singing brought her to the entrance, and she stepped outside. Another sound, a rumble of sorts, muffled nature's serenade. The cliff ... the horse's scream as she fell to her death ... Karina's own narrow escape from death. The memory of all she endured over the past several days stole her breath. She rested against the exterior cave wall.

With only one good arm, she struggled to pull on her cloak, noticing her blouse was ripped in several places, especially the sleeves, and her leather pants were streaked with grime. She couldn't imagine what the rest of her looked like. She couldn't even braid her hair like she would want. She went back inside where she untangled her hair and splashed cold water on her face.

She made her way back to the opening and gazed outside.

The mid-day sun beamed down on the rocks and sand. Hardly a tree in sight. Not surprising. Only a few plants dared to thrive in this environment. A sound like rumbling came from her right. Water sprang from a hole in the cliff-face high above her and tumbled to the chasm where the horse had fallen.

Karina took a few hesitant steps toward the abutment. Did she want to see how far down it went? Normally, heights did not bother her, but the horse's haunting cry as it dove to its death sickened her. She peered over the edge and swallowed ... a long way down.

"Should you be that close to the edge?"

Karina squeaked as she hopped back, then glared at Tristan. "What do you think you are doing, scaring me like that?"

He smirked. "I beg your pardon, Your Majesty."

"Please quit calling me that!"

"What should I call you, then?" he shouted as she stomped past him toward the cave.

She paused. What should he call her? Nothing, preferably. He should let her go. "Call me Karina."

"Fine. *Karina*, we need to get going."

When they reached the mouth of the cave, she turned on him so quickly he hesitated. "Must you take me to Faramos? Why not let me go?"

He crossed his arms. "Why should I?"

"Because it is the right thing to do!"

"Sorry, he's paying good money for me to bring you to him."

"Is that all you care about?" She marched over to the blankets and tried to roll them up with her one good arm, but the task was too difficult. She kept trying despite repeated failure, refusing to give Tristan the satisfaction of ... of what? Being dependent on him? Seeing her struggle?

He snatched the blankets from her.

"I did not ask for your help."

He ignored her protest and stared at the smoldering fire. "I have to make a living somehow."

"Surely there are more legitimate choices?"

He sneered. "We weren't all raised within the walls of a royal house."

"I did not always live in one either," she hissed.

His eyebrows lifted.

Karina spun on her heels and stormed out of the cave. Let him stew on her last words. No one had ever even hinted that she wore her position, that she thought herself better than most. He did not know one thing about her!

A short time later, Tristan followed, carrying their belongings. He piled them on the horse. "We walk from here."

"Fine."

He held up a rope. "Can I trust you not to run?"

She growled. "I gave you my word."

He tucked the rope into a bag, grabbed the reins, then led the way along a narrow ledge that wove back to where the waterfall cascaded into the ravine. The sun's beams cast a myriad of rainbows across walls of the cliff. She paused to drink in the majestic beauty.

"Get a move on, Karina."

She tore her gaze from the waterfall. "So beautiful."

He shrugged. "Simple law of nature. Rainbows are caused by the sun's reflection off the water."

"I know that. But the fact that the Creator made it to be so ..."

Tristan grunted and turned back to the path.

She sighed. How sad to not be able to see the splendor of the earth as the Creator's gift.

Beneath the waterfall, a bridge crossed the chasm. The water tumbled with terrible force into churning waters below. She gulped. A fall from this height, even into water, would be deadly. She snuggled closer to the black stallion, who snorted as he tossed his mane.

Once on the other side, a wider ledge wove its way back to a spot directly across from the cave. Within a few hours, the Barrens gave way to a forest of dead trees. Decaying branches and brush littered the ground. Nothing much changed from there as day turned into evening.

"We'll stop here for the night." Tristan tied the horse to an outcropping in a large clearing at the base of a steep mountain. "You sit. I'm going to gather wood."

When he trudged off in search of firewood, Karina sighed. Every moment since the king had died felt surreal. Was this really happening to her? Why would the Creator give her this impossible quest, only to have her fail before she even began?

Perhaps Tristan would help if he knew she had been sent by the Creator. No. He would persist in taking her to Faramos, who would most likely kill her, which would be the only sure way to keep her from completing her mission.

She pulled at one of the blankets strapped to the saddle. The longer they traveled, the more she wanted nothing more than to sleep.

The horse sidestepped her and whinnied.

"Stand still." She reached up again, but the horse pulled away.

Something growled—Karina turned, then gasped.

A large creature with heavy, dark fur and four gleaming white fangs stood on all fours at the top of the outcropping. At least half a man's height taller than she was, its bulk far outweighed her—its piercing red eyes horrifying to behold. Panic rose as a heavy boulder in Karina's chest.

A lupen.

Karina shied back against the horse, his hooves wildly stomping the ground.

The beast growled again.

She searched for a weapon. Finding nothing, she cautiously slipped the horse's reins off the stone. Something whistled through the air, then struck the lupen behind its ear. Howling, the creature swung its huge head toward the weapon's source.

"Karina, take Dom. Get away from here."

Karina scanned the area. Tristan's voice, but—where was he?

Another arrow struck the lupen. It let out a deafening roar.

"Go!"

She spotted Tristan on the mountainside, crouching behind a large boulder.

The lupen saw him too. It pushed off with its strong back legs, leaping several feet up the mountain in one bound.

Despite her injured arm, Karina managed to mount Dom and nudged him forward. The lupen stopped mid-stride and, with a growl, turned toward Karina. She prodded the horse into a gallop, and the lupen lunged from the mountainside in chase. Karina swallowed a scream.

A long howl echoed behind her, followed by two more from the hilltop. The beast was not alone.

CHAPTER EIGHT

Three lupens? Karina reined in the stallion. No matter how tough Tristan might think he was, he could not defeat three lupens. What should she do? The smart thing would be to leave her captor behind while she had the chance. She would be free to return to the temple, put this nightmare behind her, and finish the Creator's quest. She looked back across the Barrens to the way they had come.

Then again, the right thing to do would be to go back for Tristan. Good or bad, he was still a child of the Creator. And she had given her word. What if this was the only way to reach Tristan, and she turned her back on him?

On the other hand, going back was completely insane. What made her think she would fare any better than Tristan would? *I have the power of the Creator with me.* She coaxed the horse into a gallop. Hopefully, she was not too late.

The lupen chasing her had turned back toward Tristan, who was hovering behind a wall of rocks. Two lupens crested the ridge a good distance from him, but the first lupen was closing in quickly.

Karina bit her lip. *Creator, you are going to have to guide me because I cannot fathom a way to save him.*

A moment later, the horse forged its own path, circling around the lupen. With a shrill whinny, the horse bolted up the mountainside and closed in on the lupen. He did not get too near the lupen, but close enough.

When Tristan saw them, he scrambled up the stone wall onto a ledge overlooking the lupen. He must have known what the horse was doing, though Karina had not a clue. With a burst of speed, he traversed the outcropping and leapt.

Karina gasped. What was he doing? He was going to …

Tristan landed with ease behind her on the stallion. He snatched the reins from her grasp and snapped them once. The horse pushed harder.

Howls erupted behind them.

Karina closed her eyes, not daring to look.

"Nicely done," Tristan whispered in her ear.

"It wasn't me," she murmured. Aware of their nearness to each other, she arched her back.

The horse raced along the mountainside. There was no place to rest, no place to seek shelter.

Heavy paws pounded behind them. The lupens were not giving up.

"We need a plan," she hollered back to Tristan.

"Working on that."

She shivered. "There's no place to hide."

"I know."

"We don't have any weapons to fend them off."

"I know."

"What *do* we have?"

A barely audible grunt came from behind her.

The horse began to slow. The burden of two riders at this pace was too much for the stallion.

Karina patted the horses back. "Creator!" she cried, looking to the sky.

"I don't think he heard you."

A group of dead trees loomed ahead of them. Stark pillars of frail wood poked out of the ground amidst a collection of fallen branches.

"I have an idea," Tristan said in Karina's ear. "I'm going to dismount. I need you and Dom to create a distraction. Can you do that?"

Could she? She'd have to. "Yes, of course. What should I do?"

"I don't know. Run toward them. Throw stuff at them. Whatever you need to do to keep them away from me."

Great. Like she knew anything about combat strategies. Another reason she'd never make a good queen.

When they came to the copse of trees, they paused long enough for Tristan to dismount. He smacked the horse's flank, then jumped into the brush.

With control of the reins once again, she brought the horse around and stared at the lupens. The beasts had quit running but stalked towards them, heads low, sniffing out their plan. What plan was that? She studied Tristan, who crouched between the trees. He seemed to be banging something together. Flint?

Oh, fire. Brilliant.

With a sudden rush of adrenaline, Karina yelped as she nudged Dom forward. He charged. Karina continued to shout, waving her good arm like a madwoman. Her throat hurt, her broken arm throbbed, but she pressed on.

The lupens halted, sidestepping each other, eyes darting this way and that.

Maybe her idea was working.

Before they came within attacking distance, Karina urged Dom to the right, arching around the lupens.

The animals withdrew into a circle, backs to each other, their angry snarls like thunder.

The two smaller ones rose on their haunches, heads angled toward the moon. More haunting howls. The lupen leader readied to attack Tristan.

Oh, no. She still did not see any signs of fire.

"Dom, Tristan is in trouble."

The horse's flanks rippled. "It looks like we have trouble of our own."

Karina gasped as she tightened her grip on the saddle horn. "Did-did you just talk?"

"The Creator has granted you ears to hear."

"To hear …"

"The animals, of course. We are the eyes and the ears of this world."

Karina forced herself to relax and allowed a small smirk. "So I have been told."

"The lupens approach."

Karina glanced up. The other two lupens dropped to their haunches, positioned to jump. "What do we do?"

"More of the same?"

"More of the same what?"

"Allow me." Dom reared and, with a sharp whinny, took off at a run the moment his hooves hit the dirt, his guttural neighs like shouts of determination. Karina rose in the saddle and screamed at the top of her lungs. Dom headed straight for the two lupens.

Snarls proceeded futile attacks. The lupens swung their massive paws at Dom as he passed between them.

"Hurry, Dom."

Soon, all Karina could hear was the thudding of her heart. Wind tore at her hair. Her breath came in shallow gasps. Behind her, paws pounded the ground.

They were about to overtake the leader.

With a quick yank, Karina freed the full water skin tied to the saddle bag and, with a shrill cry, hurled it at the lupen. The beast shied away, slowing its gait. She maneuvered Dom between the lupen and where Tristan still crouched in the trees.

The two smaller lupens stopped behind their leader.

The wind ceased. Nothing moved, as if time had frozen ... All nature fell into silence, even the Barren's birds.

"Hi-yah!" Tristan jumped from the trees, holding branches afire in his hands.

Startled, Karina yelped. Dom whinnied as the lupen snapped at his legs. He reared and kicked with his front hooves.

Tristan hollered again as he shoved the flaming branches toward the lupen.

With a slow whimper, the lupen backed away from the flames.

"Go away," Tristan shouted. "Get."

The leader continued to back down. With a chorus of whimpers, all three sprinted toward the mountain.

"We need ... to get moving," Tristan said between coughs. "The fire ... won't last long. They'll ... be back."

"We should tie extra wood on Dom." Karina turned toward the horse. "Can you handle that, if Tristan and I walk?"

The horse dipped his head. "But is that safe? We would travel faster if I took both of you."

"Yes, but the wood would keep the lupens away from us." Karina turned to find a slack-jawed Tristan. "What is wrong with you?"

He pointed at Dom. "Were you just talking to the horse?"

"Yes."

"It looked like he might have been talking back."

"He was."

Tristan shook his head. "You're insane."

"I am not!" Karina thrust her hands on her hips.

Dom nickered. "Ask him to tell you about Annabelle."

She scrunched her forehead. "Who's Annabelle?"

Tristan's face darkened. "What did you say?"

"Uh—Dom just said to ask you about Annabelle."

Tristan stared at Dom.

The horse turned his head toward Tristan and tossed his mane about. "That's something only he and I know about—and one of many things he would rather forget."

Karina chuckled.

Tristan ran a shaky hand over his face. "I don't understand any of this."

"Quite simple, really." She folded her hands. "The Creator has granted me the ability to hear the animals."

"What kind of lunacy is that?"

"He must have thought it would be of assistance." She lifted her head. "Which it was."

He cast a sidelong glance at Dom. "We need to get moving."

The moon hid behind the passing clouds, darkening the night even more as Tristan gathered up a bundle of wood. Karina kept a couple of branches burning while she stood beside Dom, scanning the mountains for any sign of the lupens.

Tristan secured the bundle atop Dom and grabbed the reins. "Let's get out of here."

Despite the dark, they continued the trek west. Karina was not sure how much time had passed, but her body ached. Her eyelids drooped as the night wore on. Flashes of the last few days drowned out the world around her. She was dimly aware of Tristan's torch in front of her. She stumbled over a rock and fell on her injured arm with a cry.

Tristan rushed to her side, concern etched on his face "What happened?"

Karina bit back tears as she cradled her arm. "I'm not sure. I must have been so tired I did not see where I was going."

He sighed. "We should make camp. The lupens quit following us a while ago."

Dom nuzzled her hair. "Get up, child. We have no reason to fear for the moment. You rest by the rocks over there. Tristan will make a fire."

Tristan squinted at Dom. "What's he saying?"

"I rest, you build a fire."

"Figures," he grumbled but made the fire anyway.

The next morning, Tristan stood vigil over the sleeping queen. The sun had risen well above the horizon, but he hadn't wanted to wake her. She'd been through so much in the last several days. And today … well, today they would reach Faramos's fortress. But not before they crossed the river and traversed dragon territory.

Dom neighed from his resting place by a lone tree. He jerked his head a few times.

"What are you doing, you crazy animal?" Tristan rubbed Dom's side, then lifted his saddle, but the horse balked. "Dom, stand still." No such luck.

Karina yawned. "He says he does not want you to take me to Faramos."

"Is that a fact? Would he rather starve?"

Karina struggled to stand. Tristan turned to assist, but she refused his help. She gazed toward the west. A dark cloud hung in the sky, and distant thunder rumbled through the valley. "That is no ordinary storm." She glanced back at Tristan. "Dom can sense the evil emanating from there— and so can I."

Tristan considered the disheveled woman standing before him. This supposedly simple job was turning out to be more than he bargained for. As was this woman.

She could have left him yesterday—left him to the lupens. But she didn't. She came back. She and Dom had worked together to save him. Tristan let out a long breath and then shook his head. He had to bury his feelings for Karina beneath the stone that was a sorry excuse for a heart. This was a job … just another payday.

CHAPTER NINE

The bridge was gone.

Karina sat down on a rock at the edge of the Continental River. She was tired. And sore. And now this. "What do we do?"

Tristan squatted by the river bank, staring at the other side. He tilted his face toward the mid-afternoon sun. "River's shallow enough here to cross without a bridge."

"But the water's freezing!"

He shrugged. "We can take off our shoes and stockings. You can also remove whatever clothes you'd like to keep dry."

She scowled, not bothering to respond—especially when he smirked.

"When we're on the other side, our footwear will be dry, and the stockings will warm our feet quickly."

He couldn't be serious, could he?

"It will not be that bad, child." Dom nuzzled her shoulder with his nose.

Tristan knelt to remove his shoes.

Karina pursed her lips, biting back derisive comments. She was thankful for the warm sun. Back in Calliope, the snow would begin to melt as green grass poked through the winter-hardened earth. The Ice Plains never melted, though. The cold northern oceans kept the top iced over year-round. She sighed as she unlaced her dusty boots.

They tied their shoes together and slung them around their necks. Tristan grabbed Dom's reins and then nodded to Karina. "Ready?"

"No."

He stepped into the river. The rushing water only came up to his knees, which wasn't too bad for him since he had rolled up his pant legs.

Karina looked down at her form-fitting leather pants. No way to roll them up. She sucked in a breath of determination. Oh, well, they needed a good washing anyway. At the river bank, she stuck a toe in the water, then yanked it back out. "It's too cold!"

Tristan smirked. "You'll live."

She took a defiant step into the water. The cold seeped into her skin— like tiny needles stabbing her over and over again.

"If I make it out of this alive," she muttered, "I'm sending the Aletheian army after you for making me do this."

"What was that?" Tristan glanced over his shoulder.

"Nothing." She slid one foot in front of the other. "Nothing at all. This is great. Really. I—"

Something slimy slid around her ankle—and wrenched her into the water.

Before she could yell for Tristan, she slipped beneath the surface. The something dragged her along the river bed, her head hitting rock after rock. She managed to come up for air.

"Grab on to something," Tristan hollered. He splashed toward her.

Karina flailed her arms. Her nails tore as she scraped them on the rocks. Anything to hold onto. The river was deeper here, and the creature seemed determined to drag her back underneath. The water was so frigid, her skin burned. Her body ached. It was all too much. She should just let go.

No! She shook her head. Keep fighting. The Creator would not leave her here. She kicked her legs, but the beast held on.

Water filled her nose and mouth.

She couldn't breathe. Couldn't escape.

Suddenly, the beast released its hold on her leg, and her body floated to the top. She wanted to move—needed to—but her limbs refused to cooperate. Too tired. Too cold.

"Karina!" Tristan swam out to her. He slipped his arm around her and pulled her to the river bank.

Once out of the water, she curled into a tight ball.

Tristan leaned over her, his face taut with worry. "Your lips are blue." He whistled.

"Wh-what are y-you doing?" she asked as her eyelids fluttered.

"Calling for Dom. We need to get you warmed up."

Dom trotted over and nudged Karina. "I'm here. Are you hurt?"

"I-I d-don't know."

Tristan grabbed a pack from Dom's saddle. "You have a bump on your head, and I imagine your injured arm hurts quite a bit. I'm more worried about the cold. Your skin is like ice." He pulled two blankets and a brown tunic from the bag.

She shivered. "T-t-too cold. So t-tired."

Tristan pulled her up. Her legs felt like jelly, and she had to lean on him for support. He made quick work of replacing her soaked shirt with his spare tunic. Then he wrapped the blankets around her. "Karina, do not go to sleep. Do you hear me?"

"Wh-why not?" She tried to smile. Her mind wandered. "Faramos w-wouldn't c-care." She closed her eyes.

"Wake up, Karina." Tristan shook her. "Wake up! Stay with me."

She opened her eyes again. "W-with you? Why w-would I-I want to stay with y-you?"

He frowned. "I need to build a fire. Dom, can you lay next to her? Your body heat will help warm her faster."

Dom knelt next to her, and Tristan positioned her so her back rested against Dom's side. "Talk to her. Do not let her fall asleep." Tristan rushed off, out of sight.

"How are you feeling, child?" Dom nuzzled Karina's hair.

Her body trembled. "T-tired. My body hurts."

"It's trying to warm up."

"Can't I s-sleep?" She trembled uncontrollably. "I want to sleep."

Dom nickered. "As a healer, I would think you would be aware of the dangers of falling asleep."

"I-I d-don't care."

"The Creator is not done with you yet, Prophetess."

She blinked away her tears. She was no hero, no prophetess. The Creator had made a mistake. She was weak, inept—a complete failure.

When Tristan returned, he built a large fire and boiled a pot of water. "We'll camp here tonight." He tossed leaves into a cup and poured in some of the water. "This will help warm your insides." He handed her the cup. She trembled and sloshed hot water over the edges. He took the cup away, knelt beside her, and eased the cup to her lips.

As her stomach warmed, unwanted tears fell.

After a couple more sips, Tristan took her cup and moved to the river bank. He poked at the water with a stick. Was he hoping to catch fish?

Karina's shivering eased. Her whole being begged for rest, to curl up in warm blankets next to a roaring fireplace. She sighed from the depths of her distress and then closed her eyes. She pictured a side table piled with aromatic breads, savory meats and vegetables, and delectable desserts.

Instead, Tristan roasted fish on the fire and helped her eat. "Let's get you to bed. I think it's safe for you to sleep, now. Can you stand?"

"Of course I can stand," she snapped, suddenly irritated by Tristan's presence. She would not be in this mess if it were not for his greed. Gritting her teeth, she forced herself to a stand, ignoring the hand he offered. What redeeming qualities did the Creator see in this man?

He unfurled a blanket next to the fire. When she lay back down, he covered her. "Sweet dreams, Karina."

She rolled away from him and closed her eyes. This could not be the Creator's plan.

Tristan stoked the morning fire as the sun peaked over the horizon. The cool air was heavy—rain would fall soon. Not far from the river, the infamous cliffs of Tzedek towered over them, protecting them from the wind sweeping the plains above.

On the other side of the campfire, Karina still slept. Color had returned to her face. Yesterday, he'd been afraid of losing her. The feeling was disconcerting. Not his job to care about the people he hunted. Faramos would kill him if he knew.

He growled as he threw the stick into the fire. "Karina."

She didn't move.

"Karina."

She rolled over, blinking away sleep from her eyes. "What do you want?"

"We need to get going. Let's eat."

She glared at him but obeyed. Dom whinnied, and she smiled.

"I'm feeling much better this morning, Dom," she said, turning her back to Tristan. "Thank you for asking."

He sucked in a breath. The woman was impossible.

While she ate, he gathered up their stuff and strapped the gear to Dom's saddle. "I think you should ride today."

Dom nickered.

"What did he say?"

She rolled her eyes. "He agreed with you."

When they were ready to go, Tristan helped her onto Dom's back.

"Where are we going now?" Karina asked.

"The nearest path up the cliffs is back the way we came."

"How far did we come?"

He shrugged. "I'm not sure. Maybe an hour's worth of hiking."

She nodded.

He led Dom up the rocky trail. Cliffs rose on their left—a natural protective wall that surrounded three-fourths of Tzedek. As they traveled, a mist settled over them. A harsh bird call echoed through the thickening fog.

"That's just great," Tristan moaned.

"What?"

Rain fell from the sky in large, cold drops. Of all the rotten luck. Why couldn't one thing go right on this trip?

"We will have to travel through this rain. We're already late."

Karina didn't respond, but Dom whinnied.

Tristan turned in time to see Karina tilt sideways in the saddle. "Whoa, there." Tristan caught her before she fell off Dom.

Her dull blue eyes stared up into his. "What happened?"

"You swooned. Are you feeling well?"

"I—I am not sure. I'm so tired."

He helped her to a fallen log. "We can rest but only for a minute. We need to get out of this fog. I'm not sure how safe it is."

"I cannot, Tristan. I am too weak." She groaned as her eyes started to close, but she snapped them open again. She stared off behind him, her skin paling.

"Karina, what is the matter with you?" Irritation turned to worry. "Karina, can you hear me?" He waved his hand in front of her face.

Karina jumped.

Tristan whirled around, pulling his sword from its sheath. "The Creator's might!" He cringed at the sight of the largest serpent he'd ever seen. If not for the bright red star between the creature's eyes, Tristan might not have seen it through the fog. The gray snake slithered toward them in a slow, zigzag pattern, its tongue flickering, testing the air.

"Run!" He shoved her ahead of him as they took off through the ravine. Karina stumbled over a large branch, but Tristan caught her around the waist.

They came to a dead end. Large stones and a couple of trees stretched between the river and the cliffs. Tristan knelt before one of the boulders and extended his hands to help Karina. She grasped for a branch to pull herself up. It snapped, and she fell back.

Tristan caught her.

"I ... cannot," she said between gasps of breath. Rain streaked her face. "I do not have enough strength—and my arm."

Tristan nodded and sat her upright once more. She was right. This wasn't going to work.

The snake sashayed over the wet ground, covering the distance between them.

"Stay here," Tristan rushed forward, sword at the ready.

The snake halted, its tongue flickering. A voice came from it, though its mouth did not move. "I am Asharan, Guardian of the Northern Plains of Tzedek. What business have you here?"

Tristan kept his sword up. "Asharan? Faramos never mentioned you."

The snake hissed. "I do not serve evil. I was chosen by the Creator."

Karina appeared at Tristan's side. "Like Rashka?"

Tristan frowned. Who was Rashka?

Asharan turned toward Karina. "How do you know that name?"

"She revealed herself to me in Shadowed Forest."

The fog ignited with a flash of light. Tristan covered his eyes to keep from being blinded. When he let down his arm, Asharan had transformed from the large snake to an elven body, his eyes golden, his hair as white as snow.

He stepped forward. "Rashka is my sister. Why would she trust you?"

"I am Queen—"

Tristan shoved Karina to the side. "Enough." He glared at Asharan. "I do not care who you are or who you serve. Let us be, or I'll leave your dead body for the scavengers to find."

Asharan glowered. "You, I know."

Tristan took a step back as he eyed Karina. His true identity was the last thing he wanted her to know.

"Ah—so she does not know who you are, Tristan Lemur."

"Lemur?" Karina stared at the water. "That name is familiar."

Tristan rushed to speak. "That does not change what I said. Leave us." He shoved his sword back in its scabbard.

Asharan turned to Karina. "What is a prophetess doing with the likes of him?"

She blushed. "I am no prophetess."

"Ah, but the sign on your forehead says you have been blessed by a servant."

Tristan didn't see anything, but Karina touched a spot in the middle of her forehead. Enough of this nonsense. "Ignore him, Karina, and let's get moving. We need to get you out of this cold rain." He grabbed her wrist, pulling her behind him.

"I cannot let you take the prophetess any closer to Faramos's fortress."

"How are you going to stop me?" Tristan sneered but did not turn around.

Another light flashed, then disappeared. In its place, Asharan's snake form rematerialized in front of them.

"You do not understand what you are doing, young bounty hunter." Asharan bowed. Too close for comfort. "Faramos serves an ancient evil. If he sent you to retrieve a prophetess, you can trust his plans will beget still more evil. You have seen the extent of his reach already."

Tristan scowled. "I am so sick of hearing about the Creator and the evil ones. Fairy tales. My bro—" He stopped himself before he betrayed his loyalties.

"You do not believe that. I can sense your anger, but anger does not mean disbelief."

Tristan clenched his jaw.

"I beg of you, do not follow your head. Listen to your heart." Asharan glanced in Karina's direction. "Do you really wish to turn her over to the likes of him? You know him better than anyone. After the time you have spent with her, could you really do that?"

Tristan kept his gaze fixed toward the ground.

"If the woodlands speak the truth," Asharan said, "you are Queen Karina of Aletheia, are you not?"

"Yes, I am."

"Your uncle was a good king, devoted to the Creator. He will truly be missed."

Her eyes misted. "Thank you, Asharan."

"Am I to understand you will take his place?"

"If I survive this quest."

The bright light flashed again, and Asharan stood once more in elven form. He knelt before Karina. "Then, Your Highness, you have my loyalty. I will see your quest comes to completion."

Tristan did not want to listen to any more of this foolery. He growled as he drew his sword, then charged.

"No!" Karina jumped between them.

Tristan halted, his sword tip reaching her collarbone. He bared his teeth. "What do you think you are doing, Karina?"

She shoved the sword aside. "I will not let you harm Asharan."

"Do not worry, Your Highness." The elf peered at Tristan. "I do not fear his sword." Gently pushing Karina back, Asharan moved between her and Tristan. His gaze was steady. "Something tells me this bounty hunter will not turn you in. He does not want to see you slain by the dark ones. He knows what that is like."

Tristan gulped. How could Asharan know Tristan's past, read every memory? He dropped his sword. "What are you talking about?"

"You already know." Asharan spoke barely above a whisper.

Karina cocked her head "But I do not."

Asharan offered her a small smile. "That is Tristan's story to share."

Tristan paced back and forth across the rocky bank. Rain still fell, and the fog still swirled. Asharan was right. Tristan had seen what Faramos was capable of. Tristan would not kill an innocent person, but Faramos would.

Tristan stopped, glanced toward Karina, growled, then looked away. Despite the fact Faramos worried she would ruin his plans for taking over Olam, realm of the Three Kingdoms, Karina was a good person. She cared about people. She did the right thing. She had a quest.

Tristan continued to pace.

"What is he doing?" Karina asked Asharan.

"Deciding."

"On what?"

"To follow his head or his heart."

His head had warred against his heart for years. After Faramos had killed Tristan's father and ruined his mother, he'd vowed to get revenge. That quest had fallen to the wayside as he worked his way into Faramos's good graces, trying to get close enough. Waiting for the right opportunity. An opportunity that had passed many times, and yet Tristan had been unable to act. How could he kill his brother?

He balled his fists and clenched his jaw. Faramos couldn't win. He stormed over to Karina and Asharan. "Fine." He glared at Asharan. "You have no idea what this is going to cost me. This will ruin my reputation. No one wants to hire a bounty hunter who doesn't deliver."

Asharan chuckled. "I do not think you will have to worry about that."

"Why not?"

"I do not believe you will be a bounty hunter after this."

Tristan glowered and crossed his arms. Like he was good for anything else.

Asharan clapped his hands. "Shall we?"

CHAPTER TEN

"There's a bridge a couple of hours west," Asharan said, waving his hand in that direction. "From there we can head back toward Shadowed Forest."

Karina smiled. Her heartbeat slowed, and her breathing returned to normal. She was out of danger for now and so thankful to have someone else along on the quest. Bearing its burden on her own and in the face of so many obstacles had been exhausting. She looked to the man who had once seemed so strong, so unmovable.

Now, Tristan walked hunched over, his gaze only inches from his feet, one hand on his scabbard, the thumb of the other shoved into his belt. Everything about him emanated uncertainty and discouragement.

As they made their way alongside the rushing river, the repetitive echo of the water against the cliff walls began to wear on her sanity. She played with the leather of Dom's reins. "Asharan, how is it you and Rashka became Guardians?"

Asharan grinned as he tilted his head toward the sky. "Many, many moons ago, when we were barely past the age of enlightenment—er—adulthood, as you would say, the Creator charged us with protecting his creation. Elves were already caretakers of the woods, but an evil had entered the world. I do not know how he came to choose us specifically. Only that it was the highest honor to be chosen. My family was twice-blessed when Rashka and I were both called to duty."

"Like me?"

"Yes, Prophetess, much like you." The older elf smiled with an endearing crinkle at the corners of his eyes.

"You two want to keep it quiet," Tristan said in a harsh whisper. "Who knows what is watching us from atop the cliffs."

Karina bit her lip but obeyed.

They found the bridge without any difficulty.

"Wait," Karina whispered as they stepped onto the well-worn path on Aletheia's side of the river. "What's that?"

"Nothing important," Tristan murmured, pulling her along by her arm.

"No, look. Those dark clouds are hovering over a castle on the cliff's edge." She yanked free of his grasp, dropped Dom's reins, and hurried down the path. The closer she came, the more she sensed danger. Still, she pressed forward until she was directly across from the dark structure at the river's mouth.

Waves from the open sea crashed against rocks at the base of the cliff. Overhead, black clouds swirled in the sky, and lightning flashed. Winged creatures circled a staggering spire atop a dark stone fortress. Massive walls surrounded the compound.

Evil. That was the presence that had the hairs on her neck standing straight, the thing that soured her stomach—made her feel weak and afraid.

"Faramos's fortress," Asharan sighed.

Karina trembled. "Tristan wanted to bring me there?"

Asharan nodded as Tristan and Dom appeared at her side.

She searched Tristan's face for remorse. "That is where you were taking me?"

His jaw clenched, and his muscles twitched as he averted his gaze. "I'm sorry, Karina. I was mistaken."

"How could you—" She stared at the foreboding fortress. "How could you even stand to be in a place like that yourself?"

Tristan kicked a loose rock. "You'd be surprised the places I've been." He headed back to the path, away from the river's edge.

Karina glanced at Dom, then toward Asharan.

He grasped her shoulder. "Prophetess, you must remember to extend grace to him, just as the Creator has extended grace to us, time and again. Tristan is changing—give him time." Asharan smiled and then followed Tristan.

Asharan's words were wise, but she could not quite bring herself to forgive Tristan—not yet. Nor did she trust him. She glanced back to the menacing fortress, sickened by the evil emanating from that place.

Her heart was torn. How had everything become so complicated? She stared at the winged creatures. What were they? What horror would have awaited her in Faramos's fortress? She shivered as she hurried after Asharan and Tristan. Whatever her fate might have been, she now had a different future. *Thank you, Creator.*

Darkness fell, blanketing the woods with an unexpected eeriness. Tristan insisted they could not light a torch lest they call attention to themselves. The only light came from the flashes of lightning that branched across the sky, a dazzling show of might.

Karina was careful to stay right beside Asharan, feeling safest in his presence. Tristan forged the path before them, his sword extended.

"Are you sure we cannot stop for the night?" Karina whispered, rather loudly, to Tristan.

"Not until we are through these woods. It is not safe."

Maybe not. Still, her back and shoulders ached. Her legs threatened to collapse, and her head throbbed.

Tristan held up his hand.

Just through the trees—an empty clearing. Packed dirt and a few downed logs dotted the open space. She and Asharan stayed with Dom as Tristan crept to the edge of the forest line. The only sound was the remnant of the sea wind that howled through the leafless tree limbs.

Tristan eased back to their position. "I don't sense anything else out there. I think we can hurry across—it isn't very far. Karina, you can ride Dom."

She mounted Dom, then followed Tristan and Asharan in silence, her breaths shallow. They only had maybe a twenty-man span to cover.

Loud yelps rang from the treetops.

Dom reared, and Karina fell. Tristan and Asharan took up posts on either side of her.

High-pitched squeals echoed through the clearing.

A bright light nearly blinded her. Asharan had morphed into his snake form.

Yellow eyes fixated on them from behind stark bushes and from high in the trees. Eerie cackles thundered in the storm.

"Get 'em!" a voice shouted.

The cackles turned to shrieks as the creatures rushed forward, exposing their gray and green skin. Were they beasts or humanoid? She couldn't tell in this darkness. Only when the beasts were upon them could she recognize their distorted features—like goblins she had seen in books.

Karina hid behind Dom.

As the goblins approached, Tristan pushed Karina aside, swung atop Dom, and with a ferocious shout raced forward, hacking his way from beast to beast.

Asharan's snake form circled Karina, shielding her with his body. Goblins rushed him, but he swung his tail, easily knocking the predators away.

Karina could do nothing but pray.

The goblins were relentless—so many of them. Arrows flew through the darkened sky. Short swords jabbed at Asharan's tough skin. She lost sight of Tristan.

Soon, the creatures had them cornered. Trapped, with knives at his and Dom's throats, Tristan threw down his sword. At least fifty arrows were stuck in Asharan's scales. A bright light flashed, and Asharan took on his elven form again. The arrows fell away, but wounds covered his body. He sank to his knees.

Karina's eyes welled with tears. He had done his best to protect her, and now he was wounded. So much blood. She raised her chin, then pushed aside a goblin's knife and hurried to Asharan's side, placing her arm around his shoulders.

"I have failed you, Prophetess," he mumbled, his breath ragged.

"No, no, you have not, Asharan. You fought bravely. That is all anyone could ask."

A faint smile pulled at his lips. "Thank you, Your Majesty. You will be a great queen, for your heart is good and kind. The Creator has chosen well."

"Hold on, Asharan. I am a healer, I can help you."

"Dear Prophetess, the Creator is calling me home. I can hear his voice already." He patted her hand. "But do not worry, we will be watching over you." He held her gaze. "Do not forget to pray. Even at the darkest moment—there is nothing stronger than prayer."

And with a last exhalation, he was gone.

Karina closed her eyes. "Creator, welcome this faithful servant home into your waiting arms." She brushed a tear from her cheek.

"Get a move on," a harsh voice said.

Something poked Karina in the back. She glared at the grotesque goblin who jabbed a short spear in her direction.

"I said let's go."

She glanced at Tristan, his face drained of color, sweat dripping down his cheeks. He met her halfway and put his arm around her shoulders, resting his chin atop her head.

Where was Dom?

Karina let out a long sigh. She felt so—so empty. First, her uncle and now, Asharan. How many people would she lose in this quest?

The rain let up as the goblins led them toward Faramos's fortress. Thankfully, this time, they had torches to light the way, and Tristan remained at her side. She paused at the tree line and gasped. The mere sight of the fortress sent shivers up her spine. She nestled closer to Tristan, grateful for his nearness.

"I'm so sorry, Karina," he whispered.

She searched his eyes, surprised by the depth of his remorse. "I know."

Karina took the lead, marching across the bridge with her head held high. *Creator, give me strength and wisdom. I do not know what we will face within those walls, but I know you will not leave me.*

They climbed the steep incline to the Plains of Tzedek in silence. At the top, she surveyed the new land. Many years had passed since the orphan caravan had carried her across the flat plateau. Now, in the black of night, the land stretched into darkness on all sides. A hefty wind whistled through the long grasses.

A grunt came from behind, followed by a rough shove. Karina stumbled forward. *By all that's created!* She glared at the stinking goblin.

She gazed in awe as they approached the black iron gate—twice as tall as the gates of Calliope. Eight turrets lined the four walls of the fortress, patrolled by goblins in silver armor. Torchlight danced with shadows, and the lightning continued to pierce the overcast sky. The long howl of—something—came from above.

Karina turned to Tristan. "Is this Tzedek's capital?"

He shook his head. "The capital is Andor, about a half day's ride south of here. The city has fallen to ruin. Only the poorest of Tzedek's people take up residence there. This is the military stronghold."

Karina balled her hands into fists. The Creator would not let this be the end of her. She had more to do. Her quest was far from over. Let Faramos do his worst.

Once she and Tristan were inside the fortress, most of the goblins left. A squad of eight led the two of them into the castle. Inside the doors, a stone staircase with a black runner rose into the shadowed distance.

Karina's jaw dropped. How many steps were there?

"C'mon, then." The head goblin led them down a corridor on the left. "We must get you cleaned up so that you can stand before Lord Faramos."

She raised her eyebrow and glanced at Tristan.

He shrugged.

They were taken into different rooms. Karina was rushed to a cold bath. A worried-looking woman hovered near the door, so Karina did not have an opportunity to look for a way to escape. She hurried through her bath, washing off the caked mud. Not an easy task given her broken arm. Once Karina was finished, the servant gave her a dark blue dress with lace sleeves. However impractical for the cold season, the soft material was very comfortable.

She was reunited with Tristan at the bottom of the staircase. He had bathed and been given clean clothes as well—a dark green tunic and brown, heavy wool pants. At least he looked refreshed, though his expression seemed more downcast than when they parted. She craned her neck to take in the full height of the steps.

"It's really not as far as it seems," Tristan whispered.

Still too far for her. She grumbled, then began to climb before the goblins could poke her with a spear. The dark stone walls were lined with flaming sconces giving way to a line of fire at the baseboards. Hazy smoke like a light fog clouded the stairwell.

At last, they reached the door to the throne room. Flanked by four guards, two on each side, the large, ornate door had a face carved into the center. By trick of light or fear of mind, the eyes seemed to stare at Karina, no matter where she moved.

She tried to breathe through the rising panic.

"Open." The lead goblin beat his club on the stone floor, then pushed the doors inward, revealing a room bedazzled with light. Candles were everywhere—hanging from crystal chandeliers, standing on candelabras around the massive room—and a trough of fire ran in front of the far wall, behind the throne dais.

Karina gawked as the goblins shoved her and Tristan forward. At the center of the room, she turned in a slow circle. The ceiling towered above them. In the center, a round glass pane invited her to view the horrible beauty of the spire and the winged creatures circling it.

"Tristan," a voice growled. "It is about time."

CHAPTER ELEVEN

Karina spun toward the throne, tilting her head to observe the shadow cast by the fire pit. She took a step forward.

"Dismissed!" the seemingly disembodied voice shouted.

The goblins bowed as they backed toward the door. Four of them flanked the door on the inside, while the rest scampered off. The doors shut behind them.

Karina whispered a prayer. She was going to need the Creator's strength and wisdom to face Faramos.

"Well, well, so you actually found her." A figure rose from the black iron throne. He clapped his hands and hopped down from the dais.

Tristan cleared his throat. "I did."

"Very good." The man emerged from the shadow of the throne.

The first thing Karina noticed was the eye patch that overlapped the long scar stretching from his eyebrow to his chin on the right side of his face. He wore black leather, the color of his shoulder-length hair and dark eye. His smirk sent shivers up Karina's spine yet again.

"Your Highness," he said with a mocking bow. "I am Faramos Lemur. Welcome to my home." He gestured in a grand circle.

Lemur? Was that not Tristan's surname? Her pulse raced. Were they related? Karina held her head high but said nothing.

"A quiet one, is she?" Faramos elbowed Tristan in playful jest.

Tristan scowled. "Not really."

"No matter. You have finally arrived." Faramos clasped his hands behind his back as he walked in a slow circle around Karina. "She is smaller than I would have thought—younger, too. And I still cannot get over the fact the Chosen One is a mere girl." He leaned in close, and the hint of ale and smoke made her cringe. He grinned. "And to think, someone like you is supposed to topple my grand designs."

Karina's heart raced, threatening to explode. She willed herself to remain calm.

He glanced toward Tristan and laughed. "Job well done, brother!"

Brother? Karina hitched a breath. Impossible. She peered at Tristan, but he avoided her gaze.

Faramos clapped him on the back. "I bet you had fun with her on your trip."

"It was fine." He looked away. "Do I have your leave? I have other places to be, Faramos."

He had to be kidding! Karina's eyes widened. He was—he was going to leave her here?

"Of course, little brother, I know you have much to tend to." Faramos placed his hand on Tristan's shoulder. "And you shall. But first …" He ambled toward the throne, paused, then turned on his heel. "Do you want to tell me where you were taking Queen Karina?"

Tristan furrowed his brow. "What are you suggesting?"

Faramos put his hand to his ear and giggled. "A little birdie told me my goblins found you heading away from the castle."

Tristan did not so much as flinch.

"We made him," Karina blurted out. Even if Tristan was turning on her, Karina could not let anything happen to him. Not if he was part of the Creator's plan.

Faramos raised one thin eyebrow. "Made him?" He flashed a wide grin. "Made him?"

"Yes. My protector and I."

"Ah, yes." Faramos spun in a quick circle. "The infamous Asharan. He has been causing trouble on these plains for years."

"Someone has to protect the people from the likes of you."

"Oooh … I like her, Tristan." Faramos chuckled, then a menacing scowl replaced his laugh lines. "Tell me, Your Highness, how is my old friend Asharan?" He smirked. "A little hole-y these days?"

Karina glared as she pursed her lips.

Faramos faced Tristan. "I'm still waiting for your answer, brother. Where were you going?"

Tristan stood firm, holding his brother's gaze.

"Well, then, you leave me no choice. Guards!" Faramos returned to his throne as a handful of goblins entered the room. "Take my dear brother to the dungeon. Tell the keeper there will be fresh meat in the morning."

"No!" Karina shouted.

"No? *No?*" Faramos's expression darkened. "You are a long way from home, Your Highness. Your commands hold no power here. Unless you want to join my brother in the Survival Trials tomorrow, I suggest you still that tongue of yours." He signaled for the guards to take Tristan.

"I'm sorry, Karina," he whispered as the grotesque goblins yanked him away from her.

She offered him a smile of reassurance. "It will be fine, you'll see."

The massive doors closed behind them, leaving her to face Faramos alone. The only sound in the room was the crackling of the fire. Karina continued to stare at the spot she had last seen Tristan. This could not be happening.

Faramos' footsteps sounded behind her. "Be of good cheer, Your Highness. After tomorrow, you will not have to worry about Tristan anymore."

She bit back a scathing response. What did he know about anything? She turned to him. "What do you plan to do with me?"

A wide grin crossed his equally gruesome and handsome face. He spread his arms out wide. "I am inviting you to stay here as my guest."

She crossed her arms. What game was he playing? "What if I refuse your offer?"

He shrugged. "That would be your prerogative. I do promise that, if you accept, you will have chambers of your own, plenty of good food to eat, and time to stroll through the castle and surrounding area." He straightened the collar of his fancy shirt. "Not to mention exceptional company."

She wrinkled her nose at Faramos's detestable offer. "Do you not worry that I will escape?"

"Not at all," he said with a wave of his hand. "While I am giving you free movement, you will always be in the company of my best guards."

He guided her from the throne room by way of a side door. They descended a dimly lit stone staircase that opened into a private dining room. Savory smells wafted from another room.

Karina's stomach growled.

Faramos gestured toward the table. "Please, have a seat. Pray tell, what happened to your arm?"

"Oh." Karina glanced back at him as she walked around the polished wood table. Faramos pulled out an ornate high-back chair. "An unfortunate accident. No need to rehash the event." She smoothed her skirts and sat.

She scanned the room that held a fireplace on one end and a sitting area on the other—the long table where they sat was nestled in the middle. The walls were decorated with tapestries and shields.

Faramos sat in the chair next to her at the head of the table. He signaled a servant who stood beside the closed door. The man bowed and left the room.

Karina folded her hands in her lap, unsure what to think. Was Faramos trying to trick her? What did he want? She twiddled her thumbs as question after question raced through her mind, souring her appetite. Faramos's persistent stares did nothing to ease her discomfort. She did her best not to squirm, but her cheeks heated despite her efforts.

A fair-haired servant brought out a plate of greens mixed with other vegetables and spiced oil. "Roasted lamb legs with potatoes and fresh-baked breads will be the next course, sire," he mumbled.

Faramos nodded. "Thank you, good sir."

The servant looked startled. "You are welcome." He hurried back into the kitchen.

Faramos picked up a fork. "Let's eat, shall we?" He stabbed at the salad and took a bite.

Karina stared at the food. She should eat. Would he have gone to all this trouble just to poison her? Perhaps he *was* that kind of man. After all, he did have his brother hauled off to the dungeons. She gripped her fork so tightly her knuckles turned white.

When finished with his salad, Faramos turned to face her. "Karina, I have a proposition for you."

She raised an eyebrow.

"Years ago, your father attempted to negotiate the joining of our two kingdoms through a marriage union."

Karina nearly spit out her salad. "Excuse me?"

"Oh, you were much too young to remember, but Tzedek and Aletheia were on the brink of war, and your father proposed a treaty between our lands."

That was impossible. In Aletheia, arranged marriages were unheard of. Her people did not believe in them. Sure, such unions happened now and then, with the expressed permission of both the bride and the groom, but not often. Why would her father have made such a proposal? "What did my father supposedly suggest?"

"Your father promised your hand in marriage to my little brother."

Her eyes widened.

"Yes, the very same man who is now rotting in the dungeon for his sins." Faramos took a generous sip of wine.

She was at one point betrothed to her kidnapper? Her kidnapper who had done a complete turnaround and sought to help her?

"I understand your father was exiled because of this treaty."

"He was?" Karina had never been privy to the reasons for the exile, and her parents died before she was old enough to be told.

"Well, that and burning half the royal fleet as a gesture of goodwill toward my father."

"That's insane."

"I thought so as well. I never agreed with my father's alliances. The only path to true peace is for everyone to be under the same flag."

Karina snorted. "I suppose you believe your flag to be the one everyone should unite under?"

He raised his goblet. "Indeed." He took another drink and slammed the goblet on the table. "While I didn't see the wisdom of such a union back then, I do now. You are in a precarious situation, Your Highness. You are in line to be the queen, but you have no suitable husband, and if rumors are true, the former queen is refusing to abdicate her throne."

Karina sat back in the chair. She did not like where this conversation was going. "Do you wish for me to marry Tristan now?"

Faramos laughed as he waved the servants to bring the next course. They removed the salad plates and set down the roasted lamb and savory potatoes that whetted her appetite despite her disgust at Faramos's revelations.

"No, my love, I do not wish for you to marry Tristan. I wish for you to marry me."

Karina's fork clattered on the porcelain plate. "Are you serious?"

"Quite serious, Karina." He bit off a chunk of meat.

This man must be mad. He was a warlock. A warlock bent on destroying everything the Creator had built. And she ... she was the Creator's Chosen One. She slumped as the familiar pangs of inadequacy overwhelmed her former confidence. Chosen or not, she was not doing a lot of good.

"If I were to agree to this arrangement, how would Aletheia benefit?"

Faramos smiled. "Why, my protection, of course. You would become mine as would your people." He leaned in close to her, running his hand over her arm. "And I am very protective of what is mine."

As revolting as the thought was, she willed composure. "How would the marriage ceremony be performed? Our custom is weddings be held in one of the Creator's chapels before a priest—otherwise the union is not considered legal."

Faramos' features contorted at the mention of the Creator. "We do not have those same traditions here. We prefer our ceremonies to be held outside—blessed by nature and all living things. Usually the village elder performs the ritual."

Karina started to speak, but Faramos held up his hand.

"I know this must be a lot to take in for one evening. I will give you time to consider my offer. In the meantime, why don't I escort you to your room? You must be exhausted after your hard journey." He stood and offered to take her hand.

She did not want to accept him or his hand. Yet, a refusal would be deemed rude, and she must not incur his wrath, especially if she still had a chance to escape. She forced a smile and reluctantly accepted.

He pulled her hand through his arm and patted it, smiling down at her. He led her through a set of double doors into a well-lit hall. "I trust you will rest much better here than on the ground. In my experience, camp accommodations are never as comfortable as one's own bed." He chuckled.

"I thank you for being so kind as to offer me respite," Karina said through clenched teeth.

"It is my pleasure." He led her up a flight of stairs to a wide hall with blood-red carpet. Shields and various ancient weapons adorned the walls, interspersed by several doors on each side.

One set of doors, about halfway down, had a guard on either side.

"This is your room." Faramos threw open the double doors to a bedroom twice the size of her suite in Aletheia's royal house.

The room was decorated in dark blue drapes and accessories the color of her dress, which stood out against the light gray stone wall. A fireplace and sitting area framed one side, while a large bed took up over half of the opposite wall space. A handmaid entered from a door beside the fireplace.

Faramos welcomed her over with a sweep of his hand. "This is Belinda. She is here to see to your needs." He gestured to the door on the other side of the fireplace. "The washroom is in there, and you will find any clothing you may need in the wardrobe."

"I am impressed, sire. I had no idea you would be so well-prepared for me."

Faramos leaned against the door jamb, his wry smile disturbing. "Let's just say I hoped I would get the chance to woo you."

"Well, if you will excuse me, I will seek my dreams. The day has been long."

"Indeed. Tomorrow will be equally busy. We have the Survivor Trials in the morning."

"The Survivor Trials?"

"Ah, a gift for my intended's entertainment." Faramos grinned as he bowed and then shut the door.

Tristan kicked the bars of his cage. How could his brother lock him in the dungeons like a common criminal? He had no proof that what Karina had said in his defense wasn't true. And it wasn't like Tristan hadn't made Faramos angry before. He was tolerable, as long as he ended up with what he wanted.

No, something else was up. Faramos wanted to be alone with Karina. Not to kill her. That he would have done in front of Tristan, especially since he was already angry with him.

He let out a shout. Faramos had even been so cruel as to give him a cell with no windows. Oh, how he longed for a connection to the outside world, to nature. Anger would have consumed him if fear had not expelled his rage. Only a few people had survived the Survivor Trials—and there had been hundreds of players over the years. Faramos said the ancient gods determined a person's fate. If the accused were not guilty, they would survive. If they were at fault … well … a painful death awaited them.

Tristan kicked a spot free of moldy straw and sat with his back against the wall. He needed rest. Tomorrow, he would face the hardest test of his life. However, sleep eluded him. Memories invaded his mind—memories of happier times—his mother's laughter, his father's proud smile. And Faramos—Faramos as a carefree child, mischievous, full of life, but never cruel. What happened to change him?

Tristan recalled that horrid day when he, then an eight-year-old boy, and Father had returned from Aletheia. When the ship docked, a band of soldiers boarded the ship. A short battle ensued—one Tristan missed because Father had locked him in the master cabin. Tristan had managed to free himself and attained the deck just as Faramos shoved a sword into their father's gut.

Tristan shook his head. In the days and weeks that followed, Faramos insisted the deed had been necessary. He told Tristan the negotiations with Aletheia were a betrayal to the Tzedekians. His mother changed after that. She never laughed, never smiled, as if her husband's death had broken her. She died only a few short years later.

Tristan had sworn revenge.

But what could a mere boy of eleven do to a man who had turned to magic? He shivered, remembering his fear the first time he'd seen Faramos kill someone with his dark arts.

Eventually, sleep came, as Tristan resigned himself to whatever fate the ancient gods, or even the Creator, had in store.

CHAPTER TWELVE

Karina's body ached, and the feather bed did little to relieve her discomfort. Not even the burst of sunlight raised her spirits. She moaned and rolled away from the window.

"I'm sorry, Your Highness," a woman called from across the room, the voice unfamiliar.

Karina risked a peek.

Belinda stood by the open window. "It is time to rise. Lord Faramos will be sending for you in a couple of hours." She opened the heavy drapes and then meandered over to a table in the middle of the room. "I hope you're hungry. The chef made these tasty pastries in your honor."

"My honor?" She sat up in the bed, running her hand through her hair, and yawned. "What honor is that?"

Belinda giggled. "Don't be silly. Everyone knows Lord Faramos wishes a union with you. It is most exciting!"

Karina dragged herself out of bed and over to the table. "Belinda, how can you act like this? Do you not know the nature of the man you serve?"

A worried frown crossed Belinda's face, and she looked down at her shoes. "He is not so bad, m'lady. Especially when he is happy." She glanced up at Karina and smiled. "And nothing would make him happier than to have the Aletheian queen at his side."

Karina did not know whether to feel sorry for the woman or to be angry with her for not having more sense. Faramos had crushed the Tzedekians under his iron grip. They were most likely too fearful to betray him.

She took a deep breath and sat in a chair by the table. While she ate, Belinda bustled around the room. She pulled a dress and undergarments from the wardrobe. The dress resembled the blue one Karina had worn the day before, except this one was made of heavy velvet with silver and white trim.

Once she was dressed, Belinda helped style her hair in an upward fashion and painted her face in a way flattering to the Tzedekians. The effect was not much different than the courtiers in Aletheia, but her eyes were more defined by kohl and her lips were a deeper shade of red. Her reflection made her heart ache, but Belinda insisted she looked beautiful.

Karina trudged down the stairs behind the guards, fidgeting with her dress. From the sound of its name, she feared the Survivor Trials would not be fun to watch. She needed Tristan to help her escape. What if he died today? Who would help her then?

Faramos waited for her in the throne room. When did he expect an answer from her? She already knew what she was going to say. The Creator would not allow this union. Something told her Faramos was not used to being refused.

Guards pushed open the doors to the cavernous throne room. A dim light shown through the skylight, but the fires still burned behind the royal dais. Faramos reclined on the throne cushions. A petite woman stood next to him, holding a tray with a golden goblet.

When Karina entered, he leapt from his seat and spread his arms wide. "My dearest Karina. Good morn to you." He clasped her hands in his. "I trust you slept well."

Taken aback by his liveliness, she could only nod.

"That is good to know." He waved another woman over. She held out a shimmering cloak made of white fur, a kind Karina had never seen before.

Faramos took the cape from the woman and held it out to Karina. "This is for you. The seasons are turning, but I am afraid the weather is still a tad chilly in the morning." He motioned for her to turn around and then wrapped the cloak around her shoulders. When she turned back to face him, he smiled as he tied the leather strap. "You look radiant."

She ran her hand over the soft fur. "What—what is the cloak made from?"

Faramos took a step back, his half-smile alarming. "This particular garment was made from the last of the white tigers."

She gasped. "I thought those were only legends."

"They are now." He rubbed her shoulders. "And you are the most beautiful creature I have ever seen."

She pursed her lips. "Faramos, I—"

"No time for chatting, my love. We have a ceremony to attend."

"Ceremony?"

"Yes. This is a festive occasion—the Survivor Trials." He took her hand and led her from the throne room. "First, we have the sendoff. Then there is a feast, games, and dancing until we find out if the fool survived."

He led Karina out the door to a stone path that edged the cliffs. Below them, the waves crashed against the rocks, and the sea stretched to the horizon. Karina breathed in the salty air, her hopes rejuvenated with each breath. The Creator had not deserted her. Even if he should have, he had not.

Ahead, people swarmed out from the fortress and from the surrounding lands.

"How do the Survivor Trials work?" she asked as Faramos helped her over a dip in the ground.

"We drop the prisoner into a hole that leads to a maze of tunnels. If the prisoner finds his way out—there's another opening in the cliffs between Tzedek and Soter—then the ancient gods have shown them favor, and I have no choice but to let them go. In ten years, that has only happened four times."

Karina stopped. "What is difficult about the maze? There are many ways to track your path."

"There are other creatures in the maze—dangerous, half-starved creatures."

By all that was created! Karina struggled to stay upright. Faramos was going to throw his own brother into that maze?

They made their way to a makeshift dais on the edge of a huge hole. An iron bench had been placed there, adorned with dark blue and white cushions that complemented Karina's garments. On the other side of the hole, people mulled about as they laughed and chatted.

Thoughtless brutes.

Behind this crowd, another group had assembled. These people wore black clothing and stood in silence. Were they in mourning … for Tristan?

Faramos pulled her to the dais and spun her around for the world to see. "Behold, our guest of honor, Queen Karina of Aletheia!"

The peasants clapped. Some of them cheered. Those in the back did not move a muscle.

Karina felt like a piece of meat hanging in a vendor booth. Her cheeks heated.

From her position on the dais, she could see into the hole. A narrow path led along the tunnel at a sharp angle—but not so sharp as to be too treacherous if one trod carefully.

Faramos pulled her down beside him. He smiled, his eyes dancing. "Can you feel the energy of the crowd?" He leaned in. "It has been awhile since we have had the opportunity for such fun."

If she were to find a means of escape, she must humor Faramos. She hid her disgust with a phony smile. "The people do seem excited. What about you? You look happy yourself, but this is your brother."

Faramos straightened, his mood somber. "I have no brother." A moment later, his boyish charm returned. "Are we ready?"

She cringed.

Faramos stepped forward. A trumpet sounded, and the crowd quieted. All eyes were on their king. He clapped his hands, then gestured to the crowd. "Let the games begin."

The crowd went wild with applause.

A second trumpet sounded. On Karina's left, the crowd parted as a line of soldiers led Tristan toward the hole. Despite his disheveled hair, pale skin, and clenched jaws, he defied the moment, his head raised high as the procession came to a halt at the dais.

The guards bowed, but Tristan glared at Faramos.

One of the guards knocked Tristan behind the knees. He buckled forward but righted himself before he hit the ground. He glanced in Karina's direction. He seemed confused, perhaps feeling betrayed, and she longed to explain the situation. To assure him all would be well. To trust the Creator's plan.

Faramos signaled the crowd to quiet. "Ladies and gentlemen, thank you for coming. It is rare these days to have the opportunity to host these festivities. It is always a sight to see—to wonder what will happen to the hapless soul who has committed the most heinous of crimes." He pointed at Tristan without taking his eyes off the crowd. "Today, we have one of the royal trackers, but not just any tracker—my most trusted advisor, my brother."

There was a collective gasp and then the crowd booed.

Karina's heart raced. This was not right. The Creator did not save him just to have him killed.

Faramos calmed the crowd again and continued, "Tristan Lemur has decided the Creator's ways are better than the ways of his king—that the good I have done for the kingdom of Tzedek, my love and generosity are not enough. He wants to see our kingdom fall."

Mutters and shouts sounded from all sides.

Karina gripped the arms of the chair. This man thought she would consent to marrying him?

"So today, with great sorrow, I lose a brother. But it is with all humility I offer him up to fate. Maybe the Creator's ways are better—maybe this kingdom does need to fall. If Tristan survives, maybe that is a sign."

The crowd responded with muted laughter.

"Do you have anything to say, brother?"

Tristan raised his head, his eyes wide with determination. "Only that I wish I had seen the error of our ways sooner. That I had not wasted so many years tracking down innocent people for your amusement. Your heart is blacker than any I've known—you killed your own father, the man who raised you." Tristan's voice was loud and sure. "If I die today, it won't be because you were right. But rather because I deserve to die for the things I've done *for* you, not against you."

Faramos shifted his weight from one foot to the other, perhaps unsettled by Tristan's bravery.

Tristan smiled as he gazed at Karina.

Her eyes misted. This was all wrong. Wrong.

"Take him to the hole," Faramos shouted.

The guards jerked Tristan to stand.

"Stop!" Karina jumped up and rushed toward Faramos.

He clasped her hand. "Is there something you wanted to say?"

"Do not do this, Faramos," she pleaded. "He is your brother."

"Your concern for me is flattering, Your Highness, but I assure you I will be fine. I am doing what is necessary for the kingdom."

Karina shook her head. "You do what is necessary for you!" She yanked her hand from his. "You are selfish and arrogant. You crave power—and you take it without a care for the consequences. You think that I, Queen of Aletheia, and more importantly, a Prophetess of the Creator, would dare to consider uniting under your banner of hate and greed?"

Faramos' face darkened with each word. He clenched his fists.

Karina stepped closer, staring directly into his eyes. "I would rather die."

The brutal sound of Faramos's slap across her face echoed across the suddenly silent crowd.

She rubbed her cheek, a superficial sting compared to the fear in Faramos's eyes.

"Throw her in!" His previously gentle hands turned rough as he yanked the cloak off her shoulders and wrenched her broken arm. With an unreadable expression, he shoved her off the dais.

She let out a scream as her arm hit the ground. Two of the guards seized her. She straightened and glared at Faramos. "Mark my words, Faramos Lemur, the Creator is not done with you. He knows your plans, and he will bring you to destruction."

Faramos knelt on the dais, a wild look in his eyes. He leaned in close to her. "It seems to me his plan is about to die. I hope he has a backup."

Before she could retort, a guard clamped his hand over her mouth and pulled her away.

Faramos pulled on his jacket. "Now we have the pleasure of awaiting the fates of two people on this beautiful day."

The crowd cheered.

Karina ran into Tristan's arms as the guards surrounded them. They led the way to the cave-like hole. From here, the pit seemed more menacing. What obstacles would they face inside? She prayed for wisdom and peace.

They paused at the pit.

Faramos stood, apparently to pronounce official judgment. "Tristan Lemur and Queen Karina Dubrev, you are sentenced to the Survivor Trials for crimes against the crown. You are to enter this test with no weapons and no food. If fate sees fit, you will find the other side. If not, your deaths are sealed. Do not try to come back this way as the guards are ordered to kill you on sight if you do."

A trumpet sounded. The guards drew their swords, then shoved Karina forward.

Tristan swung at them. "Back off."

"Get going," a guard growled. "Both of you."

Tristan wrapped an arm around Karina's shoulders as he led her into the pit. The ground sloped down at an impossible angle, but he kept her steady as they descended toward the mouth of the cave. The further in they went, the darker the tunnel became—the light, a mere circle behind them.

"What happens when the light completely vanishes?" Karina whispered.

Tristan squeezed her hand. "I'm not sure. I've never been further than the mouth of the cave."

"Oh." She shivered but pressed on. *Creator, help us! Give us light.*

Soon, they walked in total darkness.

Karina felt for the wall of the cave, the cool stone rough to the touch. With her other hand, she reached for Tristan, and he pulled her to him. She closed her eyes, still praying.

"Karina, look." Hope etched Tristan's command.

She opened her eyes and gasped.

A blue-green light emanated from the cave walls. Karina stepped forward to get a closer look. A strange growth resembled the plain moss that covered rocks near the riverbeds, only this vegetation glowed. *Thank you, Creator.*

She turned to Tristan. "Ready?"

He shook his head. "Karina, light is going to be the least of our worries." He peered down the tunnel ahead of them. "Darkness only begets more darkness."

CHAPTER THIRTEEN

Karina stubbed her toe on a hard object and stumbled forward. Tristan's strong arms wrapped around her waist. "Thank you," she whispered as she smoothed her velvety blue dress, entirely impractical for the journey through the cave.

A skeleton lay on the floor at her feet, its bones gray with dust. The bluish-green glow revealed bits of cloth that hung in shreds from its eerie frame. She shrieked as she grabbed Tristan's arm.

He pulled her forward, attempting to hide a smile.

"What?"

"I have to admit, I was taken aback when I saw you sitting beside Faramos."

"He asked me to marry him."

Tristan chuckled. "Sounds like him."

"H-he wanted to unite our kingdoms."

"More like expand his own empire." He shook his head. "I'm glad you were able to resist."

"It was not what the Creator wanted." She stretched her good arm, feeling the pull of sore muscles. "If it had been, I am not sure I could have complied. But it does not matter now. We have to find a way out of here, so I can retrieve the armor."

"The maze itself is easy. I've seen the maps in the castle library." He knelt and picked up a smooth stone. "Like I said before, it's everything else we have to worry about."

"Like what?"

"Rodents as big as a horse—called *aqlaqs*. One got loose a few years ago, went through half a herd of sheep before the farmer was able to kill it." He used the rock to make a white X on the wall. "Aside from that, I don't know what's down here. I'm not sure anyone alive does."

"What about the ones who escaped?"

Tristan dipped his head. "They're not alive to tell the tale."

"Oh." Karina looked away, her heart torn. She knew the Creator was slowly changing Tristan, but times like this made it hard to forget what kind of man he used to be.

They trudged on for some time in silence. Tunnels branched off occasionally, but they continued to walk straight forward until they came upon the first split that forced a choice, right or left.

"Which way?" Karina peered into the darkness of both caves.

Tristan shuffled back and forth. "To the left, I think."

"I thought you said this was easy."

"Hey, I'm trying to remember." He scratched his head and then moved toward the left tunnel. "Are you coming?"

Karina stood in front of the right tunnel. The Creator would guide them, so they had to be missing something? She looked from one tunnel to the other, then back again until she realized what had been staring her in the face.

"We have to go right."

Tristan ambled back toward her. "Why do you think that?"

"It's the one with the glowing moss."

He lifted an eyebrow. "I can see why you would want to go that way, doesn't mean we should."

Karina put her hands on her hips. "The glowing moss did not appear until I prayed for light. I believe the Creator is providing a more reliable way for us than your spotty memory."

Tristan peered into the tunnel to the right. "Fine. Let's go." He pushed by her and led the way.

A peace settled over Karina. The soft glow of the moss would lead them through the maze. The dank smell did not help her churning stomach, though, and she longed for fresh air.

"Wait." Tristan held up his hand. Taking a few steps in front of her, he sniffed the air. "Something is coming."

She grabbed his arm. "What?"

"I don't know. One of the aqlaqs maybe?"

The sound of scratching on the rocks filtered through the damp air. Shapes formed in the near distance—beady eyes reflected the blue-green light.

Aqlaqs! Karina gawked at the massive rodents. While their long bodies were not quite as big as a horse, that did not make them less menacing than she had imagined. Their coarse white fur stood on end, and their light pink noses sniffed at the air. Pointy front teeth stuck out from their large mouths.

Tristan reached for his sword. "Curses! No sword." He balled his hands. "What do we do?"

He shook his head, running his tongue over his lips. "Make a run for it?"

"There are three of them, and one takes up most of the tunnel. We will never make it."

Tristan threw a rock at the closest creature. It screeched, baring its sharp front teeth. He threw another rock.

The aqlaq roared as it batted the stone away. "Lunch!" the rat screamed as it charged at Tristan, who backed up a step.

Karina gasped. What? Of course! "Wait!" She pushed her way in front of Tristan.

"What do you think you're doing?" He yanked her to his side.

"I can talk to them."

"What?"

She let out a rough sigh. "Like I talk to Dom." She turned to the encroaching aqlaqs. "Do you understand me?"

The lead aqlaq growled. "I understand you, woman, but we're a little hungry."

Karina smiled as her muscles relaxed slightly. "Praise the Creator! Please, listen to me."

"I'd rather eat you for lunch."

She pulled herself to her full height and looked down her nose at them. "I am a prophetess of the Creator, and you will listen."

The rodents cowered, their noses against the dirt, as if bowing. "W-we're sorry," the lead one pleaded. "We didn't know. Forgive us, Prophetess."

"We are on a quest for the Creator and need your help."

The aqlaq nodded. "Whatever you need."

Need? They needed to get out of here. Surely the aqlaqs knew the way to the other side. Karina glanced toward Tristan. "Want to go for a ride?"

"On that?" He pointed at the white rodent and then shook his head. "No."

Despite his objection, the aqlaqs readied themselves to be mounted, and Tristan relented.

They raced through the maze—no other creature challenged them. The aqlaqs, familiar with the moss trail, sniffed their way along the correct path. Karina resisted the urge to close her eyes. Atop the lead aqlaq, her body relaxed for the first time since entering the cave. How long had it been? Judging from her lack of energy, the time for sleep had past long ago. Still, they had to keep moving. Escape trumped everything else—even rest.

The aqlaqs came to a sudden stop. The lead rodent dipped, a signal for Karina to dismount. "This is as far as we go, Prophetess."

Karina dismounted and peered into the shadows ahead. "Is this the end of the tunnel? I do not see any light."

"It's not that far—just on the other side of *his* cavern."

"Whose cavern?"

Tristan came up beside her. "There's a who?"

Karina silenced him with a glare.

The aqlaq sniffed at the air. "Maugro's cavern."

"And Maugro is ... what?"

"A dragon."

Karina gasped.

"What?" Tristan grabbed her shoulder. "What is it?"

"A dragon."

Tristan went for the missing sword again and cursed under his breath.

Karina knelt before the lead aqlaq. "What can you tell me about the dragon?"

"Only that he doesn't fear the Creator as we do." The rodent scratched the rocky ground with his foot. "He's dangerous enough. The servants of the Creator's temple here in Tzedek had him chained in the cavern. We were put here so Maugro could not escape."

"I wish there was more I could do to say thank you."

"Farewell, Prophetess. May the Light of the Creator go with you." The aqlaqs turned and scampered into the darkness behind them.

"What did they say?" Tristan sat down on a large rock, rubbing his back.

Karina sat on a nearby rock and leaned against the cool wall. Her leg muscles ached from the long ride. "Our escape lies on the other side of a dragon's lair—a dragon the temple ensnared here. I have a feeling I will not be able to talk our way around him."

"We'll wait until he's asleep, and then we'll try to slip past him." He stood and offered to help her up. "Let's get a look at it."

She hopped off the rock. Her body swayed from lack of sleep. She rubbed her eyes and stifled a yawn. "Lead the way."

Around the bend, the tunnel narrowed, only wide enough for one person. Soon, the tunnel expanded into an enormous cavern. Karina peeked over Tristan's shoulder. The glowing moss covered the room from floor to ceiling.

The rustle of chains drew her attention. A dragon with silvery eyes, sharp claws, and scales darker than coal rested in the center of the room, iron shackles around its legs, its wings tucked at its sides.

"What now?"

Tristan shook his head. "We wait."

Karina slid down the tunnel wall. "He better go to sleep soon."

"I have no intention of going to sleep," the dragon said in a perfectly calm voice.

Karina squeaked and then slapped a hand over her mouth.

Tristan reached for his sword again.

"The dragon said—"

"I heard it loud and clear," he said through clenched teeth.

She raised her eyebrows.

"Sleep can wait—especially with the prospect of a real meal." On his feet now, the dragon arched its scaly back.

"Please," Karina said, pushing past Tristan. She stepped into the cavern and stopped. "We are on an important quest and only wish safe passage through your lair."

The dragon roared. "No one is allowed through here. If you do not wish to die, I suggest you find another way."

She had to come up with a plan, and quickly. They could not rely on brute strength, especially with no weapons. The intelligence of dragons was legendary. Was there no better option?

Karina edged forward, motioning for Tristan to follow her. "There is no other way. The other entrance to these caves is guarded by soldiers ordered to kill us if we return." She took a small step to the side, careful to stay close to the cavern wall.

"So, doomed either way," the dragon agreed.

"We would prefer your help, Maugro."

"No."

She slid a few steps closer. "Is there a way we could persuade you to let us go?"

"No." The dragon clawed at the rocky floor.

The irritating sound rattled in her head. She covered her ears and leaned against the cave wall for support. Her head felt like it would explode any moment. She could not concentrate on anything but breathing.

Finally, the noise stopped, and she was able to stand. She gave her mind a moment to refocus. "As I said before, we are on a quest for the Creator. I am a prophetess." She edged along, very slowly.

The dragon scoffed as he danced, the chains clanging in rhythm to his movements.

"You may not follow the Creator, but surely you are aware of his great powers."

"If he did not smite me when I roamed your world, I do not fear him down here."

"Smite you?" Karina dared a glance at Tristan. His face was white, but he hugged the wall as he inched alongside her. "You have been chained in a dark cavern for years. What makes you think this was not your punishment?"

"Ah, my child. That is where you are wrong. As long as I breathe, I have hope. I may be down here now, but one day I will be free."

"Run!" Tristan whispered, shoving her ahead of him. They raced for the tunnel.

Karina stole a glimpse at the dragon just as fire spewed from its mouth. Too close. Heat surrounded her, and she screamed. Something collided with her from behind, knocking her to the ground as fire blazed over her head.

"Get up." Tristan's voice was gruff. He seized her good arm and pulled her along as she stumbled to her feet.

"You will not escape!"

Something whistled through the air. The dragon roared.

More whistles—one right after the other.

Karina looked back, Tristan still pulling her along. At the far end of the cavern, the dragon reared, arrows sticking out of its chest. More arrows rushed by.

As they came to the tunnel, Karina shrieked with excitement. *Rashka!*

The black-haired elf smirked as she continued to fire arrows at lightning speed. She was so quick Karina never saw her draw an arrow from the quiver on her back.

The ground rumbled as the mighty dragon fell. Dust momentarily blocked the moss light.

Air rushed from Karina's lungs as she rushed to embrace the elf. "What are you doing here?"

Rashka stepped back and her smile faded. "I have been trying to catch up with you two," she shot a stern look at Tristan, "ever since I realized you had disappeared from the woods. I lost your trail in the Barrens. I was not sure which path he would take, but I knew he planned to bring you to Faramos." She looked away. "And then I felt my brother's death."

"I am so sorry, Rashka." Karina put her hand on the elf's arm. "Asharan was protecting me." She glanced at Tristan, a small smile warming her cheeks. "They both were."

Rashka shook her head as she stepped further into the wide tunnel. "We need to go."

They wound through the shaft for hours until they reached open air. A river rushed by in front of them, and high cliffs rose beyond both banks.

Karina fell to her knees, breathing deeply. Her head spun. *Thank you, Creator.*

"Come." Rashka placed her hand on Karina's shoulder. "We must get as far away from here as we can before day breaks. We only have a couple of hours."

CHAPTER FOURTEEN

"Here."

"What?" Tristan turned just in time to catch the hilt of the sword Rashka tossed to him. He backed away from the Barren rabbit he had hung above the fire pit.

Rashka's golden eyes glinted. A smirk crossed her face."

He lifted his chin. "I prefer to keep my skills to myself."

"You say you have changed. That you no longer align yourself with the likes of your brother. How do we know this was not a set up? Maybe you are searching for the Temple of Aletheia, not to help us, but to destroy it."

Tristan took a couple of steps toward Rashka, getting a feel for his sword by twirling it at his side. He knew neither Rashka nor Karina had any reason to trust him. This elf, though, did not realize how serious his brother had been about killing him. Faramos did not take betrayal lightly. "It's not like that."

"Fight." She pointed to the sword, then raised one of her own.

"If you say so." He held the sword up, adjusted his grip, and spun it in another quick circle.

Rashka shouted, then lunged at Tristan, thrusting her sword at his middle. She was fast, but he swept the blade aside with his own, then brought it to the ready and circled the crazed elf. Where did she get her speed?

Rashka held her sword level with the ground, her arm cocked back, and her other hand raised flat before her. An odd sight since he held his own sword at an angle to the ground. She lunged again.

Tristan deflected her thrust, but she pulled her sword back to the left and sliced toward him with lightning speed. He blocked the attempt just before the tip sliced across his chest.

She stepped back with an appraising smile. "Good."

They fell into a rhythm of strikes and parries. To his surprise, the exercise invigorated him—until Rashka swiped his legs out from under him. He landed on his back with a grunt.

She placed her foot on his chest and leaned over him. "I know your secret."

He groaned. "Which secret? I've had many over the years."

Her gaze flicked to the cave, then back to him. "One I am not sure you would want Karina to know."

He furrowed his brow. What secret could she be talking about? He'd prefer Karina knew nothing about his past. He hadn't been a good person, not since his father had died.

Tristan growled and shoved Rashka's foot away. "Do you think you can blackmail me with gossip?"

She snorted. "Nonsense. Quite the opposite. I think you need to tell Karina the truth."

He narrowed his eyes. Did Rashka really know the truth?

"I know how you know Karina—not because your brother sent you to retrieve her."

Tristan fought the memory of a petite girl who wandered the palace gardens. He had accompanied Father to Aletheia that day and had agreed to their marriage. His stomach churned with the recollection.

He bared his teeth and swung his sword in a high arc.

"Stop!"

Rashka's eyes widened, and she held her blade at bay. But Tristan brought the sword down with all his might.

Karina yanked his shoulder toward her. "What are you doing?"

He let out a shout as his sword arched in Karina's direction, unable to stop the blade's trajectory. Karina leapt out of the way.

"Woman, what do you think you are doing?" Tristan huffed. Sweat dampened his tunic, and heat burned his cheeks. "I could have killed you."

Karina pierced him with a fiery glance. "What is going on? Why are you two fighting? We are on the same side."

Rashka laughed as she returned the sword to its sheath. "We were merely sparring. I had to see what this human is worth—if he is prepared for battle."

Tristan grunted and ambled over to a makeshift fire pit. After all the fighting, his stomach demanded to be fed.

"Battle?" Karina asked.

Rashka nodded. "I hope you know you are in far too deep now, Prophetess. Faramos and his minions will stop at nothing to see you dead and the Creator's plans ruined. Not to mention there are those who wish to see Faramos succeed."

Tristan nodded in agreement as he pulled the rabbit meat off the fire.

Karina knelt at the other side of the pit. "Who?"

"People of power, of influence." Rashka sat on a large rock, elbows on her knees. "The evil that Faramos has released into our world is already taking its toll."

Karina frowned. Her shoulders slumped forward, shuddering with Rashka's revelations about Faramos's evil intentions.

Tristan held a small bowl in the air. "Come eat, Karina. You'll need your strength."

Even from across the fire, he heard her stomach growl. She accepted the bowl from him with a nod of thanks. He plopped on the ground and shook the sweat from his hair before he took a bite. The meat was gamey at best, but it was nourishment enough.

"Wait." Rashka crouched next to Karina. "Before you eat, let me heal your arm."

Karina furrowed her brows.

The elf smiled. "One of my gifts."

She held out her arm.

Rashka rubbed her hands together and then held them over the makeshift splint. A light green glow emanated from her palms. Karina let out a soft sigh as Rashka removed the bandages. "There you go."

"Wonderful. Thank you, Rashka." Karina moved her arm about. With a grin, she picked up her bowl and took a bite of the meat.

Rashka quizzed Tristan in battle strategy, inquiring as to his training, both as a swordsman and as a bounty hunter. The longer they chatted, the more pensive Karina became.

He had taken his last bite of food when she stood abruptly, handing her bowl to him. "Excuse me," she mumbled, avoiding eye contact with Rashka as she hastened toward the edge of the cliff.

What had gotten into her? He held out his hand to Rashka. "Dish?"

She raised an eyebrow. "Are you going to go after her?"

"Hadn't planned on it."

"She does not think she can complete the quest. She needs your encouragement." Rashka grabbed the bowls from him.

"I doubt that."

Rashka made her way to the river without looking back.

Puzzled, Tristan stroked his chin. Why? Why did she need his encouragement? Rashka would be a better counselor.

Karina hurried to the cliff's edge closest to the waterfall in hopes the crashing waters would drown out the clamor of insecurity in her soul. She was weak, inept. The burden of her quest weighed too heavy on her shoulders. She could not fight. Nor had she ever used a sword, except for a few sparring matches with Sam. What could she do with the Armor of the Creator? Wear it on her passage to the Lighted Realm?

She had come so close to dying, saved only by the power of her friends. What she wouldn't give to have her uncle here to advise her, or Jace—or even her father. Her heart ached at her losses. Granted, Jace was still alive, but he was not here with her. Anyone would know how to handle all this better than she. *Creator, it cannot be me. I cannot fight. I cannot be expected to lead anyone. You have to take this quest from me. Give it to Rashka. She is a capable servant, is she not?*

A gentle hand grazed her shoulder. She yelped and spun around.

Tristan locked his hands behind his back. "How are you faring?"

She turned toward the cascading waterfall, hoping Tristan did not notice her tears or sense the terror she felt. "I am fine."

"You know, Rashka and I had to create a litter to carry you because we could not rouse you. You slept the rest of the day and then a night."

She raised an eyebrow. Her body must have required the extra rest.

"Rashka says you're worried about being able to complete your quest."

Tricky vixen could probably read minds.

Tristan's hand cupped her elbow and turned her toward him. He looked down at her through captivating green eyes. "Karina, you are a most capable woman."

"Capable of getting myself killed." She tried to turn away again, but he steadied her with both hands.

He waited until she looked up at him. "Capable of turning hearts."

She gulped back the tears. Was he referring to his own reversal of intent? She had done nothing to persuade him.

He gazed into her eyes. "Karina, you are capable of so much more than you can imagine. The Creator didn't need a warrior to lead this quest. He needed someone who understands people."

"How do you know?"

He looked off the waterfall. "Because I don't think this battle can be won with an army. An army would most likely fall to Faramos's minions—he has the advantage. I remember a quote from my younger years, something my mother would read from the Creator's Letters. 'The greatest enemy of darkness is the light. The greatest enemy of evil is someone capable of love.' I believe you fit that description better than anyone else I know." He winked at her and then strolled over to the fire pit.

Karina's eyes welled with tears of humility and relief.

Tristan brought up the rear of their small caravan as they marched across the Barrens. Well, marched wasn't the proper term. Rashka led the way, her hawk-like eyes watching the skies above them, the river to their right, and the trees on the horizon. Thankfully, after three days of slow travel, they would reach River Branch before nightfall.

Karina was in the middle. She seemed more confident than she had the day before, yet still in need of his protection. He grimaced. Rarely had someone had such a hold on him. Still, the way she smiled at him since their conversation at the waterfall had made his mind reel.

He stayed to the back, giving the women their space. His instincts were better back here.

Rashka held up her hand, and they all stopped.

"What's wrong?" he asked, even as he noticed the lone figure approaching from the mountains to the north.

Rashka retrieved her bow. But there were no arrows in her quiver. What did she plan to do?

She drew the bowstring back with practiced fluidity, and an arrow appeared. It was thinner than most arrows he'd seen, with bright feathers along its shaft. Magic.

He turned back to the approaching man. Or was it something else?

Sure enough, an elf strode up to them with nothing but a sword and a small pack. His dark hair was the same shade as Rashka's, but he had more muscles than Tristan. His face drew taut over high cheekbones.

Rashka lowered her bow. "Brusho?"

"Rashka, I have found you!" His deep voice reflected joy—yet something else etched his words—something that wouldn't allow Tristan to relax.

While her bow was no longer poised to shoot, Rashka did not put her weapon away either. "What are you doing here?"

Brusho hesitated, looking at Karina and Tristan. "I sought you out after I heard of Asharan's death. I am sure your heart must be grieving."

"Indeed."

While Brusho continued to talk about his travels with Rashka, he eyed Karina in such an indirect manner, Tristan drew closer to her, his protective instincts on high alert.

Tristan cleared his throat. "Come, Karina, let's leave these two to catch up."

"What? Why?"

"Let them have time to mourn Asharan together." He stared at her for a moment, willing his meaning to sink in, and then pulled her away as gently as he could.

She looked back to Rashka, who nodded.

Tristan led Karina toward the woods as he shouted over his shoulder. "Rashka, you can catch up with us at River Branch. We'll be at the inn."

"Tristan," Karina hissed when he turned back around. "What are you—?"

"Not so fast!" Brusho warned, his voice deep, his tone commanding.

Tristan groaned. His suspicions were right. He stepped between Karina and the oversized oaf.

"What are you doing, Brusho?" Rashka lifted her bow again.

Brusho held knives in each hand, ready to the throw. His features twisted with anger—his eyes mere slits, his jaw tight. "Hand over the girl, and you two can be on your way."

Rashka gasped. "Brusho!"

"One step, Rashka, and I will kill you all. Drop the bow."

"What happened to you?"

Brusho growled. "Life happened. The world is changing, and we must choose sides. Drop the bow."

Rashka hesitated, her features hardened, but she laid the bow on the ground. "Why would you not choose the side of the Creator?"

"Because the Creator deserted me a long time ago."

Tristan watched the exchange as he slowly inched backwards. A few more steps and they'd be beyond the reach of the elf's knives.

"Unless you want Rashka to die, I suggest you cease your lame attempt at escape." Brusho glanced back toward them. "Hand over the girl, bounty hunter, and no harm shall come to you. Faramos does not wish to harm her, only to hold her until his plans come to pass."

Not likely. After they'd made a fool of him by escaping the maze, Faramos would have all their necks and not think twice. Tristan clasped Karina's hand—ice cold. He slipped his fingers between hers and squeezed.

Rashka glanced toward Tristan, her nod almost unperceivable. He squeezed Karina's hand again.

"Brusho, she is the Creator's chosen one. We cannot hand her over." Rashka took a step forward.

Brusho adjusted his stance.

Tristan squeezed Karina's hand a third time. "Run!" he whispered and spun on his heel.

Brusho's shout was cut short by a loud thump.

Karina stumbled behind Tristan. He managed to keep her steady as they raced toward the forest, never letting go of her hand.

He glanced over his shoulder. Rashka and Brusho were rolling around on the ground. Despite his size, Brusho didn't look to be any match for Rashka's speed and agility. Tristan turned back to the mission at hand, pulling Karina along after him, not daring to stop until they reached the forest.

The muscles in his legs tired, but he pushed on. The tree line was just ahead.

"Tri-Tristan," Karina gasped for air, "we need to … help … Rashka."

"She's fine, keep running."

"I—I have to—" She lost her footing.

Without coming to a full stop, he caught her.

The woods were within reach. He shot a final look over his shoulder. The two elves were circling each other. Rashka's bow was only a couple of steps away from her.

He dashed into the cover of the trees.

CHAPTER FIFTEEN

"Where are we going?" Karina picked her way through the underbrush of the woods. Branches swiped at her face and arms. Tristan, pushing through the dense foliage ahead of her, barely grunted in response. "Tristan!"

He stopped, his breath coming in labored gasps. "Karina, we can't stop right now." He glanced over her shoulder. "If Rashka doesn't defeat Brusho, he'll be after us soon. Once we reach River Branch, we can acquire horses and supplies for the rest of the trip."

"But—"

He grabbed her arm and pushed her ahead of him.

They came into a clearing where the sun shone through the trees, highlighting wild flowers and tall grasses. Karina stopped in the middle and let out a frustrated shout. "I can't do this! Do you hear me?" She threw her hands out to the side and raised her head. "You have the wrong woman. Ever since I began this journey, not one thing has gone the way it was supposed to. How can I ever hope to complete your quest?"

Tristan looked perplexed. "Who are you talking to?"

"Who indeed." Karina stomped a foot. "Because the Creator sure isn't listening!" she shouted again. Why would he place this burden on her, then let the world slowly erode her faith?

Tristan put his hand on her shoulder as he met her gaze. "Rest assured, I will make sure you get to the temple."

She blew a sigh of resignation. "I know you will, Tristan. I'm just … tired."

He nodded. Something else grabbed his attention. He cocked his head to the side. "Keep moving."

Karina obeyed without argument. The change in Tristan's demeanor since their meeting with Asharan, while not a sharp contrast, was noticeable. She could sense his guilt, his remorse, but even more so, his renewed compassion. Would he revert to his former ways after their journey was over? She shook her head. Such thoughts were better left for another time.

They traveled in silence the rest of the way. Any time she tried to talk, Tristan put his finger to his lips. They stayed off the main path, pushing through the undergrowth. At last, shouts and clamors reached them through the trees. A few minutes later, the forest gave way to a row of houses, shops, and people. Karina grinned.

"This way," Tristan whispered, lacing his fingers between hers.

She pulled her hand back but followed him through the streets. To be among decent people again put her heart at ease. Maybe the Creator had not deserted her. Her cheeks heated at the thought of the small tantrum she had thrown in the woods. Hardly becoming of a queen.

Tristan took them to the same inn they had stayed in before. Few people sat at the tables today, but a welcoming fire roared in the clay fireplace off to the left.

Ham stood behind the bar. "Tristan, you're back again." He wiped a rag across his counter as he eyed Karina and quirked an eyebrow. "What can I do for you this time?"

"We would like another room." Tristan took a couple of coins from his purse and placed them in front of the man. "And we'd like to keep our stay … private."

Ham nodded with a wink. "Very well." He tossed Tristan a key. "By the way, something of yours found its way into my stable."

Dom! In all the craziness, Karina had completely forgotten about Tristan's stallion. She breathed a sigh of relief.

"I trust you made sure he was cared for?"

He nodded.

"Thank you." Tristan flipped him another coin and led the way up the stairs to the assigned room and opened the door.

Karina had never been so thankful to see a bed. With a contented sigh, she sunk into its feathery comfort.

"Don't get too comfortable." Tristan opened the window shutter to look at the street below.

She closed her eyes, refusing to move. "I am too tired."

"I know, but we're not staying."

"What?" She eyed him suspiciously. "Then why did you bring me here?"

A smirk pulled at his lips. "Don't flatter yourself, Your Majesty."

She scowled.

"I meant this is only a ruse." He chuckled as he nodded toward the door. "We'll be camping in the woods again tonight."

Karina sat up. "But how will Rashka find us?"

"Take off your cloak."

"Excuse me?"

Tristan sighed. "We're going to leave it here."

"But it's cold in Shadowed Forest!" Karina knew she was behaving like a petulant child, but she really was overly tired. It had been a long journey, and they had not even made it to the first temple. A cloak was of little consequence. Still, this was all too much.

"I will buy you a new one. But we need to make it look like we are staying here."

"Why?"

He moved the rickety, wooden chairs about and dumped water from the pitcher into the chipped porcelain bowl.

"Tristan, stop what you're doing and tell me your plan."

He reached for the lapel button on her cloak. "If Brusho wins, he knows we're supposed to be at the inn. He will come here looking for us, but we won't be here. If Rashka wins, then it'll also throw off anyone else who comes looking for us."

"What about Rashka? How will she find us?"

"She and I have already discussed this—and she's the one who gave me the money, seeing as Faramos took everything I had. As long as you and I get to Shadowed Forest, she will find us."

Karina's eyes widened. Obviously, strategy was not her strong point. Thankfully, the Creator had sent her not one but two clever strategists to join her on this journey.

Satisfied the room looked lived in, Tristan led the way to the stable. When they walked in, a familiar whinny greeted them.

"Dom!" Karina rushed to his stall.

The horse snorted. "It is about time! I thought you two were worm food by now."

She rested her head on his neck. "I am so happy you made it back."

"As am I," Tristan said from behind them. Dom nuzzled his old friend. "We're getting supplies, and then we're out of here."

"How did you escape?" Dom asked.

"We almost didn't." Karina glanced back at Tristan. "We were sent through the Survivor Trials."

Dom nickered. "Even Mister Too-Suave-Swordsman over there would struggle to survive in there. It is a miracle you made it out alive."

"I don't think we would have if Rashka had not showed up. She is Asharan's sister and Guardian of Shadowed Forest."

Tristan led Dom out of the stall and saddled him. "Karina, are you ready?"

She nodded, and they left the stable to meander around town, collecting supplies. After purchasing some food and new weapons, they stopped at a blacksmith to secure a weapon for Karina. Tristan wandered inside the small shop, while Karina watched the bustle of people.

"Karina!"

The voice sounded familiar. She looked around. The streets were not overcrowded like in Calliope, but she could not discern any familiar faces among the people strolling the main street.

"Karina!" Someone called from behind.

She spun around.

Sam worked his way through the small crowd, waving his arms like a madman, his eyes wide with excitement.

At the sound of her name, many others turned as well. Karina swallowed and ducked from the curious stares. Did they recognize the new queen? She pushed back to the edge of the street, reaching for the safety of Tristan's presence.

"Karina!" Sam shouted again.

Tristan stepped between them, sword drawn.

She had not meant for him to mistake her leeriness of the crowd to mean she feared Sam. "What are you doing?"

"Stay back," Tristan murmured.

Sam slowed his approach, holding up his hands. A lock of his light-brown mop fell into his eyes. "Whoa!"

"Put that sword away right now!" Karina tried to shove Tristan aside, but he was too solid on his feet.

Sam stopped within reach of Tristan's sword.

"Who is this?" Tristan asked her without taking his eyes off her friend.

"This is Sam, a friend. He is a stable hand at the royal house." Tristan eased his stance but kept his sword ready. Karina turned to Sam. "What are you doing here?"

He stared for a moment. Then, with a lopsided grin, he swept her up in a tight hug. "I have been looking for you everywhere. I was so worried."

Karina pulled away. "What do you mean? Is something wrong?"

"When your squad returned, Henry said they were attacked and you were missing."

Karina cast a sideways glance at Tristan, who had not moved a muscle. "So, Anaya sent soldiers to look for me?"

Sam was suddenly intent on the dirt under his fingernails. "Not exactly."

Of course not. Why search for the traitorous niece who killed the king?

"The queen told the kingdom you had been killed."

Not surprising, really. The words still stung.

"Henry confided in me that he did not believe you were dead, but his hands were tied." Sam grinned. "I *knew* you weren't dead, so I came looking for you myself."

"You are a good friend, Sam. Thank you." She squeezed his hand.

Tristan grabbed her arm. "I don't like it here, Karina. We need to be on our way."

"Right." She turned back to Sam. "What will you do now? You cannot return to Calliope. If Anaya finds out you were looking for me—that you found me—she'll have you killed."

Sam shrugged. "I'll figure something out."

Karina looked up at Tristan, who shook his head and clenched his jaw. He opened his mouth, but she held up her hand. "Sam, you must come with us."

"What?" Tristan growled.

She ignored his resistance. "We are heading for the temple once again. With all the trouble we have had thus far, another swordsman would be very useful."

Sam glanced sideways at Tristan who shrugged and sheathed his sword.

Karina clapped her hands. "We are almost done restocking our supplies and then we will be on our way."

Tristan grunted. "Two more horses then?"

"What about Rashka?"

"She can fly, right?"

CHAPTER SIXTEEN

Darkness cloaked the world. Not even shadows could be seen. Laughter echoed through the inky-black nothingness that grew thicker with each passing moment. Louder and louder …

Tristan startled from his restless sleep. Something had awakened him—and not the nightmare. He hitched himself up on one elbow, reaching for his sword with the free arm. A low fire crackled between him and Karina.

She seemed to be fast asleep, which was a good thing. She had not rested much in the last several days. If her quest were real, she needed all the sleep she could get.

He scanned the campsite. Where was Sam?

An owl hooted in a nearby tree. Small animals scampered about in the underbrush.

Footsteps.

Tristan pushed himself off the ground, bringing his sword to the ready.

Sam ambled through the trees, rubbing the back of his neck and stifling a yawn. He scowled at Tristan. "Do you always greet people like that?"

Tristan dropped his sword to his side.

"What's wrong with you?" Sam groaned.

"I don't trust you."

Sam threw another log in the fire. "Why not?"

Tristan took another moment to survey the mass of trees surrounding them as well as the scrawny kid before him. "The circumstances that led you to join Karina's cause are suspicious."

Sam plopped down on his makeshift bed and pulled up the heavy wool blanket. "I've known Karina most of my life. She's like a sister to me. My intentions are only ever honorable."

"So you say."

Sam blew out a loud breath as he laid down with his back to Tristan.

Truth be told, the stable boy probably wasn't lying. Something felt off about the whole thing, but Tristan couldn't pinpoint what exactly.

"You are both right."

Tristan whirled around, brandishing his sword.

Rashka, in hawk form, chuckled from her perch in a nearby tree.

"I see you finally made it."

A flash of light—an elf again. She leaned her head back against the tree trunk. "Brusho is dead."

Tristan cast his gaze toward the ground. "I'm sorry."

"His fault. I told him to stand down."

"Still, he was once your friend. Like …"

In one graceful movement, she dropped from the tree. "As I was saying, you are both right."

"What do you mean?"

Rashka knelt by the fire to warm her hands. "The boy means no harm to Karina. He is a friend." She glanced to the two sleeping bodies—Karina on one side of the fire, Sam on the other. "However, I noticed footprints heading into Shadowed Forest."

"Whose?"

"Not sure. Whoever they are, they have lupens with them. I tried to track them, but either they quit following, or they are masters at covering their tracks."

Tristan swore. He didn't like the sound of that. Rashka's tracking skills were equal to his own. He gazed at Karina's sleeping form. An unfamiliar emotion took residence in his heart. She was so innocent. So … weak would not be a word to describe her. She was anything but. Still, she needed protection. He sighed.

Rashka paced the fire's perimeter. "I will take watch. You get some rest."

He turned back to her. "What about you? You must be exhausted."

"Elves do not require as much rest as humans. I will be fine."

Karina meandered behind Rashka and Sam. Her troubling nightmares had kept her awake most of the night. Dark. Soulless. Her body yearned for a more peaceful rest.

"Keep up, Karina," Tristan whispered in her ear.

She glanced up. They had fallen behind. Rashka, Sam, and his horse disappeared around a bend in the trail. She sighed as she picked up her pace.

Tristan settled in beside her, leading Dom and Karina's new horse by the reins. "Do you mind if I ask what you meant that day when you said you had not always lived in the royal house?"

Karina knew these questions would arise eventually. Still, she did not want to think about her past, let alone confess to Tristan. Yet, he deserved to know. "When I was about five years old, something happened between my father and King Pistis. I did not know then, but it had to do with whatever happened between your father and mine." She gave him a pointed look as he had yet to address anything Faramos had told her.

His ears turned crimson and his jaw tightened. But he said nothing.

She sucked in a breath. "King Pistis banished my father from Aletheia. We went to live in Soter. A few years later, we were attacked on the road to our village. My parents were killed, and I was put in an orphan caravan.

"A few months after that, the caravan crossed from Soter to Aletheia at River Branch and met with a raiding party. As far as I know, everyone was killed, and the caravan was burned. On his way back from visiting family in Soter, Aletheia's royal healer found me. I was wandering the trails, sick and dehydrated. He brought me to the royal house, nursed me to health, and took me on as his apprentice. The king took a liking to me as well, and I became his ward."

Tristan nodded. "Did he know who you were?"

"Not at the time. Before he died, though, he told me he had known for a while, but he still loved me as his own daughter. Even if—" She let out a long breath, tears blurring her vision.

"Even if what?"

"Even if I am the daughter of a traitor."

Tristan furrowed his brow. "Do you think that somehow makes you unworthy?"

She looked away. Of course, she felt unworthy. Her father's betrayal would haunt her forever.

Tristan put his hand on her arm and faced her. He waited until she looked at him. "Karina, your father's mistakes are his. Not yours." He pressed his lips together. "You are so much more than the haunted pieces of your past. Look how you overcame everything that has happened to you. You are an accomplished healer and Queen of Aletheia. Your uncle loved you. You have friends who would travel the Three Kingdoms to find you."

Tears stung the corners of Karina's eyes. "Tristan, I—"

A lone howl echoed in the distance.

She clutched his arm. "Lupens in Shadowed Woods?"

Rashka and Sam hurried back to them. "Mount up," Rashka commanded with a wave. "We need to hurry."

Tristan helped Karina onto her horse as he glanced toward Rashka. "Do you think—?"

"Yes, I do," she said as Sam pulled up behind her.

"Lupens do not enter Shadowed Forest." Karina huffed as Tristan pushed her along.

"I do not think they came on their own. This way." Rashka led them off the main path onto a smaller one. "We still have at least a half day's travel to the temple. I am not sure we can outrun the lupens."

"What do we do?" Sam pulled his sword from the sheath on his back.

Karina was not sure she wanted the answer to that question.

They climbed a small hill of stones and grass. At the top, miles of winter-deadened trees stretched in all directions. Black birds flew from canopy to canopy. The snow had almost disappeared. Nothing seemed out of the ordinary.

Rashka dismounted. "Stay here." A light flashed, and her hawk form soared over the trees.

Sam's mouth dropped open. "What in the Creator's name is that?"

Karina giggled. She led her horse to stand by his and leaned over to squeeze his arm. "You have a lot to learn, my friend."

Sam tore his gaze from Rashka. "Oh, yeah? Like you're so worldly."

"Oh, I have been to Faramos's fortress and back. You would not believe the things I have seen." She did her best impression of some of the lofty nobles.

Sam looked horrified for a moment but then chuckled.

Rashka returned in another flash of light. Her elven aura did little to hide the worry in her eyes. "There are four lupens—one of them is Brusho."

"Brusho—a lupen?" Tristan flexed his hands, his face reddening. "I thought you said he was dead."

"I—I thought he was," Rashka stammered. "They are less than half a day behind us but fast closing in."

Karina looked out over the forest. "Will we get to the temple before they catch up?"

"I am not sure, but the elders can send help if we are close enough."

Rashka led them off any distinguishable path, keeping a brisk pace through the woods. The horses plowed through the underbrush as quickly as they could. The lupens' occasional howls indicated they were closing in.

"Why would they want to give away their location?" Tristan growled.

"Brusho wants me to know," Rashka said, her tone edged with anger. "We need to separate. Tristan and I should stay back and hold off Brusho and the lupens."

"Except Sam and I do not know the way to the temple." Karina reined her horse in by a large tree.

"Sam and I could stay behind," Tristan said, "You and Rashka go."

Rashka shook her head. "Even with your experience, Tristan, I am not sure you would be a match for both Brusho and the lupens, and surely, Sam would not be either." She looked back at Sam. "My apologies."

Sam held up his hands, palms out. "Hey, I know my experience doesn't go beyond the training yard and a couple bar brawls."

Karina quirked an eyebrow, and Sam coughed, turning a deep shade of red.

"Then splitting up is not an option." Rashka crossed her arms.

Another shiver-inducing howl reached their ears.

"Let us make haste." Rashka nudged her horse into a gallop.

Their pace did not allow for much conversation, so they pushed on in silence. The trees were thicker here, blocking out most of the sunlight. They had to slow down to allow the horses to pick through the dense foliage. Karina's heart thundered as she sent up prayers to the Creator.

A longer, more guttural howl echoed, its direction indiscernible.

Rashka stopped and held up her hand.

Tristan blew out a breath. "Did that—?"

"Yes, the howl came from in front of us."

"How could that happen?" Sam peered into the trees ahead of them.

Rashka closed her eyes and took a deep breath. "They are closing off our path to the temple."

"Is there any other way?" Karina asked.

"No. Well, yes. There is only one way by land, though. The other way is by sea, but the nearest port is another two-day's journey north or south. The temple rests in the valley of two mountains at the sea's edge."

Tristan groaned. "We can't go around the lupens because we have no idea where they are."

"We will have to fight. Tristan and I will lead the way. Sam, you stay with Karina. Do not leave her side."

Sam nodded.

"If it looks like we will not win, you two continue east. Karina, do not forget to pray! As you get closer to the temple, help will find you."

"Here, take Dom." Tristan dismounted and handed the reins to Karina. "He has a soft spot for you."

Karina glanced first toward Tristan, then Rashka. She did not want to leave them—any of them. Tristan's tense jaw betrayed his fear. She placed her hand gently on his arm. "We will survive this, Tristan."

With a quick nod, he pulled his sword from its scabbard.

"Let us go, then," Rashka said as she pulled her bow from her shoulder. "Be at the ready."

The shadows in the forest deepened as the sun sank in the horizon. Darkness would descend before long. The four of them stayed close together, stepping as lightly as possible.

Instinctively, Karina reached for Tristan's free arm. Despite her earlier words, she needed to feel his strength, the assurance that everything would be fine despite the feeling her quest could fall apart at any moment.

She retrieved the dagger Tristan had given her while in River Branch. He had insisted she carry something to defend herself with, even after she told him she had never handled such weaponry. She had wanted to learn once. King Pistis had almost let her train, but Anaya would not hear of it, that teaching a lady to fight would not be proper.

"Rashka!" a voice boomed through the trees.

Karina whirled around. The brash voice seemed to come from all directions at once. The group formed a circle, their backs to one another. Tristan and Sam had their swords at the ready, and Rashka fingered the string of her bow with practiced familiarity.

"Rashka!"

"Show yourself, Brusho!"

His maddening chuckle vibrated through Karina's mind, though she could not see him.

Rashka dropped the bow to her side and turned to the group. "He is not here, he is projecting. We need to keep moving." She led them at a faster pace, dodging trees and branches.

At a clearing, she held up her hand.

Karina gasped. Moonlight filled the meadow. Beyond the clearing, four pairs of red eyes shone through the cover of darkness.

"Sam, stay here with Karina. Once the battle begins, take two horses, go around the clearing, and keep heading east. Karina, remember what I said?" Rashka asked without turning around.

Karina managed a nod.

"Good." Rashka glanced sideways at Tristan. "Ready?"

CHAPTER SEVENTEEN

Karina leaned in front of Sam to get a better view.

Tristan and Rashka stepped into the meadow just as Brusho and the lupens approached from the darkness. The long-stemmed grasses swayed with each step. Both sides sauntered toward each other like friends in a marketplace rather than enemies in battle.

Rashka stopped and leveled her bow to shoot. "How are you still alive?"

Brusho chuckled. "The mighty Faramos has magic beyond that of anyone else in the Three Kingdoms."

"What do you want, Brusho? I will not let you have the girl."

"Faramos only wants this quest to stop. Let me escort you back to Calliope, and I will not have to kill you or take the new queen back to the fortress."

"Not a chance," Tristan hissed.

Brusho smirked. "Big words from such an arrogant youth."

"We do not fear you—or Faramos," Rashka replied. "The Creator has given us a quest, and we will see it through the best we can."

"Very well." Brusho shook his head and then signaled his forces. "Attack!"

The leader of the pack let out a long howl, and the three lupens prepared to lunge.

Sam raised his sword as Karina leaned into his back.

The first lupen charged, closing in on Rashka and Tristan. An arrow from Rashka's bow stuck in the lupen's shoulder. It yelped but kept running.

"Come on," Sam whispered. "We need to get going. They're going to need help."

Karina could not tear her gaze away from the ensuing fight.

Tristan, brandishing his sword, engaged the first lupen. The beast side-stepped the blade as it fell through its arc until Tristan snatched it back, whirling to keep the lupen's teeth from sinking into his flesh.

Sam pulled Karina along behind him. He pushed her up onto Dom's saddle and then mounted his horse. They circled the fight as Rashka had instructed.

"You look a little shaken, Rashka." Brusho's harsh laughter echoed through the trees. "How do you expect to protect her against the likes of Faramos? You could not even save your own brother."

Karina's eyes welled with tears. Her heart ached for Rashka. She and Brusho had once been friends, now they faced one another in a battle to the death. Sam veered away from the clearing, but Karina craned her neck to keep from losing sight of the others.

"Faster, Karina!" Sam urged his horse deeper into the woods.

Karina followed suit. Branches whipped across her face and arms. She hissed each time one broke skin.

Rotting leaves crunched behind them. Sticks cracked. Something was after them.

"Faster!" Sam hissed.

"I hear it, I hear it," Dom grumbled.

Karina patted his neck. She dared not look over her shoulder. The sounds were terrifying enough. Her heart beat in rhythm to Dom's gallop. Karina was weary—mind, body, and soul. Her friends were going to die.

She was going to die.

Creator, do not forsake me! Please, do not let me die out here. I have not completed the task you have given me. She repeated her silent plea over and over. Still, the lupen drew nearer.

After what seemed like hours, the forest gave way to an open field at the edge of a mountain. Heaving for breath, Dom came to rest behind Sam's horse. Karina surveyed the area around them. The steep rock face offered no place to hide … no place to run. Sam pulled his horse in a southerly direction along the mountainside. Dom galloped after him.

A howl echoed through the rocks as the lupen broke free of the tree line. Karina's heart skittered. What should they do? The lupen could overtake them here.

Dom halted without warning.

Karina nearly fell but held fast to the saddle horn. "Dom?"

He flicked his head.

Atop a small rise was the largest white cat Karina had ever seen. Its face alone was bigger than half her body. Its fur was snowy white with thin, black stripes.

Karina gasped … a legendary snow tiger.

Sam grabbed her reins and brought the horses about, giving them a clear view of both the cat and the lupen. He dismounted, switching his sword point from one creature to the other.

The lupen had slowed. Judging from its heavy breaths and awkward limp, this lupen must have been the one Rashka injured. It growled as it broke into a full run.

Dom reared, and Karina slid off his back.

Sam adjusted his stance, ready to strike.

A blur of white flew past them and barreled into the lupen. Both creatures tumbled to the ground in a mass of fur and power.

Tristan wiped his free hand across his sweaty forehead. One lupen downed by Rashka's arrows. One had disappeared. That left one more to conquer. He wanted to go after Karina. If a lupen was tracking them, what chance did she and Sam have of reaching the temple by themselves?

But the remaining lupen circled him, eyes hungry with vengeance and hate. Its tongue now hung out to the side. Overhead, faint wisps of morning light reached into the clearing. The lupen's eyes did not seem as red in the brightening sunlight.

Out of the corner of his eye, he saw Rashka's slow advance on Brusho. They were arguing, but Tristan couldn't make out what they were saying over the growls of the beast wanting to make a meal of him.

He turned back to the lupen. Time to end this. He sheathed his sword and withdrew daggers from the pouch attached to his belt. He threw one of them straight at the lupen's head. The lupen dodged, and the knife ricocheted off its leg. With a guttural growl, it charged. Paws pounded the ground.

Tristan threw a second knife ... it caught the lupen in the shoulder. Though in obvious pain, the creature kept moving toward him. Tristan threw a third dagger. This one sunk into the lupen's chest, near its heart. It howled as it reared on his hind legs. Tristan threw the remaining knives into the beast's gut, and it staggered into the clearing. He drew his sword, and with one massive swing, slashed the lupen's neck. The beast whimpered as it finally sank to the ground.

Tristan wiped the blade across the ground and glanced toward Rashka's battle.

Brusho was no longer there. In his place was another lupen. Was that his shapeshifter form? Rashka stood perfectly still with her bow poised to shoot. Other than the shapeshifting, had they moved while Tristan fought the other lupen?

Tristan swung his sword in a circle and then took a few practice swings. "Rashka?"

"Stay out of this, Tristan."

"It looks like—"

"I said no!"

Brusho crouched in attack position and growled. "Let the boy play, Rashka."

Tristan narrowed his eyes at the lupen, pressing his lips together.

"Stay back." Rashka warned.

He let out a sigh but kept his blade at the ready. Just in case.

"Let us end this, my love." Brusho crouched even lower.

"As you wish." Rashka pulled the bow string back. An arrow appeared, long and thin like the last, but this one had a black shaft and feathers.

With a roar, Brusho leapt off his haunches.

Rashka waited.

Tristan's eyes widened. She was going to get herself killed.

Brusho bounded toward Rashka, fangs bared.

She kept her stance.

He let out a ferocious roar just as he lunged.

Rashka released the arrow, and time seemed to cease as it arched through the air.

Brusho opened his jaws, ready to tear his victim's flesh, but the arrow found its mark in his open mouth, then exited through the back of his head. The monstrous beast fell at Rashka's feet.

"Ignorant fool," she snapped. She nudged Brusho with her foot. "May the Creator judge you better than I."

Tristan exhaled and shook his head. Their fight was over.

Rashka smiled. "Nicely done, Tristan."

He nodded. "Not too bad yourself."

"Pity I could not make him see the error of his ways."

Tristan didn't know what to say, so he kept silent. They had downed two lupens and an evil elf. What next?

Karina!

"Come, Tristan. The battle is not over yet. We need to catch up with Karina and Sam."

"My thoughts exactly."

Karina hit the ground hard. The impact jarred her right shoulder, and black dots danced across her vision. She looked up as the snow tiger pounced on the lupen. The creatures tumbled backwards, rolling for several spans. Karina scrambled to her feet. Pain ripped through her shoulder.

The tiger let out a roar as it swiped a giant paw across the lupen's face, continuing its unrelenting attack with tooth and claw.

Karina cringed, whirling away from the gruesome sight. The sound of tearing flesh turned her stomach.

At last, the lupen's dying cries faded away. All was quiet. Sam wrapped his arm around Karina as they faced the magnificent creature—their protector.

Crimson streaks stained its fur. The tiger had protected them and now wore the consequences on its coat. Karina's eyes filled with tears. She shook her head. She was acting ridiculous. The blood was the lupen's, not the tiger's, and would wash away.

The tiger backed away from the lupen and turned toward them. A flash, like lightning.

"What in the—" Sam breathed.

In the tiger's place stood an ethereal woman—an elf with long, white hair the color of the tiger's fur and fathomless blue eyes. She wore a white dress that matched her pale face.

I am Kona, Keeper of the Temple. Welcome, Prophetess.

Karina bowed in acknowledgment.

We have been expecting you for some days now.

"Do you hear that voice?" Sam asked, a hint of confusion in his voice.

"I—I am s-sorry," Karina stuttered. "I was delayed."

"All is well, Prophetess." Kona smiled. "But let us not tarry here. There is much to be done, and time is short." She looked from Sam to the horses and back to Karina, then frowned. "Were there not more to your party? Where is Rashka?"

Karina averted her eyes. She could only hope their friends had fared as well. "Rashka and Tristan stayed behind to battle the other lupens and a dark elf. Rashka wanted to make sure we—I—made it to the temple."

Kona nodded and gestured for them to follow as she led them around the mountainside.

Sam's eyes still seemed twice their normal size as he hurried behind Kona. He cleared his throat. "So, can all elves shapeshift?"

Kona smiled. "No. Shapeshifting is a gift from the Creator when we are called to his service."

"Then how did a dark elf obtain such power?" Karina asked as they resumed walking.

"I assume you refer to Brusho. He used to be in the service of the Creator—Guardian of the Barrens. At one point, Faramos managed to capture him. We do not know what happened while he was in prison, only that he was tortured at length. Understandably, he was not the same after his ordeal. Sometime later, his family was murdered." Kona frowned. "You can imagine what that does to someone."

Indeed, she could. Karina's heart broke for what she and Brusho had been through. Tears moistened her tired eyes. Where would she be if she had thought the Creator had deserted her? She shuddered to even think on it. In another life, she might have turned out much like Brusho, or like Tristan when she first met him.

They came to a broad ravine. Strangely, the bridge did not seem to reach the other side, as if incomplete. Across from them, a mountain shot up to the sky with sheer cliffs at the base. Why construct half a bridge?

Kona walked out onto the bridge without hesitation.

Sam stopped at the edge to look this way and that. "Where does the bridge go? It just stops."

Karina shrugged.

Dom stomped his feet. "Are we sure she is who she says she is? What if this is a trap?"

"I believe she is who she claims to be."

Sam scowled. "Were you talking to me?"

She pointed at Dom. "No, I was talking to him. He wanted to know if this was a trap."

Sam's jaw dropped, and he looked like he wanted to ask more questions but could not quite form the words. Karina tried not to laugh.

Dom stomped at the ground. "With your leave, Your Majesty, I will find Tristan. No telling what kind of trouble he has found himself in without me."

"Of course. Please, bring him back safely."

"I will do my best." Dom trotted back the way they had come.

Karina avoided Sam's dumbfounded expression. He would get used to this strange new world soon enough. Gathering up courage, she stepped out on the bridge.

CHAPTER EIGHTEEN

The bridge stretched before Karina, ending at the cliff face. Could magic have made the door to the temple look like the rest of the rock? If so, how disappointing. She had imagined the temple would be a beautiful construction of gold surrounded by lush green trees and the softest grasses. Wildflowers and animals and …

Karina shook her head. She was not usually prone to fanciful thinking.

Sam followed closely behind her as they made their way across. He gasped. His whole body stiffened.

She glanced over her shoulder. "What?"

He stared straight ahead and clung to the rail. "I made the mistake of looking down."

Karina couldn't resist a peek. The ravine had plunging cliffs on both sides that dropped into a dark, dense fog. She could only imagine what lay beyond. She kept her gaze on the stone in front of her.

At the other side, Kona paused. "Come now, Prophetess." She took a couple of steps, then disappeared.

Karina gawked.

Sam took a step past Karina. "Where did she go?"

She shrugged as they hurried after the elf.

When they reached the far side, Karina realized the bridge did not, in fact, disappear. A trick of light hid the sharp turn as it passed between two mountains. Cliffs of dark stone rose up on either side of them, the gap wide enough for the bridge to pass through. The dank smell of moss permeated the air. Karina grabbed Sam's hand and led him along the twists and turn, Kona remaining just beyond their line of sight.

Above, Karina could barely distinguish the wisps of dawn, but the shadowy path before them was lit with torches. The firelight glinted off polished rock. Water trickled down grooved patterns in the walls.

"Kona!" Karina called out.

"You are well, Prophetess. Not much further."

A few more turns, and the bridge straightened. Ahead, light filtered in from the edge of the mountains. Kona waited there, her hand resting on the bridge rail. Her white hair tumbled about with the rush of wind that swept the cliff path.

"Welcome to the Temple of Aletheia, Prophetess." With a wide gesture, Kona ushered her off the bridge.

Karina stepped onto a stone path that led into the valley below. A silver spire reached toward the heavens. The entire temple was elegantly constructed of white stone and silver, with giant archways and ornately carved trimming and surrounded by shimmering snow that sparkled in the morning sun. Shoots of green worked their way to the surface, in defiance of the lingering winter, to hail the beginning of spring. An inlet of water, perhaps from the sea, wrapped around the temple on three sides, creating an island shadowed by towering mountains.

Karina could hardly breathe. Such beauty hidden between these mountains. The wintery smells reminded her of Calliope, of home.

Kona slipped her arm through Karina's, leading her to the temple.

"Do you know why I am here?" Karina kept her gaze fixed on the path.

"Yes, I do. The Creator warned me he would send his Chosen One to retrieve the armor."

"And there is some sort of challenge I must complete?"

Kona's features tightened, her smile disappeared. "Yes, there is, but you do not need to worry about that right now. Let us get you inside, for you are most wearied. I think food, a bath, and rest is much needed. Do you agree?"

Food? Rest? Karina sighed. Nothing sounded better.

They came to another bridge that crossed over the stream. From there, the path wound up to a massive archway with elegant wooden doors. Ancient words were carved along the top of the arch.

Karina pointed toward the words. "What does that say, Kona?"

"Enter all who seek his name in truth and faith."

"Truth and faith," Karina repeated, the words rolling off her tongue. Of course, she had faith, and she tried to be honest in everything she did. What would this temple hold for her?

Kona led them through a large hall of giant silver columns. Several arched doors of refined wood lined the side walls, and in front of them were two winding staircases that met at a landing on the next level.

"The sanctuary is at the top of the staircase." Kona pointed to the double doors at the top. "But, come, let us get you two settled first."

"Kona?"

The priestess turned to her.

"What about my friends?"

She smiled. "I have a feeling we will see them soon."

Kona was right about the food and bath. Karina stepped from the luxurious hot water and wrapped a drying cloth around her body. She crossed the sun-warmed stone floor to her bedchambers. The mid-afternoon sunlight fell across the large bed aligned against the opposite wall, brightening the pink and yellow room.

A dark-purple dress with blue accents hung on the door of the wardrobe to her left. Next to the garment was a white nightgown. She slipped the gown over her head, snuggling into its warmth, and grabbed the rose-colored robe behind it.

The room smelled like a kitchen on a cold winter's day. On the round table in the center of the room, she found two trays. One held a plate of savory meats and roasted vegetables, the other was set with separate platters of fruits and pastries. A goblet of warm milk stood between the trays. Karina plopped down in the chair, staring at the delectable foods. Her mouth watered at the sensational smells.

"Are you devouring the food with your eyes alone, Karina?"

Karina gasped and jumped out of her chair. Sam stood in the doorway, chuckling. She grinned. "More like savoring the sight."

Sam uncrossed his arms and stepped into the room. "How are you doing?"

"I am feeling refreshed." She sank back into the chair. "But exhausted at the same time. I intend to eat and then let the bed swallow me whole."

"It is good to see you have your sense of humor back. Do you need anything from me?"

She shook her head.

"Then I'm going to retire until they call us to the sanctuary. Do you know when that will be?"

"Kona said it would not be until Rashka and Tristan join us. At least the dinner hour."

Sam stretched his arms over his head as he ambled back out the door. "Great! That affords me a nice, long nap."

Karina redirected her attention to the feast before her and scarfed down the lamb and vegetables like a starving lupen. Who cared about manners when nourishment had been sorely lacking on their adventures?

When she had her fill, she downed the rest of the milk and sat back with a satisfied sigh. It took all her energy to crawl from the chair over to the bed. She pulled back the dark-pink satin coverlet and slipped between the sheets. The pillows were stuffed with the softest feathers she had ever known. In moments, she drifted off to sleep.

Karina stood before the mouth of a massive, red-stone cave. She furrowed her brow. There was no red-stone anything in Aletheia. Where was she?

Tristan stood next to her, rubbing his chin. The high sun shone off his dark hair when he tilted his head toward her. "You ready?"

"No."

"How about now?"

She groaned and shot him an annoyed look. "I suppose there is no reason to keep waiting."

He held out his hand to her, and she grasped it. With a deep breath, she took a step into the cave.

Just inside, the mouth opened to a large cavern with a fire pit in the middle. The flames danced, casting shadows on the cave walls. At the back of the room were two paths. Above one path was the word TRUTH ... above the other, FAITH.

"Is this the temple quest?" Karina asked Tristan.

He gave her an odd look. "Yes. We have to retrieve the armor somehow."

She nodded. The words echoed in her mind as she read them again. "Did they say which way we are supposed to go?"

He quirked an eyebrow. "What's gotten into you? The elders gave us that crazy riddle, but that was it."

"Riddle?"

"Don't ask me to remember it. I'm just here to protect you."

"Well, I have no recollection of how we even got here." She sat on a boulder by the fire. "Think, think, think." She stared at the words.

Tristan stood behind her but said nothing.

"Do you suppose …" She did not know what to suppose. "Maybe …"

"Don't try to overthink this, Karina. The elders said you would know the path to take."

"Well, it does not help that there is a huge gap in my memory, now does it?" She groaned, and her head drooped. Why the Creator thought her capable of anything was beyond her.

She looked up again. Faith—faith was something she already had. Maybe she needed truth. What truth, she did not know. But assuredly faith was something she already possessed. "Let's go with truth."

"Very well, my lady," Tristan said with a smirk. "I'll follow your lead."

She rolled her eyes as she stood.

They approached the Truth passageway together, and Karina felt a sense of peace. But something else as well. Something foreboding. How could she sense both at the same time?

"Here we go." She took a deep breath and marched through the opening. "See, I figured faith is something—"

An unearthly scream interrupted her. She spun around.

A pile of smoking ash sat just inside the tunnel. Tristan had disappeared.

Karina screamed Tristan's name as she sat up in bed, the dream too real. Bright sunlight shone in the crystal windows on her right.

Footsteps thundered down the hall. The door flew open.

Tristan rushed in with his sword at the ready. "I'm here, Karina."

Karina yelped and pulled the covers up around her neck.

Tristan scanned the room, then opened the door to the wardrobe and peeked into the washroom. "Why did you scream my name?"

"Uh …" She searched her mind for a reasonable answer but could not find any. Her cheeks warmed. "I was—I was dreaming. You died."

He chuckled. "I didn't realize you cared so much."

She grabbed one of the pillows and threw it at him. "I do not."

"Your secret is out now."

She crossed her arms. This was ridiculous. She groaned as she straightened. "Where is Rashka? Did she arrive as well?"

"Rashka is fine. She and Kona went off somewhere."

"When did you get back?"

"Not long after the noon hour." Tristan sat in one of the wooden chairs beside the round table. "Dom found us and brought us in."

Karina suddenly felt uncomfortable. She was in her bed clothes, in a bed. She tried to pull the covers even tighter as she avoided eye contact with Tristan.

He coughed as he stood again. "Well, it does not look like you are being attacked. I was on my way to wake you when I heard you scream. One of the priestesses says we are to convene in the sanctuary in one hour."

"One hour?" Karina pointed toward the door. "Out!"

Tristan's face lit up as if amused. He held his hands up. "I'm going. I'll be back for you in one hour."

CHAPTER NINETEEN

Karina adjusted her deep purple dress and smoothed her dark waves with another quick glance in the mirror. *Acceptable.* She then slipped on the pair of soft wool shoes she had found at the bottom of the wardrobe.

Someone knocked on the door, and she hurried to open it.

Tristan let out a soft whistle. "You look beautiful, Karina."

Unaccustomed to his compliments, she ducked her head to hide her blushing cheeks. "Thank you, Tristan."

He bowed. "May I escort the queen to the sanctuary?"

"It is only polite," she teased but accepted his extended arm.

"Have you had time to explore the temple?"

She shook her head. "Kona took me to my room where I bathed, ate, and fell asleep."

"You clean up nicely, Your Highness."

She groaned. "Please do not call me that."

They came to the end of the hall, and she peered through the open door into a large room with silver columns. In the middle of the room, Kona, Rashka, and Sam waited for them. Her friends had bathed and been given fresh clothing as well.

Rashka bowed as they approached. "It is good to see you made it to the temple, Your Highness."

Karina released Tristan's arm and grasped Rashka's hand. "No need to be so formal, Rashka. After all we have been through, we are friends."

"The elders are waiting." Kona gestured toward the stairs at the other end of the room. "Shall we?"

Karina followed behind the others, staring at the large, silver doors at the top of the stairs. What awaited her up there? What tasks would they bestow upon her? Would she be worthy?

Sam took her hand, looped it around his arm, and then gave it a gentle pat. "It's good to see you looking so charming once again."

"Stop it!"

"What? It's the truth." His eyes twinkled.

She nudged him with her shoulder but allowed him to lead her up the stairs.

By the time they reached the top, the doors to the sanctuary were open. Karina held her breath as they crossed the threshold.

The sanctuary glittered with the light of a thousand candles. The windows high on the towering walls allowed the final rays of daylight to add their glow to the gathering. A hint of cinnamon filled the room. Along the sides, two rows of intricately carved chairs faced each other. A dark purple runner traversed the expanse of the floor leading up to a raised dais and three throne-like seats etched with silver.

Cloaked in white, much like Kona, priests and priestesses, both human and elves, sat facing each other. Each wore silver bands around their upper right arms. For the moment, no one sat upon the dais.

Kona led their group up the aisle. The temple priests bowed their heads as Karina passed. She attempted to return the gesture, but her nerves were in such a frenzy she was unsure she made any such actions.

At the foot of the dais, Kona turned to address the congregation. "Everyone, please welcome Karina, the Prophetess, Queen of Aletheia. And we also welcome her friends, those who have traveled with her as companions and protectors."

At Kona's behest, Karina turned as applause filled the room. She nodded to acknowledge their appreciation.

Kona held up her hand, and the room fell into silence. "Presenting the Trium!"

A door off to the left opened, and two men and one woman entered, all wearing long white robes like the one the Servant of the Creator had worn. A silver circlet, adorned with a large ruby in the center and a smaller sapphire above it, rested on their heads. The Trium stood in front of the lectern on the dais and bowed to the those present.

Karina bowed in return.

The Trium took their places—a female elf on the left, a male human on the right, and a male elf in the center who smiled as he glanced toward Karina. "Welcome, Prophetess, to the Temple of Aletheia. We are most excited to have you in our company this day." He turned to the rest of the group, his white hair swishing with each movement. "I understand the journey came at great cost to you as well as to each of your friends."

Tristan and Sam exchanged glances, but Rashka did not move.

"For your loyalty to Prophetess Karina, I thank you." He bowed his head to them, and they returned the gesture. He faced Karina, his smiling blue eyes so much like Kona's. "I am Lucian, Head Elder of the Temple. Do you know why you are here?"

Karina wet her lips. *Creator, do not let me make a fool of myself.* She took a deep breath. "Garon, Servant of the Creator, visited me on a mountainside. He said the Creator had chosen me to stop the impending darkness by gathering the Armor of the Creator. Each of the three kingdoms—Aletheia, Soter, and Tzedek—has two pieces of the armor. At each kingdom's temple, I am to complete a challenge to retrieve pieces of armor."

Lucian nodded. "That is true. Though there are two challenges." He looked at her friends. "And one of you shall accompany her."

"Excuse me, sir," Karina waited for the elf to face her. "What sort of challenges?"

The red-haired female elf leaned forward. "I am Vyra, Elite Servant of the Temple. I am sorry, Karina, but we cannot divulge the nature of the challenges. We can only tell you that you must choose one person to enter with you."

The human male cleared his throat. Experience showed in the wrinkles around his eyes and in the graceful graying of his hair, but he still looked spry enough to give Tristan a workout in the arena. "I am Paul, Elite Servant of the Temple. Indeed, the challenges are sacred. We will have something of assistance to you when the time comes." His eyes twinkled. "We have the utmost confidence in your ability to face the quest before you. The Creator would not have chosen you otherwise."

Lucian stood. "The challenges will begin mid-morning tomorrow. In the meantime, I invite everyone to the dining hall for a celebratory dinner in your honor."

The Trium descended from the dais and led the way across the sanctuary. Karina and her friends followed, the priests and priestesses trailing behind.

The dining hall was a noisy, cheerful place. Great stone fireplaces graced three of the four walls. Three rows of long wooden tables with benches along each side were set up in the middle of the large room. Servants hurried about, lining each table with trays of food.

The Trium ushered them to a longer table set perpendicular from the rest. This one only had benches on the side nearest the wall. The Trium sat in the middle, and Lucian gestured for Karina and her friends to be seated on either side of the Trium.

Rashka grabbed Sam's arm. They sat next to Vyra, who embraced Rashka as a friend. That left Karina to sit with Tristan next to Paul. She bit her lip. She did not like to sit apart from the crowd, but to refuse her assigned seating would be considered rude.

Paul nodded when they sat down. "Greetings, Prophetess."

She bowed her head. "Thank you for welcoming us to your temple."

"This is the Creator's temple, my child, but he is most happy to share it with you."

Her cheeks warmed at the slip of her tongue. She glanced toward Tristan, who was staring at one of the fireplaces. "Tristan, are you all right?"

"What?" He turned to her, dazed, as if he had been deep in thought. "Oh, yes, I'm fine."

The meal was delicious and consisted of a selection of meats, pastries, vegetables. The whole feast rivaled the best celebrations at the royal house. The people talked and ate and laughed. Several came up to introduce themselves to Karina. By the time the festivities ended, she could barely keep her eyes open.

Tristan nudged her with his elbow. "Perhaps I should escort you to your room before you fall asleep in that bowl of pudding."

She offered a thin smile. "That would be nice."

They bid their goodnights to the Trium and to their friends and then made their way out of the dining hall.

"Are you worried about tomorrow?" Tristan asked as they walked across the great room.

"Yes. I like to be prepared for what lies ahead. Unfortunately, I have no idea what these challenges will hold for us."

Tristan nodded. "I can see how that would be unsettling. Do you know who you'll choose to go with you?"

She stopped inside the hallway door and faced Tristan. Grasping both of his hands, she looked up at him. "I was going to talk to you about that."

He raised an eyebrow. "Yes?"

"I want you to go with me."

"Me?" He laughed. "Not Rashka or your old buddy Sam?"

She shook her head. "Call it a feeling, but I think you should be the one."

The laughter left his eyes. He coughed as he stepped back. "I don't know, Karina."

What could she say to him? He had every right to be concerned. If her dream was any kind of vision, one of them may not make it out alive. She pursed her lips. "I know you're afraid, but—"

He raised his head as he narrowed his eyes. "That's not it."

"Remember my dream earlier?"

He scowled. "The one where you thought I died?"

"Yes." She stepped back, wetting her lips. "In the dream, you went into one of the challenges with me."

His lips pulled into a half-hearted smirk. "That's where I died?"

"Well, yes." Karina let out a frustrated sigh. "You did, but you died because we made a mistake. Please, Tristan, I know you are supposed to face these challenges with me."

"Still …" He looked deep into her eyes.

She could see his compassion, his need to protect her, and she smiled. The Creator had worked a miracle with this man. Once an aloof bounty hunter, now a changed man.

"Hey, wait up!" Sam dodged the silver columns with Rashka close at his heels. "We wanted to know what your thoughts were about tomorrow."

Karina fidgeted with the sleeves of her dress, but she looked them straight in the eye. "Tristan is going with me."

"Oh." A crestfallen expression crossed Sam's face, then he quickly broke into a smile. Karina's heart went out to him, her best friend … one who had been her protector since her return to the royal house.

"I wish you well, Karina." Rashka embraced her. "The Creator's might be with you tomorrow—both of you. For now, we should all get some rest."

Karina nodded.

Rashka and Sam went on ahead to their rooms while Tristan led the way to her door.

"Where is your room?" she asked.

"I'm sharing with Sam."

Her eyes widened. "Really?"

"Apparently only you women are special enough to deserve your own rooms."

Karina giggled.

Then silence fell between them. She wanted Tristan to say something, anything, but he just stood there. Did he hear the thunderous beating of her heart? Her cheeks warmed.

"Good night, Karina," he said, finally.

"Good night, Tristan." She ducked into her room and shut the door before her emotions got the better of her senses. She plopped in the nearest chair. The way her skin hummed when he was near …

Tristan might be a changed man, but could she trust him with her heart?

CHAPTER TWENTY

Sunlight shone through the crystal windows, warming Karina's face. She snuggled against her pillow and reluctantly opened her eyes, forcing herself to leave the comfort of her soft bed to greet the day, even if somewhat belatedly. She sat up and looked around. A snow-white dress hung on the door of the wardrobe. No one else was in the room. Where did these clothes keep appearing from?

She scrubbed her face, hands, and arms in the washroom, then braided her hair on both sides, positioning them into circle around her hairline. Ignoring the butterflies in her stomach, she donned the simple white dress.

When she stepped out of the room, Tristan ambled toward her in a white tunic and leather pants. From the pained expression on his face, he was not comfortable at all.

She bit her lower lip to keep from grinning. "White is a good color on you."

"Don't even start," he growled. He offered her his arm, which she accepted.

"Am I not to leave my room without your escort now?"

He shook his head. "No. I'm just trying to be polite."

She mimicked his furrowed brow and growled back. "Right."

He ignored her teasing.

In the great hall, the Trium stood beside the open entrance while many of the priests and priestesses meandered around the base of the stairs. Kona, Rashka, and Sam, also dressed in white, stood by the Trium. Rashka's raven hair stood out against her white dress, so like Karina's. Sam's tunic and pants were also like Tristan's.

"Here she is!" Lucian waved them over. "We can go now."

Karina shrunk back. "Go?"

"Have no fear, Prophetess. The challenge begins out by the sea." He offered her his arm. "Come."

Karina let go of Tristan's arm and accepted Lucian's escort.

He patted her hand in a fatherly fashion. "We believe you will accomplish great things, Prophetess. I am confident you will complete this task."

He led the group from the temple to a path that crossed the inlet.

The air was crisp and the sky clear. Karina gazed at the beauty of the snow-capped mountains and the green valley before them.

Lucian angled toward another path leading through the mountains. At least this one was not a bridge, much to Karina's relief, but it was just as winding. The rocks were a lighter shade here, not the same dark stone as on the other side. A constant swooshing of waves echoed along the stone walls.

"Why are we headed to the seaside?"

Lucian smiled at her. "There is a cave at the bottom of the mountain."

"A cave?" Karina nearly choked on the words as her mouth went dry.

"Yes."

Her nightmare replayed in her mind. Distracted, she almost lost her footing on the dirt path.

"Careful, Prophetess." Lucian regarded her with concern.

"Karina, is everything well here?" Rashka caught up to them, her face contorted in a worried frown. Tristan and Sam were behind her.

"I am fine, Rashka. I need to watch where I am walking." If her laugh rang hollow in her own ears, how much more did her phony attempt at good humor seem insincere to her friends?

"If you are sure ..." Rashka's brow wrinkled, but she said nothing more.

The path took a turn downward, and the sea stretched before them. Karina breathed in the salty air. King Pistis had never allowed her on the boats in the harbor at Calliope, but she used to wander the banks while he visited with the ship captains about various military and trade matters. She loved the wind on her face, the way the vast expanse of water heightened the marvel of the Creator's creation. She was a single grain of sand in his ocean, but he still knew her.

Sunbeams ricocheted off the water, blinding her for a moment, and then they turned from the path onto a rocky beach. A mountain loomed just ahead. She gasped at the massive opening in the red rock face—as in her dream.

At the mouth of the cave, Lucian faced the crowd, his long, white hair tossed around by the breeze. "Greetings, my fellow servants! What a glorious day this is. The one promised to us has come to seek the sacred Armor of the Creator. The Prophetess Karina."

Everyone looked on with bright, smiling faces.

Lucian motioned for Karina to join him at his side. "Prophetess Karina, which of your friends have you chosen to enter with you?"

She cleared her throat. "Tristan Lemur."

"Very well." Lucian nodded. "Tristan, do you accept her request?"

"Yes, I do."

"Then please step forward and place her arm in yours."

Tristan smiled as he came to Karina's side. He took her hand and kissed it gently, then wrapped it through his arm. Karina prayed she had made the right choice.

"Let us listen to the reading of the Word of the Creator." Lucian stepped down from the rock, and Kona stepped up. She unrolled a tattered scroll. "It is my honor to read the words of the Creator written by the first Elder of the Trium:

> To whom I have chosen, fear not. For I have protected my armor. To wield its power requires virtue, and I must ensure you are prepared, and so have placed my armor behind this challenge. The bearer of the Belt of Truth must look deep within and know himself, for only when truth of self is known can the truth of others be known. The Shield of Faith protects the one whose faith is pure. Though you may worry about your circumstances, trust in me. Finally, where there are two, only one may enter. Each challenge offers clarification … each challenge offers guidance … each challenge offers a righteous power.

Kona stepped down from the stone.

Karina was so dizzy she could barely stand while she contemplated the meanings of the riddles. Belt of Truth? Shield of Faith?

Lucian stepped up again. "Let us pray for the Creator's guidance." Everyone bowed their heads. "Creator, we come to you with humble hearts. You are the Great Creator, the one with knowledge of all things. You have chosen Karina and Tristan for your quest, and we ask that you give them the strength and wisdom needed to complete their challenge. In the Creator's name."

A chorus echoed off the cliff. "In the Creator's name."

Lucian made a sweeping gesture, "And now for the gifts."

Paul stepped forward, a long leather bag strapped over his shoulder. He removed it and smiled as he handed the pack to Karina. "Inside you will find everything you might need for the journey—food, water, and basic tools. No one has been in these caves for a long time, and we wanted to be sure you would be prepared."

Vyra walked over to Tristan and gave him a pack as well. And then she held out an old sword, rusted from disuse. Tristan's lip curled as he accepted the weapon.

At last, Lucian presented Tristan with a large, orange stone set in a gold ring. "This is the sunstone, a token of faith from the Creator's servants." He bowed and then stepped away.

"Am I supposed to protect Karina with this?"

This time Lucian's smile resembled a smirk. A rebuke? "You may only take these items."

"What about me?" Karina asked. She might not know how to use a sword, but if there were dangers ahead, she should at least have some sort of defense.

Kona came to her side and offered her the Blessing of Three Kisses. "You have need of nothing else."

"A warning before you enter." Lucian glanced toward the cave, then let his gaze fall on Karina. "The way is not as easy as it seems. Beware— for a wrong decision can be dangerous, even deadly. You are under no time constraints, so think through each decision. Remember, the Creator's words *where there are two, only one may enter.*"

Karina nodded. The fate of the world depended on her ability to accomplish this task. Her—the daughter of a traitor and an accused killer. She looked up at Tristan, who offered a wink of encouragement. No help.

He led her to the mouth of the cave. She stared at the massive opening that towered above them, at least four times their size.

Tristan rubbed his chin. "You ready?"

"No." The words echoed through her mind with a vague sense of familiarity.

"How about now?"

Karina shook her head. Too odd. Was her dream even a dream? A vision, perhaps? Should she not heed its warning? Tristan would not meet his fate if she could help it. "Let us begin."

They entered the cave. As in her dream, a fire pit crackled in the middle of the room. At the back were two tunnels, each with a word written above it. She recognized the strange language. One side had the word TRUTH, and the other had the word FAITH.

Karina trembled as she caught her breath. Whatever happened, Tristan could not go in the entrance marked TRUTH. She sat down on one of the stones by the fire pit.

"What's wrong?" Tristan knelt beside her.

"My dream from yesterday. You and I were here, in this place, exactly as it is now. With those tunnels there." She pointed. "We chose the way of truth, but as we passed through the entrance, you dissolved into a pile of ash."

"That doesn't sound very good."

"I do not know what we are supposed to do."

Tristan straightened and surveyed the small room. "The answer is simple."

"Oh, really?"

"Yes." He walked to the other entrance. "We take the path marked FAITH. I don't die—all is well."

He did make sense. But something about that plan felt off. She followed him to the tunnel marked FAITH. The closer she got, the faster her heart beat.

Tristan grabbed her elbow. "What is it, Karina?"

She stopped. "I'm not supposed to go in there." She stepped back from the entrance. The word TRUTH jumped out at her from the other tunnel. Her challenge would be met on that path. *Where there are two, only one may enter.* Those were the Creator's words, and she took them to heart. "We have to go separate ways."

Tristan frowned. "What?"

"That is what Lucian warned us about."

Tristan followed her back to the fire pit. "What do you mean?"

She paced back and forth in front of the fire. "'Where there are two, only one may enter.' There are two of us. Only one can enter each tunnel."

Tristan spun her to face him. "I'm not letting you go anywhere alone."

"You do not have a choice." She gently removed his hand, raised her chin, and marched toward the archway marked TRUTH. "This is my path. If you follow, you will die." She pointed to the other path marked FAITH. "I have a feeling if I were to go in there, I would die too."

"I don't like this." Tristan crossed his arms. "Splitting up is never a good thing."

"The Creator is with us. He will protect us."

"Easy for you to say," he mumbled. Finally, he threw up his hands in surrender. "As you wish. But I don't have to like this."

"Fair enough."

Tristan glowered and sauntered toward his path.

As he walked away, Karina doubted her decision. Her legs turned to jelly. "Tristan?"

In a second, he was by her side. She leaned into his warmth, his assurance. When she pulled away, his expression was one she had not seen before. His jaw muscles were tight, his eyes seemed large in the firelight.

He traced the line of her jaw with his finger. "Be careful."

She nodded, afraid to speak.

He cupped her chin and brought his lips to hers. The warmth of the moment, a new sensation, sent tingles through her body. She pulled away, dazed.

"I mean it, Karina. Be careful."

"I will," she whispered.

Tristan crossed into the FAITH tunnel—and nothing happened.

Karina let out a long breath and smiled. After a glance at the open sea at her back, she hurried to the TRUTH tunnel.

CHAPTER TWENTY-ONE

Torch flames flickered and danced, chasing shadows on the slick walls. When the light from one torch grew dim, Karina would cross into the light of another torch. If no one had been down here in a while, who had lit the torches?

The musty air was cool and damp. How often did anyone venture these tunnels? Did anyone ever come down here? Or was it a place reserved for the chosen ones? Sand on the stone muffled her footsteps, and her own breath whispered in her ears.

How was Tristan doing? Was he scared or nervous? Probably not. He was like that. Defiant just to be defiant. What could he possibly be afraid of?

The sloped path led deeper into the mountain. The walls closed in, leaving a narrow path for her to walk. Her senses tingled, the hairs on her neck rose with each passing moment. Something was coming.

Karina's strength waned on this endless trail, her legs weakened from exhaustion. Had she gone the wrong way? To her relief, the narrow passage soon merged into a brightly lit room where more torches lined the walls in sconces above her head.

Across the way, two large boulders stuck out from the reddish-brown stone. Human forms stood beside each boulder, but Karina could not see their faces from where she stood at the edge of the tunnel. Were they friends or foes? She swallowed the growing lump in her throat. A weapon of some sort would be helpful in moments like this.

"Enter, Prophetess," a gravelly voice commanded.

Creator, be with me. Karina took a deep breath and stepped into the room.

The torches blazed more brightly, highlighting a well in the middle of the room. With each step she took, the strangers in white-hooded robes moved toward the well. They stopped at the edge, across from Karina. Was it her imagination or did one of them shift away from the other?

The one on the left raised his head, and the hood fell back.

Karina's knees buckled. "Father!"

The figure's dark hair was smoothed to one side, and he smiled at her through kind eyes—eyes she remembered from so many years ago. She wanted to touch his face. Tears filled her eyes. Yet he did not respond.

The other person raised his head as well. Karina did not recognize him. He wore a sash decorated with suns, like the priests of the Creator. "Greetings, Prophetess."

Her mouth parted slightly before she remembered her manners. She bowed her head to him. "The Creator's blessing be with you."

"And with you." He gestured behind him to the boulders. "You have a choice to make. Behind each stone is a path. Only one will lead you to the next part of the challenge, the other leads to certain death."

"How do I choose?"

Father came alongside Karina and squeezed her shoulder. "Do you have to ask? I can escort you to the next part, and we'll talk. I cannot tell you how proud I am of you, Karina."

She plastered on a smile. Her heart was torn between relief, seeing her father after so many years, and pain, knowing how his mistakes had affected her life. "I—I am not sure."

He hesitated. "Of course. I understand." He dropped his arm, shook his head, and rejoined the priest on the other side.

Karina bit back her tears.

The priest glared at her father, then turned to Karina and motioned for her to follow him to the boulders. "Long ago, the Creator set these boulders here for a reason. There is much power in the sacred armor, and the belt can only be trusted to one with utmost integrity. Though you do not know me, Karina, know that the Creator put me here to ensure you make it through safely."

"For all she knows, you're a demon in disguise." Father pulled her toward his stone. "Karina, I know I have disappointed you in the past."

Indeed. She opened her mouth to speak, but he held up his finger.

"The Creator knew of your disappointment, and he sent me here to make it up to you." He knelt before her and took her hand. "I am sorry, Karina. Look, you do not have to do this. I am proud of the person you've become. Your mother and I look down on you and smile." He let out a sorrowful sigh, the likes of which sucked the joy from Karina's heart.

He grasped both of her hands in his. "But we know this is too much for you. Let me get you through this challenge alive, and then we can get you out of this quest. You have been through so much already. While I am not surprised you made it this far, I fear there are far worse trials ahead. Instead, let us go back to Calliope, where it's safe. I have so much to share with you."

How wonderful that would be. Karina hugged her father.

He pulled away but kept his hands on her shoulders. "I want to tell you the truth about what happened between my brother and me."

The priest stepped in. "The Creator does not make mistakes, Karina. He chose you for a reason. He has a plan for you. Do not mistake hardship for failure or disfavor. No matter what, he is always with you. You know this."

"Of course, he is always with her." Her father turned to Karina with a big smile. "But I am not. I have but a short time in the Three Kingdoms before I must return."

Father's words echoed in her head. He loved her, and he was proud of her. Any good father would want what was best for his child. Maybe he was right.

"Search with your heart, Karina." The priest clasped his hands together. "Our words should hold no weight."

She peered at her father and then at the stranger. She wanted so much to go with her father, to spend time with him, to tell him about her life, to hear about his. On the other hand, the priest was right. The Creator had a plan for her. Whether she saw this quest as a blessing or a curse, it was a quest only she could complete. No one else could take her place—be the Creator's chosen prophetess. In the Creator's eyes, she possessed what was needed to carry this burden.

He saw her when she had cried as they left the castle after her father had been banished.

He saw her on the road to their home in Soter when the mercenaries murdered her parents.

He saw her all alone after the bandits burned the orphan caravan and killed everyone but her.

He saw the moment she resolved to forget her past, forget who she was, and to accept a home in the royal house, despite what they had done to her father.

After all he had seen, he still chose her.

He saw her as a leader. He saw her retrieving the armor. Even when no one else did—even when no one else understood—he saw her.

Today was no different.

Creator, thank you for being the God who sees me. Even when I feel alone or afraid, you never leave me. I know you have given me this quest because you see something in me that I have not been able to see. I know now who I am is not dependent on who my father was, or what he did. Who I am is a reflection of you in my life. Show me what it is to live in your light.

A scream interrupted her prayer. She glanced up.

Her father's face contorted as another scream erupted. His skin sagged, melting like candlewax. Hollow red eyes blazed from behind a haggard skull.

Then he evaporated into thin air.

Karina closed her eyes and exhaled. *Thank you, Creator.* She turned to the priest, who offered her his hand.

"Well done, Prophetess."

Tears pricked the corners of her eyes. "That was not my real father, was it?"

The priest shook his head. "A demon meant to lead you astray."

She nodded.

He swept his hand in a wide arc, and the boulder rolled away from the second tunnel. He walked with her to the edge. "You have faced the truth of who you are, Karina. Now that you have accepted your place, the Creator can show you how to see others—to understand their hearts. Be careful, though. There is nothing more deceitful than a human heart. There is also nothing else that fills us with more hope and possibility."

Why must everyone speak in riddles? She bowed her head. "Thank you, priest."

He offered her the Blessing of Three Kisses. "The Creator's *wisdom* be with you."

"Thank you." She waved as she strolled into the tunnel to face the path before her. Her heart ached for the missed opportunity with her father. Though her head knew he was a demon, her heart yearned for a time when she could let her father know she had forgiven him. Still, she warmed at the knowledge that the Creator deemed her worthy of this quest.

Before long, her stomach began to gurgle. She fished through her pack and pulled out a two bread rolls and a hunk of cheese. She slumped against the cool wall of the tunnel and nibbled on her snacks. Despite how long she had been in the cave, the water inside the skin remained cool, sweet. The nourishment and rest refreshed her, and she was ready to continue.

The tunnel twisted this way and that for some time. Why so winding a trail? Did the Creator make it so long to weary her? To test her endurance? She sighed with frustration and pushed forward.

At last, she found the next cavern, a square-shaped room. Three tunnels led from each of the other walls. In front of each opening stood a crimson-robed figure. As Karina entered the room, each form stepped toward the middle. The demon's deception hung fresh in Karina's mind. She eyed each figure with suspicion.

"Greetings, Prophetess." An old woman with a gnarled face smiled up at her. "You are most welcome here."

A man pushed back his hood to reveal a handsome face and thick, blond hair. He bowed. "We are honored by your presence."

"You have faced the truth of yourself, now you must face the truth of others." A small girl, no more than ten, peeked out from under her hood. She had a scar over her right eye.

The old woman stepped forward. "Where the light shines, so shall you find the Creator. Where the darkness closes in, there he is as well. Set your sights on him alone, and he will not steer you wrong." And with that, the old woman hobbled back to her tunnel.

The young man bowed and then glanced toward the old woman. "What she speaks is truth, but this quest requires more than the Creator's blessing. It requires skill and discernment. Knowledge is power—a power you will need to defeat the enemy. My path leads to your prize and all the knowledge that goes with it." He bowed again and retreated.

"They don't know what they're talking about." The little girl tugged on Karina's arm and wiggled her finger, asking Karina to stoop down. "I may be small, but don't let that fool you. It is important you understand what is at stake. The Three Kingdoms are depending on you—the evil coming is darker than any our world has known in many centuries. Do not forsake us. Choose to follow me." She peered back at her tunnel. "In courage lies your true path."

Karina pursed her lips. They all presented an excellent argument for their path. The old lady reminded her of the importance of the Creator's presence. The handsome man offered knowledge that would help her defeat the evil. The young girl added that she couldn't let fear hold her back. How was she supposed to choose? She doubted the girl could be more than a puppet, for she was too young. The old woman did not even look real. A demon in disguise perhaps?

She had already faced the truth of herself. So, she surmised, she needed more truth. Truth came from knowledge. "I choose the second path."

"Is this your final decision?" they asked in unison.

"Yes."

The man bowed once more. "Prophetess, right this way."

Karina followed him to the second tunnel. A dry, earthy scent wafted from the opening. *I hope this is right.* She shook her head. She had to have faith. The Creator would guide her.

So why did her stomach churn when she stepped into the darkness?

The torches were few and far between in this tunnel, which seemed to drag on in one, never-ending turn to the right—like she was spiraling downward. The further she went, the further apart the torches were. Should she go back? She chastised herself. Like the priest had said, hardship did not mean failure. She had to have more faith.

Soon, the space between the torches became so dark she could barely see the distant light ahead. *Creator, help me! I'm scared.*

She reached a place of total darkness. The light from the torches had vanished. The air was completely still. Her ragged breaths reverberated off the walls. Surely, when she rounded the corner again, there would be another light. She took a step forward.

Stop! The voice was loud, urgent.

Karina yelped and jumped back. She clung to the wall. That voice seemed to have come from her right as if speaking directly into her ear. Yet, she did not sense the presence of another being. She took a small step forward and then another, her back against the cool stone. She put her foot out, feeling for sturdy ground. But she found no such safe place.

Instead, her foot slipped over the edge. Instinctively, she flung her body to the right, landing with a thud, her legs half over—what? A cliff? She turned and felt the ground. Flat on her stomach, she inched forward slightly, enough to peer into the darkness. There—far, far below her—was an orange river, the heat so intense fire seemed to burn her cheeks.

She heaved a sigh. She had come very close to death. She backed away, blood pounding in her head. "Creator, oh Creator." She sagged against the tunnel wall. "Thank you."

A loud screech echoed from somewhere down below.

Go!

CHAPTER TWENTY-TWO

Tristan hurried along the passageway. His legs were numb, his back hurt, and his temper was on the verge of exploding. Every muscle in his body tensed, each nerve on high alert as he pushed deeper and deeper into the mountain. He imagined the tons of stone and dirt falling on top of him. He had never been one to follow tunnels that led away from the light.

Torches lit his way now, and he was thankful for that much guidance. The old sword banged against his thigh with each hurried step. The ridiculous sunstone felt heavy on his left hand. "Of all the most useless tools—a ring?"

What he really wanted was *his* sword … or at least his daggers. Even a bow and arrow would be nice. Hopefully, he wouldn't have to use the useless weapon the Trium gave him.

The torchlight began to fade. Darkness closed in on him. Tristan stopped. Air brushed by his ears, but that was all. He retraced his steps to the last torch and yanked it from the wall.

Karina was clearly out of her mind, choosing him for this challenge. The Creator wanted nothing to do with Tristan Lemur, and that was fine with him. He didn't need faith. Faith didn't pay for food. Faith didn't keep people from dying. Faith was a crutch for fools.

Still, hadn't it been Karina's faith that endeared her to him? He pictured those beautiful blue eyes, the color and depth of the cold Aletheian Sea in the summer. The feel of her lips on his …

He smiled, then pushed thoughts of the Prophetess aside. Whatever lay ahead, he was sure it wasn't going to be a jaunt across the Green Plateau. How long had it been since he'd ridden across the famous fields of Tzedek?

The only light now was from the torch in his hand. An oppressive black emptiness pressed in on all sides, and beads of sweat formed across his forehead. Even his hands were clammy. *Maybe I should go back.*

He shook his head. Not a chance. No way was anyone going to call him a coward. But he didn't know where he was going or what was down here. Perhaps that was part of the challenge—not knowing, yet facing whatever came his way?

He tripped, and the torch flew from his hand. It thumped against the damp wall of the cave and then dropped to the ground. Before he could scramble to reach it, the flame snuffed out.

The cold dark fed on his mind. No walls. No floor. No way out.

Tristan tried to breathe. *Nothing. No air.*

His heart thundered like a stampede of wild horses. He leaned back against the wall, sweat soaking his tunic. He shut his eyes and clenched his fists.

Light shone through his eyelids, and he dared to peek with his right eye. He was surrounded by the lush green grass of his homeland. In the distance, waves crashed in quick succession on the cliffs of Andor. Across the field, by an old apple tree, stood a woman with dark-red hair. He strode toward her, soaking in the familiarity of his home. The woman—he knew her. Mother.

This wasn't a trick. It was a memory. He remembered this day—right after his father had died. He approached his mother with the realization that she was much taller than he was. Of course. He had only been eight when his father was killed.

"Tristan." Her voice was tender. She smiled, her eyes shining. But there was still a touch of sadness behind them. "Where were you?"

He remembered he had wandered into the woods alone.

"You were lost. I found you." She took his hands in hers. "Walk with me."

His breath caught in his throat. "Where are we going?"

"You have important business to attend to, my son. The Creator has plans for you."

He groaned. "I'm mad at the Creator."

"Tristan Richard Lemur, I will hear no more of that from you."

"Why not? Where was the Creator when we pleaded for Father's life?"

She shook her head, red curls bouncing around. "His time was over. The Creator is always with us, no matter what we have been through."

"I'm still mad at him."

She chuckled as she leaned to his level. "I am sure he understands. He still loves you, though. When you're ready, he will forgive you. All you have to do is ask."

The scene faded, replaced by another. He stood in his mother's bedroom—two years had passed. His mother rested peacefully in her bed, buried under the covers, her round face too pale against the soft pink pillows. Her chest rose and fell with a steady cadence.

He stepped forward, bumped into a chair, and winced. He hadn't meant to disturb her.

His mother blinked the sleep from her eyes. "Tristan? There you are." She patted a spot on the bed. "Come, sit and talk with me. I was praying."

"Praying?" He jumped up on the bed next to her. "Why were you praying?"

"I asked the Creator to take care of you." She looked away. "And your brother."

He swallowed. Life in Andor had gone from bad to worse ever since Faramos assumed Father's throne. Through his dark magic, he'd brought all sorts of evil creatures into the realm. Tristan shuddered.

"Why do we need him? We've got you!" He leaned over and hugged his mother.

She laughed. "Yes, you have me for now. But I won't always be here, Tristan. The Creator will be with you, even when I am not. He has a plan for you."

"Why are you saying this stuff?" He could still feel the tears in his little-boy eyes.

"I do not have very long before I go to the Lighted Realm." She squeezed his hand. "I want you to know someone will always be here for you. The Creator will never leave you."

He closed his eyes, wishing that were true. Not in his experience. He'd seen too many good people corrupted, too many innocents die. The world was a dark place where people put their hope in a god, who if he existed, no longer cared.

When Tristan opened his eyes again, his mother was gone. Instead, the heavy darkness devoured him once again. He willed his senses to calm and his heart to slow. He pushed himself off the wall and reached for the other one. It was further than he remembered. He took a few stumbling steps forward before fear gripped him again. He blew out a breath as he dropped his head between his knees. He could do this. Karina was counting on him.

A flood of light burnt his eyes but only for a moment. He straightened to find himself on the Green Plateau. Another memory. All around him, life thrived. Grasses tussled with the wind, meadow birds called as they chased each other through the sky. However, on the horizon, a darkness hovered over the new fortress. If he remembered correctly, this was only a few years ago.

"My, how you have grown, Prince Tristan."

He spun around. An older elf with long, white hair and eyes the color of late-summer wheat stood behind him. "I know you." Then, he hadn't recognized the elf by name. Now he knew the figure had been Asharan.

"Come, we have much to discuss."

What kind of trick was this? "I'm not going anywhere with you."

Asharan smiled. "I mean you no harm, young prince. Please?"

Tristan narrowed his eyes but followed. He could more than hold his own against an old elf, if it came to that. "Where are we going?"

Asharan shrugged. "The Creator will guide us."

Tristan didn't want to quarrel with the elf but succumbed to the bitterness in his soul. "I suppose you want to convince me to reclaim my faith."

Asharan shook his head. "I do not need to."

"No?" With a raised brow, Tristan fell in step next to Asharan.

"No. You already have faith, but you are not ready to accept it yet."

Asharan acted as if he knew Tristan. He knew nothing of Tristan's life, what he had been through to get to where he was. What he had done.

"I know you struggle with your past as well as your present. Even as a bounty hunter, you have morals that set you apart from the other miscreants and mercenaries out there."

Tristan looked down.

Asharan faced him. "You have a good heart, Tristan. You always did, but you have lost your way."

Lost. That's exactly how he felt—all the time.

"The Creator does not look at your past deeds, Tristan. He looks at your heart. If your heart is repentant, he will help you. Remember that."

The older elf offered him a smile, but then he began to fade, along with the rest of the plains.

As Tristan's sight returned, he realized he was no longer in the dark. Torches lined the wall of an open chamber, bigger than any arena he had been in before. His jaw dropped. How had he ended up here?

Scattered around the room were skeletons—some with armor, some without—all decayed and dusty. In the middle lay the most gruesome beast

Tristan had ever seen. A humungous dragon slept peacefully among the sordid destruction.

Not just any dragon, for Tristan had seen a few at Faramos's fortress, as well as the one he'd faced with Karina at his side. No, this was an ancestor of those modern beasts. Twice the size, this creature had scales like armor and a razor-sharp tail. The beast's red color reflected the flames of the torches. Supposedly, these dragons had teeth like swords and eyes sharper than any hunter. And they could not be slain—only an act by the Creator himself could destroy these abominations.

Tristan exhaled a long, deliberate breath as he clutched the hilt of the old sword. Was this his challenge? To defeat an ancient dragon with nothing but a sorry excuse for a weapon? Maybe one of the other fallen men had left behind their sword.

Careful not to make a sound, he crept along the side of the chamber, stepping over bones and other debris. He dared not inhale too quickly for fear he would wake the dragon before he had a proper defense.

He found a skeleton entombed in armor. Tristan slid his rusty sword from the scabbard. He poked around the bones looking for any sign of another sword. Nothing.

He moved on to the next skeleton where an old wooden shield covered half the body. As he leaned it against the wall, the skeleton shifted, and the bones disintegrated into a pile of dust. Tristan froze. He waited for the sound of movement behind him but only heard the soothing breath of the slumbering dragon.

He continued circling the room, finding nothing of use. Not even a decent dagger. He hurried back to retrieve the shield—the only shield—from the wall where he had placed it. His foot caught on a stray stone, and he tumbled forward, arms extended. His sword hit the ground with a crash and slid away from him. He closed his eyes, his forehead on the rough stone. Idiot. He rolled to his side and stopped.

The dragon's gaze fell on Tristan as a snort of dark smoke came from its nostrils.

Tristan swallowed hard. Beads of sweat formed at his temples. He needed his sword. Keeping an eye on the dragon, he scurried along the wall. The growing light in the beast's belly warmed the room. Shouting an obscenity, Tristan dove for the sword provided for him. He turned just as the dragon rose up on all fours.

Tristan scrambled back until he hit the wall. He might be a trained bounty hunter, but he was not a dragon slayer. He did not stand a chance against this monster without decent weaponry—and even then … His hands shook. Without taking his gaze off the dragon, he grabbed the shield.

The dragon reared back its ugly head and then expelled a fire hotter than the black sands of the western volcanoes. Tristan dropped his sword to hold the shield with both hands. He could feel the heat blazing across the wood like the panic racing through his body. The wood and metal heated quickly, burning his fingers. He persisted—scorched hands were better than death.

When he believed he could hold out no longer, the barrage ceased. He tossed the burning shield aside and picked up the sword, swearing as the rough wood rubbed against his blistering flesh.

The dragon swung its tail, and Tristan managed to dodge the razor-scaled appendage aimed at him. On the return swing, he stepped to one side to avoid the scales, but the fleshy part of the dragon's tail batted him against another wall, and he fell to the ground. Pain raced through his entire body. Dazed, he sucked in breath after breath, then opened his eyes.

The hulking tail flew at him again, but he rolled out of the way.

Tristan scrambled to his feet and retrieved his sword. When the dragon reared back again, he hurled the dull hunk of metal at the dragon's heart. The sword clattered against the scales and fell uselessly to the floor. *So much for that plan.*

He searched the room for something else to use. Nothing.

He dodged the next firestorm, staying ahead of the heat. Sweat dripped into his eyes, his hands were clammy. His battered body protested. No way could he keep this up. Time was running out.

The fire's glow glinted off the sunstone ring. He stared at the stone. What could he do with this ornament? He punched his right hand toward the dragon.

Nothing happened.

He pressed his lips together. Maybe the ring required a spoken command to activate its power. He held his arm out again. "Die!"

The ring did little more than reflect the torchlight, probably giving the beast a good laugh.

He raised his right hand. "By the Creator's might!"

Nothing.

The Creator had deserted him now as he had when his parents died.

The dragon roared, demanding Tristan's sacrifice.

Weary from running, Tristan stumbled. With what little strength he had left, he picked himself up. This time, when the tail came at him, he couldn't maneuver quickly enough. A scale caught him in the thigh, tearing through the muscle to the bone. Tristan rolled to the ground, his vision clouded. Pain seared through his body, worse than anything he'd ever known. Even torture at the hands of mercenaries did not compare to this.

Once more, the dragon reared back its head.

Tristan bowed his head. He had failed.

I am sorry, Karina.

CHAPTER TWENTY-THREE

Karina scrambled to her feet. The voice inside her head urged her to move faster.

Another screech came from the pit.

She raced along the path, though she could barely see. What was behind her? She did not dare look. Blood pulsed through her body.

Faster. Faster.

The sound of beating wings echoed through the tunnel—more than one set.

Where had she gone wrong? The first part of the challenge had been all about her faith in the Creator and his plan for her. Would not this challenge expand upon what she had already learned?

Another high-pitched cry came from behind her, closer this time.

Creator, I need your help!

She rounded the corner. The previous cavern opened before her. Relief flooded her veins. Her legs collapsed beneath her, and she fell to her hands and knees.

Another screech came from the tunnel.

Karina turned.

A gigantic bat, with two long, sharp teeth and piercing red eyes, swooped to the opening. Another bat dove in behind the first. She shielded her head with her arms. The bats shrieked … a splat … then another splat … then silence. She peered through the gap in her arms. The bats slid down an invisible barrier, their bodies crumbled on the ground.

She shivered.

"You have returned, Prophetess," the old woman crooned.

Karina stood and brushed the dirt from her not-so-white dress. She let out a breath. "Indeed."

"Not many have made it out alive after having made the wrong choice," the man said—the one whose path Karina had chosen. "You must have a strong faith."

The little girl nodded. "Now which path will you choose?"

Karina stared at the old woman and the little girl.

She remembered the old woman's words: "Set your sights on him alone, and he will not steer you wrong."

Karina forced a slight smile. How could she have been so stubborn? *Creator, how do I choose? You must guide the way for me.*

The eyes of the man and the little girl glowed red. Their faces contorted, and the flesh melted away—like her father's image in the first test.

Karina shook her head. She had not relied on the Creator to guide her. Lesson learned.

The woman reached out her withered hand. "Looks can be deceiving, so can words. You have to rely on the Creator to show you the truth of others."

"I promise to remember that in the future."

The old woman led the way to the correct tunnel.

"The Creator's blessing on you, Prophetess. The Three Kingdoms are counting on you." A white light momentarily blinded Karina, then the old woman disappeared.

Karina took a deep breath. What lay ahead of her now? She grabbed an apple from her knapsack and savored the first sweet bite before gobbling the rest.

On to the next leg of the challenge. She threw the bag over her shoulder and then took a hesitant step forward. Hesitant? What kind of fresh start was that? The Creator chose her. Despite all her iniquities, despite her failures and mistakes, he chose her.

With head held high, she strode into another long tunnel. She made her way down a plummeting, narrow path, taking small steps to avoid falling to certain death. She swiped her forehead. This would be the never-ending quest!

The air was even cooler here, and there was more distance between torches. Her mind wandered to the different tortures that could await her at the next step in this challenge. She shook away her doubts. This was the right way. The Creator wanted to reveal his power to her—his gift. And he wanted to be sure she could wield the power, or rather she would understand that she could. He already knew she could.

The path evened out and widened considerably. Ahead, she could make out two tunnels. Not another choice! A hooded figure stood between the paths, his presence solemn and unmoving. Should she be fearful or welcome the company?

"Good evening, Prophetess," a male voice said from beneath the white cloak. "I see you have made it this far."

She tilted her head in acknowledgement, unsure of how to respond.

"You have faced the truth of yourself and the truth of others." He held his hands out at his side, gesturing to the two paths. "Your final task is quite simple. Only one of these paths is the right one. The other leads to certain death. You must choose."

She looked down the left path, alit with torches. An even brighter light came from around the bend. To her right, the tunnel was identical down to the brighter light beyond a turn. "Do you know which way I am supposed to go?"

The strange man nodded.

She bit her lip. "I do not suppose you can tell me?"

He shook his head.

"No, of course not." She paced between the tunnels. *Creator, you brought me this far, do not leave me now. What am I supposed to do? Which is the right path?*

Warmth emanated from the man. She could feel a peace wash over her, and she embraced it. She silently asked the Creator's blessing once again. A light shone before her and then faded to the left before disappearing completely.

Her jaw dropped. "Did you see that?" She pointed toward the left tunnel.

The man smirked. "See what?" With a flourish of movement, he removed his cloak, revealing his identity … Garon, the Servant of the Creator … from the mountaintop.

Karina stepped back. "You!"

"Greetings, Prophetess. You seem to be coming into your powers in your own right. You could sense who I was. The Belt of Truth will enhance that power within you, a mighty weapon indeed, that can be used for incredible good or unspeakable evil."

She furrowed her brow. "What do you mean?"

"What you sensed in here today is but a miniscule glimpse of the power of the belt. With the Belt of Truth, you can see inside to someone's soul. You can see their past and their present. You can see their heart and sense their intentions. A suitable tool for a prophetess such as yourself."

She thought on all she had learned to this point. "So, essentially, the belt keeps people from being able to lie to me?"

The servant shook his head. "No, it does not work quite like that. They can still lie to you, and part of the belt's power is to reveal to you they are lying. But it goes so far beyond that. It is something you will have to experience for yourself to fully understand."

Karina smiled, more from politeness than comprehension.

Garon laughed. "Do not worry, Prophetess. The Creator will guide you, and I may see you yet again if the Creator sends me to your aid."

"Thank you." She bowed her head slightly and turned to the left tunnel.

"May the Creator's blessing be with you, my child." And then he was gone.

Karina puffed her cheeks. Part of her wondered if she even wanted this responsibility now. Had she not been through enough already? She shook her head. Doubt was a useless emotion. She straightened her shoulders and then made her way down the tunnel as the path twisted to the right and then to the left. She tired of these narrow passages. Still, the light grew brighter with each turn.

Finally, she came upon a set of golden doors. Each side had a sun, the symbol of the Creator, etched in the top half. The doors glowed with such brilliance she had to cover her eyes. It was time. She moved to open the doors, but they swung open before her. Karina peered in but could see no one.

She entered another small, well-lit chamber resembling one found in a castle. Torches hung on the wall, but an iron chandelier full of lighted candles also hung from the stone ceiling. On the far wall, a pedestal sat on a raised platform. A dusty, faded-purple rug led from where she stood to the fixture. Tables lined the other walls with trinkets of every kind—goblets and daggers, shields and jewelry. Many were gold or silver and embedded with precious stones. Karina blinked several times at the beauty stored in this room. Not that she would know what to do with a treasure such as this.

She should find the belt and leave.

She moved across the carpet, still enamored with all that glittered on the side tables. A shiny gold tiara capped with crimson stones caught her eye. Intricate carvings of leaves and vines encircled the crown. Karina placed her hand over her heart. Stunning. Would she be wrong to try the tiara on? She glanced back at the pedestal that most likely held the belt. What harm could be caused by a quick look?

Better not. She sighed. Her quest was not a crown, nor was it what she truly desired. Still … she gazed back at the tiara. Something her father said niggled her conscience. *A person is not the sum of their possessions; they are the sum of their character.* She turned away from the jeweled temptation.

With a deep breath, she approached the pedestal. Humbleness seemed an inadequate description for the emotions she felt. She was about to be entrusted with one piece of the Creator's sacred armor.

The belt looked nothing like what she had envisioned. The thick, braided leather was a dark shade of purple, with half of a pewter sun at each end that linked together to clasp around one's waist. When someone said the word armor, Karina imagined a metal suit piece. Could this meager piece of worn leather be considered armor? She glanced around the room. Maybe she had the wrong item. Maybe there was something else.

She held the belt in her hand as she circled the chamber, glancing at the trinkets on the tables. Nothing seemed to resemble a belt. With raised eyebrows, she surmised she must have the right piece after all.

She looped the belt around her waist. Though it blended well with the dirty white fabric of her dress, there was a certain demure beauty about it. She waited for a moment. Nothing happened. She didn't feel any different. *Creator, did I make the right choice?*

The sound of stone rubbing against stone interrupted her prayer. Off to the right of the pedestal, a doorway opened.

That must be the Creator's answer.

Back into the tunnels she went. She traversed more turns and bends for what seemed like hours. Though this maze did not create choices, she still felt lost. At last, a distant white light clashed with the dim yellow glow of flames from the torches. She was almost there.

She came out of the tunnel at the same chamber where she had begun her challenge. There were the two entrances with the words TRUTH and FAITH written across the top. She had emerged from the TRUTH path— the same way she had entered. How was that possible?

Though the fire had gone out, wisps of smoke indicated it had not been out for long. Where was Tristan? Had he already gone outside? She glanced toward the FAITH tunnel. What challenges had he faced? Was it anything like hers?

She'd had to own up to the truth about herself in a way she had never been able to before. She may be the daughter of a traitor, but that fact did not define who she was in the sight of the Creator. Who her father was did not determine her path in this world.

Sunlight spilled over the rocks as she exited the cave ... its warmth on her face, a welcomed pleasure. She raised grateful hands to the Creator.

For the first time, she noticed she was alone on the beach—not another soul, human or elf, in sight. She turned back toward the cave. Same entrance. So where was the crowd of priests and priestesses? Where were Rashka and Sam?

She should probably wait for Tristan. He could not be done already. He would not have left without her. What if he were hurt? What if he did not pass his test? How would she or anyone else ever know?

Karina returned to the fire pit and stoked the embers with dried sticks she had found at the mouth of the cave. She sat on one of the larger stones and bowed her head, asking the Creator to protect Tristan, to open his eyes to the faith he so desperately needed.

A vision of Tristan battling a dragon engulfed her. She gripped the stone. Tristan lay in front of the dragon, battered and bleeding, writhing in pain. The dragon reared back its head.

The echoes of her scream reverberated through her head. "No!"

How was it he even saw her? Tristan cringed at the reflection of horror in Karina's expression. He wanted her smile to be the last thing he saw. Instead of peaceful beauty, her face grayed as she screamed. "No!" she shouted, reaching for him.

He shook his head. Delusions from the pain? As his mind cleared, he focused on the torches hanging from the red-stone walls. The dragon roared as it swung its head from side to side. It opened its mouth and spewed more fire.

With a loud groan, Tristan forced himself to roll toward the beast, the only way to ensure he would not burn. The dragon tried to back away, but it was too clumsy to maneuver within this chamber. It stretched its neck ... the fire still too close for the creature's comfort. It shrieked, flailing its wings.

Spent of his will to fight, Tristan let out a long breath. He had lost too much blood. The pain had dulled—that, or his mind blocked out the intensity. He felt as if he were enveloped in thick fog. All he wanted was to sleep.

The roar of the dragon cut through the haze, feeding his fear.

He was going to die.

Here, in the heart of a mountain, all alone.

He closed his eyes. He wasn't ready. For once in his entire life, he was not ready to die. Acknowledging that fact sent a fresh shiver through his body. With a rush of adrenaline, he pushed himself up on one leg and hobbled to his excuse of a sword.

If he was going down—

The tip of the dragon's tail caught him on the other leg. Tristan howled as the razor-sharp scale tore half his muscle away. The force knocked him against the rough stone. Darkness encroached on his vision. He could not breathe, as if a large stone were crushing his chest.

No, he couldn't die here. Alone.

Creator, can you hear me? Please, forgive me for being so stubborn. I need you now. I know I don't deserve your help, but I ask for your mercy.

A sudden warmth filled him. No longer numb, white-hot pain seared, followed by stiffness, like lying in a hot bath after a hard battle. The relief so great, tears fell—tears he initially resisted but now allowed to wash his spirit and heal his broken body.

He opened his eyes. A shimmering light surrounded him. He looked down. The ring Vyra had given him glowed like a tiny sun. He held up his hand to admire the beauty—and power surged through him.

The dragon's thunderous roars captured Tristan's attention as the monster dove toward him, teeth bared. Tristan thrust out his arms, a senseless attempt to stop the enormous beast. Still, he'd made his peace with the Creator.

If this was his time …

Karina would accomplish her quest without him. The Creator would see to that.

The dragon screeched as if in pain. Tristan covered his ears to block out the vibrating howl. The monster reeled back, then burst into flames. A second later, it was a pile of ashes on the chamber floor.

Tristan dropped his arms to his side. He surveyed the room, then glanced at his ring. The glow faded, and the sunstone returned to normal.

Shield of Faith.

Tristan smirked. *You're a clever one, you know that?* He twisted the ring two times. Shaking his head, he wiped the dirt from his hands and then made his way back up the tunnel, leaving the sword behind.

As he wandered back up the path, he thought about how much his life had changed since he'd met Karina. She had reached out to him, despite the things he had done to her. He had kidnapped her, by all that was created! Yet, she'd stayed with him when the lupens attacked. And with one word she could have had Asharan kill him … yet didn't.

All of that had led him here, to this moment. The Creator knew what it would take to bring a former prince turned rogue back to the path of righteousness. The Creator knew what it would take to restore his faith. Tristan felt humbled by the swiftness of the Creator's response. He had reached out in prayer, in the heat of the moment, when he had nothing left, and the Creator was there. Right there.

The setting sun pierced the dim passageway as he came out of the tunnel, the sudden brightness blinding him for a moment. When he moved out of the rays, he could see again. Karina stood by the fire pit in the middle of the room. Her hands were on her hips, her eyes were shining.

She knew.

When he smiled, she ran into his open arms, tears on her rosy cheeks. "I saw everything," she mumbled into his tunic as he held her tight. "I saw you."

How could he explain the overwhelming emotions roiling in his soul?

She stepped back. "You found your faith again."

"I did." He reached for her hand. "And thank you for helping me."

She grinned. "You are most welcome."

"So, what now?"

"I imagine we rejoin the others and return to the temple."

He led her out of the cave and stopped. "Where is everyone?"

CHAPTER TWENTY-FOUR

Karina stood on the rocky shore with one hand shading her eyes as she stared at the dark blue water. The salty air was refreshing, and Tristan's presence behind her sustaining. She placed her hand on the belt now clasped around her waist.

"So, what happened to you?" Tristan asked.

She turned to him. He sat on one of the larger rocks, throwing stones into the ocean. At first glance, he appeared to be unscathed by his experience, but the layers of grime on his skin and his torn clothes proved otherwise. His countenance had changed … a sense of peace … a man no longer at war with his heart.

Karina sat next to him on the rocks. "I learned to accept who I am."

Tristan raised an eyebrow.

She looked away. "I know, it sounds silly. But I have based my worth on the mistakes my father made, instead of trusting in the Creator and his plan for me."

"And the belt?"

She glanced down at the purple leather adornment with its pewter sun. "Since I realized the truth about myself, the belt helps me see inside others and realize the truth about them. Or something like that."

"A powerful tool, indeed."

"That's what the servant said."

Tristan tilted his head toward the belt. "How does it work?"

"I am not sure … what about you? What happened?"

"I fought a dragon, and it almost killed me." His tone seemed empty of emotion.

Karina offered a half-smile. "I saw."

Tristan held up the sunstone ring. "Apparently, this is the Shield of Faith."

"A ring?"

He gazed at the ocean as he rubbed his palms against his pants. "When things got bad, I finally reached out to the Creator. The ring glowed—I was healed. The dragon attacked, then burst into flames. That's what happened, but I can't explain how."

Karina thought *her* experience was draining. She reached for Tristan's hand, but he pulled away and stood.

"My stubbornness almost got me killed," he growled, "and endangered your quest."

She rested her hand on his shoulder. "But you survived. That is all that matters."

He shrugged.

"Tristan, I want you to know something." She held her breath as he turned to face her. "I forgive you."

He quirked an eyebrow.

"I forgive you for everything that happened before. For kidnapping me, taking me to Faramos—all of it. You were not the same person then, and I would be wrong to hold that against you. So, I forgive you."

He clenched his jaw. "Thank you, Karina."

Awkward silence prolonged the moment as they stared at each other. Karina glanced up the mountain path. "Do you think we are supposed to wait here, or are we to return to the temple?"

"I'm not sure." He followed her line of sight. "We've been out here for a while, though. Maybe we should head back. I'm starved."

She nodded and followed his lead. They made their way back into the mountains. The stone wall rose up on either side of them. As dusk fell, a chilling wind breezed through the winding pathway. Karina wrapped her arms around her body to stay warm.

Tristan remained silent, his pensive expression like one who tried to solve the world's problems on his own.

She cleared her throat. "Do you feel any different?"

"Different, how?"

"I mean, we went through quite an ordeal. We had to come to hard realizations to acquire the pieces of armor. Surely, we are not left unchanged."

He shrugged. "I don't feel much different. It's more like—like you said earlier—knowing my place."

"I don't feel much different either. Free from my self-doubt but still worried about what is to come."

"We have a long fight ahead. I don't expect that part is going to change." He put his arm around her and pulled her close. "No worries, for now."

"I was thinking, though, if it took prayer to make the ring work, maybe that is how I'd make the belt work as well."

"It's possible."

"May I try it on you?"

Tristan recoiled and stopped in the middle of the path. "No!"

"Please? I need to figure out how to use the belt before it becomes necessary."

He shook his head with such vehemence there was no doubt as to his opinion of the matter.

"But …" She let the word die on her lips. As a former bounty hunter, Tristan probably preferred his past remain his secret. She bowed her head. Her cheeks heated. "I am sorry. Please forgive me."

He locked his hands behind his back as he picked up the pace. Karina hurried to keep up with him.

As they approached the Temple, music drifted across the salty sea breeze. Torches flickered along the dirt path, as if applauding their return. She clasped the worn belt around her waist. They had been successful. The oppressive weight that had held her down for years had been lifted.

Savory smells teased Karina as she strolled through the arched double doors. Her stomach gurgled. When was the last time she had eaten? The white marble shone in the glowing light of the wall sconces. Joyful chatter from the dining hall bounced off the walls.

Tristan ushered her into the crowded room. When they entered, someone shouted, "Here they are! "The cacophony of voices halted, and a hundred sets of eyes turned toward the open doors.

Karina froze under the scrutiny. She gripped the sullied skirt of her formerly white dress and stared at her dusty sandals. These people were dressed in ceremonial finery, and she appeared before them in rags.

"You have returned!" Lucian pushed through the crowd, seeming ethereal in his gold-stitched white robes. "I am pleased to see you were successful." A twinkle in his eyes, he glanced back at Tristan. "And in one piece at that."

Tristan grunted as he pulled his arms behind his back.

"You two should retire to your rooms and change into more fitting attire," Lucian said with a sly grin. "I look forward to hearing about your adventures."

They hurried to their rooms to change. As the hour grew late, Karina returned. Her freshly braided hair hung over her shoulder, and she was dressed in a purple silk gown she had found hanging in her wardrobe.

Tristan immediately swept in to claim her arm. "Would you do me the honor of dancing with me? I am tired of all the questions."

Karina faked a smile. "My, you do know how to flatter a lady."

He looked dumbfounded. "My apologies. I meant no disrespect."

"Just tell me you know how to dance!"

He waggled his eyebrows as he dragged her to the middle of the floor. With a quick twirl, they joined the other couples.

Karina grinned up at Tristan when he raised his hands. She splayed her hands before his—close, but not touching. They circled each other in rhythm with the other dancers. First to the right, then to the left. They eased around each other with graceful movements. She danced away until their arms were fully extended and then spun back into his arms.

She tripped over his foot, but Tristan caught her with ease. She gazed up at him.

"And you were worried about *me* not knowing how to dance," he teased. He snatched her up so quickly her breath left her, and she stared into his emerald eyes, now so full of life. His head tilted toward hers.

Her vision clouded …

> She stood on the edge of the mountains where they overlooked the sea. Thick clouds shrouded the sun and turned the water to a dark gray. In front of her, three large ships with dingy white sails and a black flag bearing Faramos's image clung to the shoreline.
>
> The world spun. She found herself on the other side of the mountain range. Shadowed Forest spread before her. Though she could not see very well as night closed in, she could hear crashing through the brush. A lone lupen howled, and then the night was overrun with eerie echoes as more lupens joined in chorus.
>
> She shivered.

Tristan shook her shoulders. "Karina! Karina, are you ill?"

She blinked rapidly. "What—what happened?"

"I don't know." He steadied her as she swayed.

"I think I had a vision."

"Of what?"

A shout echoed above the crowd. Three men rushed in, red-faced and breathing heavily.

"We're going to be attacked!" one of them cried.

Oh, no. Karina straightened.

Lucian, Vyra, and Paul made their way through the crowd.

"C'mon," Tristan whispered as he clutched her hand. They followed the group to a meeting room.

"Tell us what happened," Lucian demanded. He nodded to Karina and Tristan as they entered, and Paul closed the door behind them.

A large table, surrounded by fourteen chairs, took up most of the room. A fireplace was at the far end. Tapestries, depicting the Creator's sun and his miracles, decorated the remaining walls.

The three men sunk into cushioned chairs. Though their labored breathing had returned to normal, sweat still ran down their faces. The burly one, who had spoken earlier, cleared his throat. "We were on patrol on the far side of Shadowed Forest—near River Branch. We saw several companies of Faramos's army entering the woods."

"I thought this place was hidden?" Karina asked.

Lucian balled his hands. "It is, but it is not spelled. Someone with the right knowledge and persistence could find us."

"How do you know the soldiers were Faramos's army?" Karina asked.

"His forces are unmistakable, Prophetess," Vyra explained. "He's the only one who employs goblins, lupens, and dark elves."

"And I saw the goblins and lupens," one of the men said.

"What do we do now?"

A knock sounded at the door. Paul opened it, and Rashka and Sam rushed in.

"What is happening?" Rashka asked.

Sam stood off to the side, his gaze on Karina. His worried look reminded her of the time she'd gotten her foot stuck between tree branches just a few hours after Jace had reprimanded them for climbing trees. What had she dragged him into?

"Faramos has sent his army to the Temple," Lucian said. "And we are not equipped to handle an attack of this kind."

Lucian continued talking, but Karina could not concentrate. Surely the Creator would not let his temple to fall to the likes of Faramos? Her stomach rumbled, and a fire burned within, warming her blood, giving her renewed strength. She took a deep breath and willed herself to calm down. The situation required a clear head, not one clouded by emotion.

"We will have to escape to Calliope by way of the mountain inlet and the sea," Lucian said.

"No!" Karina shouted.

The room fell silent, and for the second time tonight, all eyes turned to her.

"Karina?" Tristan put his hand on her shoulder.

She shook her head. "We cannot use the inlet."

"Why not?" Lucian's glare revealed his doubts.

She bit her lip. Would they believe her vision? She sucked in a deep breath. "Faramos has ships on the sea. They are not far from here, awaiting the command to attack. And his army spreads at least a half day north and south on the forest side. They will not attack for at least three days' time—maybe more."

"How do you know?" Sam asked, wide-eyed.

She swallowed.

"The Prophetess has spoken." Lucian glanced toward Sam, whose ears reddened. "We cannot evacuate. We will have to stand and fight." He then nodded to Vyra and Paul, and they hurried from the room. Lucian sighed as he eased into a chair. "We will fight, but I fear we may not win. Only by the Creator's miracle could we survive this."

"We need to send for reinforcements." Karina paced alongside the table. "Calliope will send an army to protect its temple if I command it."

Lucian arched an eyebrow. "I thought you did not want to be queen."

"I cannot change who I am, even if I wanted to, which I do not."

He laughed. "Very well, then. What do you suggest?"

"We need to find a way to send a message to Aletheia's royal house. Captain DeMarco will send the army."

Sam shook his head. "Everyone thinks you're dead. Any message from you will fall on deaf ears."

Tristan stepped forward. "Does the message have to come from Karina? Lucian could just as easily send one."

"True." Lucian nodded. "But how would we get it out?"

Karina shrugged. "Could we send scouts?"

Tristan shook his head. "There would be no assurance they would get through. We would never know if one succeeded in their mission to Calliope."

Karina groaned.

Rashka put her hands on the table. "We can go."

"We?" Lucian raised an eyebrow.

"Karina and I."

The room buzzed with objections.

Rashka sighed. "I can transform and fly us out of here."

Karina stifled a laugh. "I am not sure your hawk form could carry me."

Light flashed, and a large griffin stood on the table. Its claws scraped at the wood as it flapped its wings.

Karina stared at the monstrous beast that could very well be their salvation.

"But, wait." Tristan stepped between Rashka and the group. "If Karina goes, how do we know Anaya will not have her thrown in the dungeon?"

Karina shook her head. "In the event of my death, Captain DeMarco would become king. Anaya has no power anyway."

Tristan let out a breath, and his shoulders slumped.

Lucian stood. "Very well, make your preparations quickly. You must leave as soon as possible."

Tristan and Sam followed Karina to her room. Tristan slammed the door behind them. "I do not like this, Karina. You can't go alone. Plus, you're exhausted."

"I will not be alone, Tristan," Karina rifled through the wardrobe and found suitable riding attire. "Rashka will be with me."

Tristan let out a long sigh. "I know, but—it's not the same."

Karina stepped inside the washroom, then poked her head back out. "You mean, she is not you." He looked crestfallen, and Karina felt disappointed as well. "She will take good care of me."

He glared at the floor.

Sam growled as he slouched in the chair by the side table. "I don't like the idea of you going back to Calliope right now. The queen is going to be furious."

Karina laughed. "Let her be furious. She is not the queen any longer, and I am the rightful heir." With that, she shut the door to the washroom and changed her clothes.

The men continued arguing in her bed chamber. They both wanted nothing more than to protect her, which she appreciated. The Creator had surely blessed her with loyal companions for this journey.

She emerged from the washroom, knotting the end of her braid.

Tristan rose from where he had been leaning against a window sill. He held out the dagger he had given her when they rode from River Branch.

River Branch. Could it have been only three days ago? She closed her eyes for a moment, while she massaged her temples. She was so tired.

Tristan cleared his throat. "I know I still haven't had time to teach you to use this, but just in case, you need something."

"Thank you." She stuck the dagger inside her riding boot. The weapon did not make her feel any more protected but taking the knife would ease Tristan's mind. She patted the Belt of Truth at her waist—it did not make her feel much safer either.

CHAPTER TWENTY-FIVE

Karina left her bed chambers, Tristan and Sam at her heels, giving her tips on how to handle different situations, then arguing with each other on how she could best protect herself. When they entered the front hall, she spun on her heel and held up her hand.

"Enough!" She looked from one man to the other. "I know you want to ensure my safety, and I am grateful to have such good friends. But please. I trust the Creator will see my journey is completed quickly and safely. In the meantime, you two need to focus on how you can be of service here. The Trium will need swordsmen like you."

They both stared at the ground.

"Of course," Sam mumbled. "You're right."

Tristan shoved his hands into his pockets.

"Very well, then." She turned back around.

Rashka and Lucian met them at the temple doors. "Ready?" Rashka asked.

Karina nodded. "How long will it take us to reach Calliope?"

"We should reach the royal house by mid-morning."

Tristan grunted. "Are you sure you want to travel at night?"

"The darkness will hide us as we travel over the army. It will be safer."

"No falling asleep!" Sam interjected with a slight grin. "Hang on tight."

Karina stifled a giggle. "I will be fine."

"Let us pray." Everyone bowed their heads. "Creator, we come before you this day to offer thanks for your past protection, and we ask your continued protection on your prophetess and guardian as they make their way across enemy lines. May their journey be swift and fruitful. In the Creator's name."

"In the Creator's name." They all repeated.

A light flashed as they opened their eyes. Rashka had shifted into her griffin form, ready to leave.

Karina trudged over, but her gaze strayed to Tristan, his smile, encouraging. What she really wanted was for him to sweep her up in his arms like he had done after his challenge. Right now, she was weary. She could use his strength.

He must have sensed her need, because he pulled Karina aside. "You must be careful," he said, his face close to hers.

She nodded, not trusting herself to speak.

"Do not try to be a hero if you get into trouble. I mean it."

Again, she nodded.

He searched her eyes as if he wanted to say more.

"Tristan?"

He pulled her into an embrace and rested his chin on the top of her head. She inhaled his spicy scent—a mix of sable and figs. He stepped back and held her at arm's length. "Go," he whispered. He ushered her ahead of him, turning to Rashka as he walked by. "You better keep her safe."

Rashka dipped her head in acknowledgement. "Let us ride!"

Karina gripped the griffin's feathers as Sam helped her mount.

"I'm ready," she said to Rashka, and, in turn, nodded to Tristan, Sam, and Lucian.

Rashka strode out the temple doors. The sun had fallen well below the horizon, cloaking the valley in darkness. A dense layer of clouds blocked the moonlight.

"Will you be able to see?" Karina eyed the spot where darkness covered the mountaintops.

"My night vision is perfect. You have nothing to fear, Karina."

She swallowed hard, praying Rashka was right. "Let us go, then."

Rashka squawked. She took a few running steps, then leaped into the air.

Karina gasped and leaned forward as far as she could. The cold night air whipped her cloak. She dared not let go to wrap it around her.

Rashka flew in large circles around the valley as she climbed higher in the sky.

Karina wanted to shut her eyes, but she could not, enthralled by the view. The mountains blended in the darkness, giving the appearance of a natural fortress overshadowing the valley. A sign of hope—everyone would be well until she returned.

At last, they rose above the mountain tops. Aletheia spread before them in muted shades of black and gray. Far below, Karina could distinguish orange dots of fire amid the forest along the mountains sheltering the temple. She looked off to her far right, to the sea. The ships were not yet visible, but she knew they were there.

Free of the mountains, Rashka flapped her powerful wings and increased their speed.

They had not traveled far when Rashka telepathically spoke into Karina's mind. *We have company.*

Company? Karina surveyed the sky in front of them and to their sides but could only see darkness. She glanced behind them. Nothing. She leaned in closer to Rashka's head. "What do you mean?"

A fireball flew past, fizzling in the frigid air. Karina cast a glimpse over her shoulder once more. She could make out two winged creatures in the distance. Another fireball barreled toward them.

"Watch out!" Karina squeezed her eyes shut.

Rashka dodged the flames.

Karina bit her lip to keep from screaming. "Were those—were those dragons?"

Yes. There is nowhere for us to hide, we will have to outfly them.

"Can you do that?"

I have never tried in griffin form.

"Would it not be better to hide amongst the trees?"

When dragons have fire to burn us out?

Karina groaned. "You are right. Out-flying them seems like the only option."

Rashka pushed harder.

Karina looked back again. The dragons were gaining on them. "Hurry, Rashka!"

Her powerful wings pumped even harder.

Karina longed for a bow and arrow. Sitting here on Rashka's back made her feel helpless. All she could do was to hold on tight.

The two great beasts split apart and flanked Rashka on either side.

"What are we going to do?" Karina's heart beat faster than Rashka's wings.

I am not sure. It is hard for me to fight …

One of the dragons turned its head. From here, Karina could see its belly glow. She buried her head in Rashka's feathers. *Creator, please do not let us die!*

Rashka suddenly slowed. *Hold on, Karina!*

She gripped Rashka's golden feathers until her knuckles turned white.

Faramos had a swarm of dragons circling his castle. Why had no one considered the possibility he would storm the temple with them? She sat up, more angry than afraid. She refused to let Faramos win.

Rashka advanced with lightning speed. The second dragon reared back to avoid the fireball thrown by the first dragon. While the second dragon was still off its stance, Rashka clawed its delicate wings—shredding and biting. The dragon roared, his belly glow building even as Rashka attacked the other wing.

Both Rashka and the dragon descended rapidly. Rashka stopped mid-air, but the dragon plummeted to the forest below, turning on to its back as it neared the ground. Its mighty jaws opened. Liquid fire spewed straight up.

Rashka maneuvered away from the cone of heat.

"Where did the other dragon go?" Karina looked around but found no sign.

Right—

The roar came from above them. Karina ducked as the dragon sloped toward them.

Rashka tried but could not outfly the beast. Its claw struck her side, and she dove into the trees. Karina struggled to hold on, unable to breathe.

Overhead, the dragon circled.

Rashka thumped into the trees. She moaned as Karina dismounted. A flash of light, and Rashka's natural form sprawled out upon dead leaves and leftover snow.

Karina knelt at her side. "Where are you injured?" She noticed the huge gash in Rashka's arm and the lesser wound on her side. "By all that is created!"

"It looks worse than it is, I am sure." Rashka tried to chuckle but winced at the effort.

"You lay back and rest."

"I cannot." She tried to sit up. "There is a dragon still searching for us."

Overhead, the beast soared high in the air, but it did not seem ready to attack.

"Let me tend to your arm." Karina poked and prodded for a minute. The dragon's slash had torn through muscle. If conditions were more ideal, she could stitch the wound. Right now, she must stop the bleeding.

She pulled off her cloak and ripped it into long strips, wrapping a few of them around Rashka's arm to stop the bleeding, then took two more strips to fashion a sling for Rashka's arm.

Karina finished tying the knot for the sling. "Are you not able to heal yourself, like you did my arm a while ago?"

"Our healing powers are for others, not for ourselves."

Karina glanced upward at the still-circling dragon. "What do you suppose he is doing?"

Rashka's eyes widened. She jumped to her feet and grimaced as she jostled her arm. "We need to go."

"What do you mean? You need to rest."

"The dragon—he is not just wandering around up there."

"What is he doing?"

"He is a beacon." She gazed toward the trees behind them. "Something else is coming."

Karina gasped. "By all that is created!"

"Whoever—whatever it is, they are not close enough yet. If we hurry, we can retain the advantage."

They tore through the trees. Though most likely in considerable pain, Rashka kept a quick pace. Karina admired her ability to keep going no matter the circumstances.

After they had ran a good distance, Karina paused to lean against a tree. Her legs were numb, her breath short. Sweat ran down the middle of her back. "Rashka!"

Rashka slowed and turned. "Come on, Karina. We cannot stop."

"I—I cannot run anymore."

Rashka hurried back and grabbed her arm. "You do not have a choice. We do not know what is coming after us." She squinted up at the dragon. It continued to circle them overhead though they had covered quite a distance. "But I can guarantee you, whatever is coming, we cannot fend off on our own."

"I vote for climbing up in a big tree and resting until morning."

Rashka smiled. "That would be nice. Not sure how hidden we would be from the dragon. Let us go now."

Karina groaned as she pushed herself away from the tree and followed Rashka.

They reached the Ice Plains about mid-morning. The early sun showered the snowy, flat land with sparkles. If Karina were not so worried, she would have enjoyed the beauty of the clear morning. In the distance, the towers of the royal house rose before the Western Mountains.

"What are we going to do?" Karina plopped on a log off the trail. "If we attempt to cross the Ice Plains, there will be no place to hide."

"I have already considered that, and there is only one thing to do." Rashka breathed deeply, then shifted back into griffin form.

Karina shook her head. "There is no way you could carry me in your condition."

I do not intend to. I am going to distract the dragon and find out what is following us. You are going to run for as long as you can. Try to keep a steady pace. It will take at least a half a day to cross the plains on foot, even at top speed. Stay strong. Hopefully, the soldiers will notice and come to your aid.

A faint rustle came from the direction of the underbrush behind them. Rashka motioned for Karina to move behind a tree, then lifted herself up above the trees. The staccato beat of hooves sounded from the trail ahead. One set. Karina pressed closer to the tree, not daring to peer around. She closed her eyes, as if doing so would make her invisible to whatever evil approached.

The hooves slowed as it reached the tree line. Whatever it was stopped, quieted for a moment, then pawed the ground.

"Karina?" A familiar voice. "Karina, come out."

She peeked around the tree. "Dom!"

He nickered as he turned to her. "You are safe. Praise the Creator."

She nuzzled his nose. "It is good to see you, friend." She called to Rashka.

Rashka landed at their side. *Dom, what are you doing here?*

"Tristan sent me. He said one of the scouts saw dragons pursing you. He wanted to come with me, but Lucian said that would not be wise. Are you aware you are being followed?"

Karina pointed to the sky. "The dragon is tracking us. We do not know what is following us, though."

"A group of goblins and elves. They are riding lupens."

Faramos's assassins, most likely. This is not good. We will stick with the plan, but now Dom will carry you across the Ice Plains.

Karina nodded.

Dom, you must ride as fast as you can. You are in the open with no place to hide.

Dom tossed his head. "Karina, get on."

Karina mounted and grabbed the reins.

Rashka dipped her head. *I will keep the dragon distracted for as long as I can. Hopefully, if I get him off course, he will lead the assassins away from you.*

"The Creator's might go with you." Karina forced a smile.

And with you. Rashka squawked and took off above the trees.

Karina patted Dom on his side. "Ready?"

"As ever."

"Let us go."

Dom charged across the Ice Plains. The sun did little to warm the crisp air. Snow crunched beneath the horse's hooves. The freezing wind numbed Karina's cheeks and fingers. A shout came from behind them. She craned her neck to get a good look. A cluster of goblins and elves appeared at the tree line. She gulped. Above Shadowed Forest, Rashka battled with the dragon.

"Faster, Dom!" she shouted above the wind. Sweat coated Dom's flanks, but he pushed on.

They stayed well ahead of the assassins, even when Dom's energy waned. She did not want him to push so hard, but their situation was dire. Thankfully, the assassins were not gaining on them.

She spoke into Dom's ear. "Let us take a rest."

"We—cannot."

"We must. If you die, all is lost." She pulled on the reins.

Dom huffed but slowed to a stop, and Karina dismounted. "We need to keep moving." Dom pulled at the reins. "We will take an easy pace for a few minutes while I catch my breath."

"Fine."

They hurried on in silence … far from the calming forest sounds. No bird calls. No animals rustling in the underbrush. The only noise, the crunch of snow under their feet. Karina shivered as the cold pricked her skin like a thousand needles.

"What happened to your cloak?"

"I had to use it to bandage Rashka's arm," she mumbled through chattering teeth.

"Sounds like you two had quite the adventure."

Karina laughed. "You could—"

An arrow whistled by, then stuck in the ground in front of Karina.

Dom reared back.

"Whoa, boy!" Karina pulled on the reins and reached out to smooth Dom's mane. Behind them, the assassins were closing in. Most were on the backs of lupens, carrying bows and arrows.

"Get on, Karina."

She vaulted into the saddle and tightened her hold on the reins as Dom broke into a gallop. Her heart thundered in rhythm to the pounding of his hooves. Arrows soared past them. Karina leaned forward and turned her attention toward Calliope, the city gates now in view.

Dom stumbled forward, and Karina fell, rolled a few feet and then landed on her back, breathless. She blinked, unable to move. The ground quaked as the stampede approached. She wanted to move, but she could not. She closed her eyes. *Help!*

A loud squawk sounded above the noise. Karina rolled to her side to look behind her. Rashka dipped low to the ground. With her great claws, she attacked a couple of goblins, carrying them upward before dropping them. They thudded to the ground.

Karina sighed with relief. She hurried over to Dom. He had managed to stand again, although an arrow stuck out near his tail. "Can you run?"

"Yes. Hurry."

"Do I need to take the arrow out?"

He shook his head. "Get on."

As soon as Karina mounted, Dom charged across the snow.

The city gates were closer now, and Karina could see them open. They were waiting for her. She was safe! A line of soldiers on horseback raced through the opening. Tears filled Karina's eyes.

Home!

CHAPTER TWENTY-SIX

The line of soldiers split as they approached, circling Karina on both sides. Six soldiers surrounded her, while the others raced on to meet the enemy. Rashka continued to dive into the enemy squad.

"I am King DeMarco, and I demand you tell me your name."

King? Karina managed to sit straight in the saddle and stared at *Captain* DeMarco.

His eyes widened. "Your Majesty."

She raised an eyebrow. "Am I? Seems to me you were all too happy to step into my rightful place."

He bowed his head. "We thought you were dead."

"You mean, Lady Anaya wanted me dead." She dismounted, and the soldiers followed suit. Her pulse raced, and she balled her hands into fists. "Rumor has it, even when I was missing, nobody sent out search parties."

Captain DeMarco's cheeks reddened, and he looked away.

"Why was no one sent, Captain DeMarco?"

"We did send two search parties into Shadowed Forest. When they returned, the queen said—"

"Last time I checked, *you* were my steward—not the *former* queen."

He cleared his throat. "My apologies, Your Majesty."

She handed Dom's reins off to one of the other soldiers. "See that he is well taken care of—his wounds tended to. Then he should be bathed and given an extra measure of oats. He has traveled far and hard."

The soldier glanced toward Captain DeMarco.

Karina's eyes widened. "Now!"

The soldier hurried away with Dom, who chuckled, a sound more like a nicker to the untrained ear.

"May I?" Karina nodded to Captain DeMarco's white and gray stallion.

"Of course." He helped her up.

"We have much to discuss, Captain. We will meet in the throne room in one hour." Without looking back, she rode into Calliope and up to the royal house.

Shouts of shock and excitement echoed throughout the courtyard. When she dismounted at the main entrance to the royal house, servants and friends surrounded her, showering her with hugs and words of relief and encouragement. Her heart melted at the greeting. She was not sure what she had expected upon her return, but this show of affection brought tears to her eyes. Still, this was not her homecoming—not a real one anyway.

She excused herself, using her long journey as the reason, and promised to give details at a later time. In the royal house, she found more of the same welcoming but hurried to her room. She shut the door behind her and breathed a sigh of relief.

She went to the wardrobe to select a dress. Empty. Where were her clothes? She marched over to the vanity ... also empty of her personal items. *Of course. Why leave my things when you tell everyone I am dead?*

She hurried into the washroom and scrubbed her face, neck, and arms. A variety of hair pins still lay on the vanity, so she re-braided and pinned up her hair. She caught her reflection in the mirror and cringed. Though her face was clean, her riding habit was torn and dirty, but a change of clothes would have to wait.

A knock sounded at the door. Mauri rushed in and greeted Karina with the Blessing of Three Kisses. "Praise the Creator, the rumors are true! I did not dare believe my ears but had to see for myself if you are really here."

Karina hugged her long-time friend. "I am so happy to see you. Oh, you would not believe the stories I have to share!"

"You must tell me all about it."

"I cannot right now, I fear. Come with me to the throne room. I have much to discuss with *Captain* DeMarco." Karina did not much care for sarcasm but could not help herself as she considered the ridiculousness of the situation.

"So, you heard he was named king?"

She plopped down on the edge of the bed and sunk into its feathery softness. How she wished she could take a long nap. She yawned. "He introduced himself as such before he realized who I was."

"Did you also know he married Lady Anaya?"

Karina straightened. "What? When?"

"On the Sabbath of the last moon cycle."

"King Pistis had not been gone twenty days!"

Mauri shook her head. "Lady Anaya has changed—even before you left, she had not seemed like herself."

Karina recalled the confrontations with the former queen after the king's death.

Mauri leaned in close. "If you ask me, the queen has more power these days than the king. King DeMarco bends to her will on most everything."

That did not surprise Karina in the least. The way the captain sputtered and tripped over his words earlier showed a lack of confidence. "Then we shall see what transpires in the throne room."

Creator, I better be prepared for a fight. A peace settled over her. She could do this. Be the queen, that is—with the Creator's help.

She and Mauri walked side-by-side on the way to the throne room. Mauri filled her in on other activities in the castle—the growing army, less regard to charity for the poor and displaced, the increase in taxes.

"But I have not even been gone that long! What is going on around here?"

Mauri gave her a half-smile. "At least you are back now. I know you will rule with the same kind heart as your uncle."

Karina sighed. "That is just it. I do not intend to stay. I have only come to ask for help."

"Oh." Mauri looked at her feet. "I thought you were—"

She placed her hand on Mauri's shoulder. "I assure you, when my quest on behalf of the Creator is over, I will return and rule as King Pistis desired. But I cannot until this evil is defeated."

They strolled into the throne room.

Captain DeMarco was already seated on the throne with the queen next to him. A crown replaced the helmet from earlier. Karina pursed her lips. *Of all the nerve!* Soldiers in black armor lined both sides of the deep-purple rug leading to the throne dais. Mauri hung back by the doors, but Karina strode down the aisle with her chin up.

Captain DeMarco and Lady Anaya graced the gold cushioned thrones. Light filtered in from the crystal windows at the top of the room. Tapestries with purple and burgundy backgrounds boasted the accomplishments of the past kings of Aletheia.

Anaya tilted her head. Her dress was black, as if she were supposed to be in mourning. But for whom? She cared not for Karina, as shown by her actions. And it could not be for King Pistis, because he was barely cold in the ground before she remarried. "I see you have returned."

Karina nodded. "I have."

"What is it you wish?"

"The Temple of Aletheia needs assistance."

Anaya quirked a perfectly shaped eyebrow.

She took in a deep breath. "Faramos's forces have discovered its location and are moving to destroy the temple in hopes of stopping my quest."

Anaya narrowed her eyes. "And how did they divine such information?"

Karina gazed toward the floor. These things were not her fault, per se. If she had not been given this quest …

Anaya shook her head. "As I suspected. What exactly would you like us to do?"

"Send the army. This is Aletheia's sacred temple, and they need your help."

"Impossible! The tenuous peace between Aletheia and Soter and Tzedek has been threatened by these developments. We need the army here to protect Calliope."

"If we do not defeat Faramos, his evil will spread. Our world will not survive."

Captain DeMarco cleared his throat. "The queen has spoken, and her words are wise. We need to protect ourselves."

"Do you not trust the Creator to do so?"

Anaya laughed. "He does not speak to us all so candidly as you, my child. The rest of us must fend for ourselves."

Karina growled. This was impossible. She smoothed her dress and raised her chin, stating her purpose as clearly as she could. "I am here to take my place as queen."

Anaya sneered. "It is too late. A new king has already been named."

"But not before a fair search for the rightful queen was given."

"We were assured you were dead."

Anger boiled in Karina's blood. She took a breath to keep from screaming. "You were not. The knight told you I was missing."

Anaya looked away for a moment, then quickly met Karina's glare once more. "What knight is that?"

"The one who told Sam, which is why he sought me out."

"Sam? Who is Sam?"

"You know very well who he is."

Anaya shook her head. "King DeMarco has already decided he is not abdicating, nor do I wish him to." She rose from the throne and took a step forward. "I am sorry, Karina, but we have no room for murderers or traitors here."

Karina gaped. The word *traitor* stung … but not because her father's mistakes had caused her pain. "Do you insinuate that I murdered King Pistis?"

Anaya scoffed and stepped down from the dais. "I have no need for insinuations. Jace has proven that my beloved husband was poisoned. You killed King Pistis, so you could take his throne. That is a betrayal. Not merely to your uncle. You have robbed Aletheia of their king."

"That is a lie!" *Creator, I need your help. What is going on? They cannot take the throne from me under these deceitful conditions. What happened to my aunt to make her hate me so?*

An odd feeling surged through her. Her senses tingled, and she became aware of everything around her—from the smallest breath to the slight movement of air in the room.

Anaya glared at her, and Karina met her gaze. Then everything was made clear.

> Anaya as a small girl, sitting on her father's knee, giggling, and then standing over his grave a few years later. Following her sister to the royal house to visit the reigning queen. Falling in love with King Pistis the night of the annual costume ball. The joy of marriage followed by the despair over each stillborn child. The loneliness, the pain, the confusion. Screaming for the Creator's help but finding only more sorrow.
>
> A dark fog covered the images. Darker and darker as the years went by. Hatred took up residence. Anger. Resentment. All surrounding a young girl the king took in as his ward. Anaya's belief that since his queen could give him no child, the king found one of his own.
>
> The queen stirring a packet of white dust into the king's mid-morning tea.
>
> The images faded to black. In their place was a pair of blood red eyes.

Karina cried out as she stumbled backward.

"What is wrong with you, traitor?" Anaya demanded.

"N-nothing. I fear I am more wearied than I thought. May we take up this discussion later, after I have rested?" She turned to march down the aisle.

"Stop!" Captain DeMarco's voice echoed through the great hall. "Guards, arrest this woman for treason."

Karina spun around. "What is this?"

"You are being taken into custody for conspiracy and murder." He looked down on her, but she could see the remorse in his eyes. He no more agreed with her aunt than she did. Yet, for whatever reason, he would not stand up to her.

"You cannot do this!" Mauri rushed forward, tears streaming down her cheeks. One of the guards restrained her.

Karina held up her hand. "Stay back, Mauri. Do not worry." She stared at Captain DeMarco. "The Creator knows what really happened. He will see that everything works out for the good of those who trust in him." She looked back to Mauri. "And I do trust him."

Mauri quit fighting the guard, but her sorrow remained evident.

Anaya lifted an eyebrow as a smile curled her lips.

And Karina kept her chin held high as two guards led her from the room.

She knew the way to the dungeon by heart, as she knew her way around the rest of the castle. They passed the front hall where the grand staircase rose to the second floor, into another wing, past the kitchen, then down a winding, stone staircase.

At least the guards seemed apologetic for their actions. "I do not know what is going on here, Your Highness, but I wish we didn't have to lock you in here," one of them said as he opened the cell door.

"Then do not! Let me go. Come with me. We can stop the queen."

He shook his head and gestured for her to enter the cell.

She bit her lip as she peeked inside. Rough stone walls, dank straw on the floor, cobwebs in the corner. She shuddered, but the guard gave her a gentle nudge. The door closed behind her. Rather than turn around, she stared out the barred window at the top of the far wall. A view, at least.

"I really am sorry, Your Highness." He turned the lock, then retreated.

Karina thought of her friends. The last time she had seen Rashka, she was fighting off assassins despite a wounded wing, and Dom had been led off to the stables. But what about Jace and Henry? Did they know she had returned?

What was Tristan doing right now?

CHAPTER TWENTY-SEVEN

Tristan paced the bridge that linked the two front turrets of the temple. Karina should have returned by now. What was taking so long? Surely the dragons hadn't foiled their plans. Dom hadn't even returned yet.

He spun his sword with restless energy. More than anything, he wanted to go after her, to be assured of her safety, to provide protection. He ran his free hand over his scruffy face.

"You're not worried, are you?" Sam sauntered over from one of the turrets.

"She should have been back by now."

"The Creator will take care of her."

Tristan sagged against the cold stone of the bridge rail. "My head knows this, but my heart is not listening."

Sam nodded. As if he understood. "You love her, don't you?"

Tristan shoved Sam's shoulder. "Of course not!"

Sam grinned. "It's pretty obvious."

He turned back toward the forest. Love? That wasn't a word he had ever considered. Definitely not something he'd wished for. Love? The word did not roll off his tongue at all. What kind of love could a bounty hunter expect? Yes, he believed in the Creator's power to redeem. But he could no more be the man Karina deserved than a lupen could avoid killing its next meal.

Did he *love* Karina? Of course, he did.

"It is hard to trust those we care about most to the Creator."

Maybe. Tristan stared out over the tops of the trees. Somewhere in the distance, beyond the curve of the world, lay Aletheia's royal house. Hopefully, Karina was safe within those walls. And if the Creator saw fit, that is where she would stay—away from this mess.

"How long do you think it will be before the attack?"

Tristan sheathed his sword. "Can't be sure. My guess is that they'll attack at night, when the lupens and goblins will have the advantage."

Sam nodded. "The scouts say they spotted the ships Karina predicted."

"I know. This fight is going to be a nightmare." He tossed another glance in the direction Aletheia's royal house. "Hopefully, Karina will send an army."

Karina rested against the rough stone of the cell. The sun had begun to set, and only faint wisps of daylight made their way inside the dim cell. Her stomach growled for food. Yet, the thought of eating revolted her. The normally sweet-smelling hay strewn about had turned rancid. She wrinkled her nose as she shoved a clump away with her foot.

"We found your friend," a guard called through the tiny, barred window in the door. The lock clicked, and the door swung inward.

Another guard entered, carrying Rashka in his arms, and laid her gently on the floor. She was unconscious. "I found her on the battlefield. She's alive, but barely."

Rashka had a new wound in her side, most likely from an arrow. The arm with the large gash was no longer in a sling, and the bleeding had resumed.

"I know we are prisoners, but can you get clean cloths and a bucket of warm water?"

"Certainly." The guard nodded and turned to leave.

"Thread and a needle from my bag in the healer's quarters would be nice as well."

"I'll see what I can do." With that, he left.

While he was gone, Karina examined Rashka's body. Other than a few bruises, she had no additional wounds. Likely, Rashka overexerted herself during the battle, causing more blood loss.

Another soldier brought her dinner—a slab of unseasoned meat, crusty bread, and a mug of ale diluted with water. She ignored the despicable food, despite her stomach's rumblings, and held the mug to Rashka's lips. She forced a couple of sips, then laid her back down.

The first guard, whose dark hair framed gray eyes, returned with supplies. He laid a bag of clean cloths and a bucket of warm water beside Rashka's body. He placed Karina's bag of healing supplies by her side. "Henry told me to bring as much as I could."

"Henry? Where is he? I need to speak with him."

The guard shook his head. "The queen has forbidden him to come down here."

"What?" Karina took a deep breath, held it for a moment, and then exhaled slowly. The guard's thin smile was of little comfort.

"I did not know what else you might need, so I threw a few bottles of herbs and such in here as well." He gestured toward the door. A second guard entered and placed blankets and clothes for both Karina and Rashka in the corner of the room.

Karina's jaw dropped. "Th-thank you."

The guards bowed their heads. "We may be following orders by keeping you here, but we want you to know that we—and others—do not hold to what is going on," said the first guard. He glanced toward Rashka. "And from what I understand about elves, they're supposed to be forces of good, guardians appointed by the Creator himself. This just isn't right." He turned back to Karina again. "We'll be back to check on you. Let us know if you need anything else."

She nodded, grateful for the good people of Calliope. "Thank you," she said again—all she could think to say.

The guards left, and Karina turned her attention to Rashka. With practiced movements, she cleaned both of the wounds and sewed them up. Rashka stirred once when Karina first pricked her with the needle, but Karina used an herb mixed in the ale to put her back to sleep. With some of the other herbs, she concocted a salve to both ease the pain and prevent infection. She used the clean cloths to wrap the wounds and put Rashka's arm back in a sling.

The work was tiresome, and the dim daylight had now disappeared as night descended. At one point, the dark-haired guard brought in a couple of lanterns and set them on either side of Rashka. Karina laid out one of the blankets on the floor and asked the guard to place Rashka on the blanket. Karina covered her with the rest of the blankets when the guard bid them good night.

Satisfied her friend would sleep through the night, Karina quickly changed from the torn mess she was wearing to the nice, if impractical, dress the guard had procured for her. She sat in the corner and picked at the leftover dinner. Ignoring the meat, she slowly chewed the bread. Her mind whirled … confusion battled with overwhelming fatigue. She needed a plan. She needed to get out of here.

Too soon, though, she surrendered to her dreams.

Karina awoke the next morning to the rattle of plates being placed on the stone floor. She opened one eye to see a different guard from the dark-haired one the night before.

He glanced up. "So, it is true. You have returned."

She nodded, unsure of what to say.

"I'm glad to hear it. Things have not been the same since Captain DeMarco became king, especially with Anaya at his side." He coughed. "Begging your pardon, m'lady. I did not mean to speak ill of your aunt."

Karina offered him a knowing smile and leaned forward. "What is your name, solider?"

"Ben, m'lady."

"Ben, what do you mean when you say that things have not been the same? Have things not been well?"

"Not exactly." He paused a moment and blew out a breath. "But they have been getting worse. Seems the nobles are more concerned with protecting themselves than doing what is in the best interest of the people."

"I see." Much like what Mauri had said yesterday. "Thank you, Ben."

He bowed his head, then left.

She shuddered, recalling what she had seen in Anaya's soul. Anger and hatred born from years of sorrow and resentment. The ancient evil had taken hold of her long ago and, like a slow plague, rotted her insides until she had no room left in her heart for love—not even for her husband.

The thought that King Pistis's legacy had been undermined sickened Karina. She longed to see the restoration of all he had accomplished—something she could only do if she were queen. Thankfully, if—when—the Creator brought her through this quest, he would still be with her as she took the throne. Then she would undo the harm caused by Captain DeMarco and Anaya.

Rashka stirred under the blankets on the far side of the room. She groaned as she moved her legs. When she tried to sit up, a gasp escaped her lips.

"No, no." Karina hurried to her side. "You need to rest."

"Karina?" She moaned, pain evident in the creases around her eyes. "Where are we?"

"We are in the dungeon. My arrival was not welcomed by the new king and his bride, formerly King Pistis's queen. They have usurped the throne."

Rashka let out a sound somewhere between a cough and a laugh. "That is a strange family you have, Karina."

"You will get no argument from me." She retrieved the plates of food. "Here, try to eat some bread. You need to keep your strength up."

"What happened to me?"

"I am not sure. I would guess you were injured on the battlefield. You were unconscious when the soldiers brought you in here. I stitched up your wounds."

Rashka nodded. "Thank you. I can tell you are a skilled healer." She winced as she tried to sit up again. When Karina attempted to stop her, Rashka held up her hand. Finally, she sagged against the stone wall and accepted the plate of food.

While they ate, Karina explained how her interaction with Captain DeMarco and Anaya led to their imprisonment. Rashka shook her head. "Captain DeMarco sounds like the type that would let a queen rule through him."

"I never would have thought that before now. He was very competent as the Captain of the Guard."

"Maybe—but he still had someone to report to. Some people need to be held accountable, to have someone guide them—even if they are leading others."

That much was true. Maybe he only stepped up when he had to prove himself to someone, like King Pistis. Karina sat up on her heels and pushed away the plate of half-eaten food.

The day wore on with little action. The guards brought meals at the appropriate times. Karina checked and redressed Rashka's wounds, which were healing quite nicely. The sun had set again, casting the cell into darkness, save for the meager light coming in from the window. No one came to relight the lanterns.

Rashka drifted off to sleep, and Karina followed suit.

> Karina stood on the edge of a cliff. A monstrous beast made of molten fire roared at her from a deep ravine. When it reached up for her, it was almost as tall as the cliff. Fear clutched her stomach while her heart raced. A sound like buzzing hurt her ears. What could she possibly do against something this big? All she had in her hand was a staff.
>
> *Command it.*

The words came out of nowhere, and Karina stepped back from the edge and scanned the area. She was alone. Command it? Why would a monstrous beast listen to her?

Command it to retreat in the name of the Creator.

Surely it was not as easy as that. Was it? She crept back to the cliff's edge to peer into the ravine.

When the beast saw her, it spewed fire.

Karina rolled out of the way, then stood again. Command it? Fine. What was she supposed to say? She licked her parched lips. "Be gone!"

The beast paused for a moment, and then a menacing smirk crossed its face. "Be gone? No, I think I will stay. You look like a tasty meal." He chuckled.

She took in a deep breath, praying for the Creator's help. "In the name of the Creator, I command you to return from whence you came."

A vicious sneer replaced its terrifying smirk. "No."

A power rose up in Karina she had never experienced before. She shouted, "I am the Prophetess. You will do as I command. In the name of the Creator, I command you to return from whence you came."

The monster roared in anger, swiping a massive hand at her.

Before it could strike, the ground beneath rumbled as the sides separated. The beast shrieked as it was pulled into the abyss below.

Karina awoke with a start. She blinked against the darkness in front of her. The heat from the fire still singed her cheeks.

Rashka groaned as she turned to face Karina. "Are you well, Karina? You called out in your dreams."

She nodded, though Rashka could not see her. "I am. It was just a nightmare. I think."

The sound of jostling keys and light footsteps filled the corridor outside the cell.

"Karina?" a voice whispered.

CHAPTER TWENTY-EIGHT

That voice …

Karina rose from her spot in the corner and took a tentative step toward the cell door.

"Karina!" came the harsh whisper again. Keys jingled in the lock.

Her eyes widened. She rushed over to the door as it swung open. "Jace!"

Her mentor, the royal healer, pulled her into a tight embrace. "Oh, my child, I have missed you. I apologize that I was not able to follow Sam in search of you. It would have raised too much suspicion, and I was of better use here where I could keep an eye on the queen."

He pulled away, and she took in the sight of him. There were a few more wrinkles around his blue-gray eyes, and his gray hair was longer than she remembered, but he was still the same Jace.

"It is so good to see you."

Someone cleared her throat.

Karina peeked over Jace's shoulder. Mauri beamed, tears in her eyes again. Karina laughed as she hugged her handmaid. "Mauri!"

"We could not leave you down here," Mauri sobbed. "I am so sorry, Karina."

"Hush-hush. I am well, Mauri. No tears."

"Come, come," Jace waved her through the door. "We will have time to catch up later. Right now, we need to rectify a horrible mistake."

"What is that?"

His lip curled. "Making the cowardly captain king."

Karina paused. "Wait. I cannot leave Rashka behind."

Jace waved at two guards outside the dungeon cell. "Take this woman to my quarters and put her to bed."

The men helped Rashka to her feet.

"I want to go with her." Karina's heart was torn between her old friends and her new one.

Rashka nodded. "Go with them, Karina. The only way we are going to get the army we need is if you take back the throne." She protested when one of the guards swept her up in his arms, but his strength proved greater than Rashka's resistance.

Karina was still doubtful. How many times had King Pistis said the fate of the many was more important than the fate of one? She had never liked that saying—people, individual people, were important for they made up the many. Despite what he said, Karina could not count the times King Pistis had gone above and beyond to help just one person—including her.

"I will find you as soon as I can."

Rashka nodded. "I look forward to hearing all about your adventure."

Karina smiled and then hurried after Jace and Mauri while the soldiers carried Rashka in the other direction, toward stairs that led up to the hall to the kitchen.

She caught up with Jace. "Where are we going?"

"We are going to the throne room," he said as they reached the room at the bottom of the stairs. At least two dozen soldiers were assembled in four straight lines. Their black metal armor gleamed in the golden light from the fireplace at the side of the room.

"What—what is this?" Karina tucked a loose hair behind her ear and surveyed the faces of the men. Some were familiar, some were not. A few nodded or smiled.

Mauri clapped her hands, a huge smile on her face. "Some of the soldiers have pledged their loyalty to you."

"To me?" Her eyes widened.

Jace nodded. "Many are dissatisfied with the current status and are willing to follow you. Your reputation precedes you."

Karina's cheeks warmed. She did not know what to say. Her hands were clammy. How could people put so much trust in her? What if she were no better than Captain DeMarco?

"Jace, what exactly has happened here?"

He lowered his head for a moment and then met her gaze. "When Captain DeMarco became king, he swore to uphold King Pistis's legacy. However, after marrying that dreadful woman we once again call queen, he changed. Together, they withdrew all charity for the people, they raised the taxes, the army was called in full force to protect the royal house. People are starting to go hungry because the soldiers have been told to stock for war. If anyone dares to question anything going on, even members of the court, they are immediately executed."

Karina gasped. "Executed?"

"There's more."

She shook her head. "I have heard enough for now. We will correct this grievous error on my part, and then we can begin to mend the damage that has been done." Her eyes welled with tears. She must not let emotion overtake her senses.

"You could not have known, Karina." Jace patted her arm.

A soldier stepped forward and removed his helmet. Henry! She resisted the urge to fling her arms around him. Had it really been so long since Tristan had kidnapped her?

"Your Majesty, there are another five dozen men awaiting you in the throne room."

She nodded. "Thank you, Lieutenant Mason, for your loyalty." Henry's eyes sparkled at the use of his title. She turned her attention toward the rest of the men. "Thank you all."

Henry bowed and then ordered his men up the stairs.

Jace pulled Karina's hand around his arm. "My child, I have never been prouder of you."

"Neither have I," Mauri said.

Karina glanced back at Mauri and the handful of soldiers who protected the rear.

"I just hope I can do this," Karina said as they climbed the stairs. She let out a long sigh. "This is not what I expected when I returned to Calliope. I knew Captain DeMarco would be made king, since I was assumed dead—however deceitfully—but I did not expect he would abandon the values that made King Pistis great."

"It is sad, yes." Jace sighed.

"What will happen?" They paused at the top of the stairs, and she looked at Jace. "I mean, once I am in the throne room?"

"I fear you will not make it that far," a voice boomed through the hall.

Karina gasped as she let go of Jace's arm.

"What is going on here?" Captain DeMarco demanded, his face dark with anger.

The soldiers immediately moved into a defensive position in front of Karina, every hand on the hilt of their sword.

The gesture brought tears to Karina's eyes. She stared at the ranks of soldiers behind Captain DeMarco. Their armor matched that of the men loyal to her. Who would be able to tell the difference in battle? Her throat constricted with the thought. A battle inside the royal house would not settle this dispute.

Captain DeMarco cleared his throat. "Well? Someone had better speak up." He glanced away from them when Anaya appeared at his side.

Karina had not noticed Anaya's wan appearance before. Her sallow cheeks and austere hairstyle intensified her severe appearance. The form-fitting, fur-collared black dress was far different than her usual attire.

Jace nudged her. She peered at him, and he inclined his head toward the captain.

"Me?" she mouthed, and he nodded. Her heart raced, and her vision blurred. She was not prepared for this. She must take back her throne ... but how? *Creator, please direct my words.* She stepped forward.

In front of her, the soldiers shuffled as an uneasiness covered the hall. They were waiting—somewhat impatiently—for her directions. She had to act fast or risk losing their confidence.

Her soft footsteps echoed in the deafening silence as she maneuvered her way through the line of guards until she emerged from the group. With a deep breath, she straightened her shoulders and lifted her chin.

"Well, well." Anaya smirked. "Look who thinks she is all grown up."

It was now or never. "Captain DeMarco, you are hereby relieved of your duties as my steward. I am the rightful heir to the throne, both by blood and by King Pistis's declaration, which both you and my aunt were witness to."

"She is lying," Anaya snapped, pointing a bony finger in her direction.

Karina continued, hoping her voice did not waver. "Furthermore, if you step down quietly, I am willing to show you mercy for your crimes against the throne." She paused. The muscles in her face relaxed. "No one has to die here today."

Anaya stepped forward. "You do!"

Captain DeMarco glared at his wife, who huffed and smoothed her dress.

"As you can see, Captain DeMarco, those loyal to me outnumber your soldiers."

He scoffed. "They do not."

"Such a wild imagination," Anaya cackled. "Attack!"

The double doors to the great hall swung open, clanking against the stone wall. More soldiers filled the entry hall. They filed in front of Karina and then faced Captain DeMarco.

Karina pushed her way through once again. "Please, I do not want a battle in my father's house."

"Your father was a traitor," Anaya said, hatred evident in the slits of her eyes.

"Both my father and my uncle tried to protect the country they loved. A country I love." She faced the other soldiers. "Since King Pistis died, the kingdom has fallen far away from the values he fought so hard to maintain. And now the Creator has entrusted me to lead our people back to where they once were, to end their suffering."

Anaya's face reddened. "But—"

Karina held up her hand and silenced Anaya with a glare.

"I will not hold any soldier at fault today. This situation is a case of misguidance. If you return your loyalties to King Pistis's royal line—to me—then I will show you and your families mercy. You will always be welcomed in Aletheia and in Calliope."

"This is ridiculous." Anaya took another step forward and turned to the soldiers. "We will not stand for this treason. If King DeMarco will not put a stop to this, I will. Attack!"

No one moved.

"I said attack!" she screeched.

Captain DeMarco shook his head, his eyes fully expressing his sorrow. Letting out a prolonged sigh, he knelt on one knee, head bowed.

Karina held her breath.

One by one, the rest of the soldiers followed suit, until all the soldiers on Captain DeMarco's side of the room were kneeling before Karina.

"All hail the true queen!" Captain DeMarco shouted.

"All hail Queen Karina!"

Karina closed her eyes, dizzy with relief. No blood would be shed today. At least not here. Her kingdom was safe from Anaya's tyranny.

"No!" Anaya drew a dagger from her sleeve, her eyes wild as she rushed at Karina.

Before she could dodge Anaya's attack, Captain DeMarco stepped between them, sword raised. Anaya refused to yield. In the moment before the sword pierced her body, the captain looked away.

She shrieked in pain. "William?" Her breath rattled as she staggered back, yanking the blade from her body. It clattered on the stone floor amid a chorus of gasps. She pointed a finger at Karina. "You will regret this, traitor." She turned around, stepped forward—then disappeared into thin air.

Karina covered her mouth, unable to move. What had happened? Where did Anaya go? Karina surveyed the confused faces as soldiers removed their helmets. When her gaze landed on Jace, he shrugged.

Tears filled Karina's eyes. Anaya was gone. They were all gone. Anyone she had ever called family. Gone. Grief tore at her heart. Her knees threatened to buckle. Jace steadied her, and the warmth of his touch gave her strength. She had reclaimed her rightful place as queen. Now she must be strong so that her people would trust in her—trust in the Creator's choice.

She took a deep breath to keep from breaking into sobs. She stepped forward and put a gentle hand on Captain DeMarco's shoulder as he retrieved his sword.

Tears streaked his cheeks. "I am so sorry, Your Majesty."

She shook her head, afraid to speak. Instead, she embraced him, for they had both lost someone dear to them.

Later the next morning, Karina met with Captain DeMarco, Jace, and some of the lieutenants in the great hall. She had dismissed the soldiers to their homes and then retired to her room where Mauri had helped her to bathe and change into more suitable attire.

Now, she sat on the throne, dressed in a silver-lined, blue-velvet gown. Though fancier than she preferred, both Mauri and Jace insisted she needed to dress like a queen, at least while she was in the royal city. She wished Tristan, Sam, and Rashka were here with her. Their guidance meant more to her than she had realized. They would know what needed to be done.

As if it were a personal gift, the doors opened to usher in the elven guardian. Rashka made her way slowly to the throne dais. She hobbled with the use of a stout cane, but she had bathed and been given fresh clothes as well. Her raven-black hair had been pulled back from her face and tied with a leather strap.

Karina rushed to embrace her friend.

"Careful, Your Majesty. I am still a bit sore." She accepted the hard-backed chair Jace brought over for her. "I hear Aletheia's rightful queen now sits on the throne."

Karina's cheeks heated, but she smiled. "Now there is much to be done." She returned to the throne and turned her attention to Captain DeMarco. "I meant what I said about not holding this misunderstanding against any of the soldiers. However, I am afraid I can no longer keep you as Captain of the Guard."

His eyes widened.

"I still need a capable officer, one who knows the art of warfare, since I do not. You have made mistakes, but you also proved your loyalty—at a great cost to you. You are welcome to continue to serve in the guard as a lieutenant, but Henry Mason will be promoted to Captain of the Guard."

He looked away.

"I know you can—and will—make better decisions. Do you still wish to serve?"

Lieutenant DeMarco straightened. "Yes, Your Highness."

"Very well. Please find Captain Mason so I can inform him of the changes." She stepped down from the dais. "The sacred temple of Aletheia is about to be attacked, if it has not been already. I need as many soldiers as we can spare. Ready the men as soon as possible. We leave before nightfall."

CHAPTER TWENTY-NINE

Tristan tried to rest. At least, that's what he was supposed to be doing. He hadn't wanted to retire to his chambers, but Lucian had insisted, claiming Tristan would need all the energy he could muster for the night ahead.

He scoffed. Energy? He needed focus. Karina had been gone for four days now, and he could not think of anything else but her. Where was she? Was she safe? When would she return?

A trumpet sounded outside his window. Groaning, he rolled off the bed and pulled on a tunic, trying to ignore the overwhelming guilt that hit him every time he thought of Karina. His growing need to protect her confused him. His place seemed to be at her side.

Another call of the trumpet sent him scampering out the door. He smacked into Sam in the hallway. "What's with the trumpets?"

"The enemy breached the bridge on the other side of the mountain. Lucian has called us to the sanctuary." They bypassed the men and women who barely passed for soldiers. Most of them were archers, as Lucian had explained that was all they had ever needed.

Day had given way to night as they stepped inside the large sanctuary. People hunched over a large table as they argued and pointed at a map. Tristan elbowed his way through the crowd. "What's going on?"

Lucian glanced up. "There you are. The attack has begun. Faramos's army is attempting to cross the bridge. I have several soldiers along the mountain, taking them on with bow and arrow, but the enemy is powerful. It is only a matter of time before they reach the temple."

Tristan ran his hand through his hair. Was Karina on her way? He sighed. They could not count on her. "Why don't you burn the bridge?"

Vyra's eyes widened. "What? Impossible. That route is our only way in or out except by the waterway."

"Exactly." Tristan pointed at the map. "If we burn the bridge, we will cut off more than half of Faramos's forces. It's at least a day's march north or south to get to the sea."

"But we will also cut off any escape route." Lucian sighed as he sat in a stiff-backed chair. "And what if Karina and her army get here—they would have no way to help us."

Tristan blew out a breath. "I know, but I think it is a risk worth taking, don't you? We don't know when reinforcements will arrive—*if* they are even coming."

Lucian stroked his chin as he studied Tristan. "There is wisdom in your words, but it is an awful risk." He stood. "Let it be done."

"Lucian!" Vyra put her hands on her hips. "Is it not best to try to hold them off for a while longer?"

"If we had another flying shapeshifter to go out and see if Karina's army were on its way, you are right, that would be best. But we do not. This will protect us from the enemy's overwhelming numbers." Lucian nodded to Tristan. "Since this is your idea, the task falls to you and Sam. I will send a couple swordsmen with you. The archers will cover you from the sides of the mountain."

Tristan gave a quick nod.

"Go ... hurry."

Tristan dragged Sam from the sanctuary.

"What were you thinking?" Sam hissed as they hurried out of the temple.

The moon had risen high in the sky, only partially hidden by passing clouds. Bonfires burned on either side of the trail to the temple. Archers and swordsmen alike warmed themselves by the fires, from which there was no laughter or chatter. A heavy solemnness pressed against his soul.

"I was thinking Karina would want us to do whatever it took to save the temple." He found a stack of torches by one of the larger fires in front of the temple. "We stand a better chance if we only have to worry about half the ranks." He picked up two torches and tossed them to Sam.

Sam looked doubtful, but he didn't question Tristan further.

Tristan grabbed more torches, then turned to find Paul approaching with two swordsmen behind him. He stopped and bowed his head. "Lucian informed me you needed two swordsmen. These are the best in our guard, and they are at your disposal."

Tristan eyed the two men and wondered what *excellent* translated to on the battlefield. "Very well. Thank you. Do you have oil or another flammable substance?"

Paul looked pensive. "All we have are the drums of oil for the lamps."

Tristan pointed to the swordsmen. "You two go with Paul and get the oil."

Paul bowed again and hurried back to the temple with his men.

"What's going on in that head of yours?" Sam asked. The flames from the torch cast shadows across his face.

"We need a fast-moving blaze. The easiest way to do that is to wet the wood with oil. We can light the fire from a distance without risking injury to ourselves."

When the swordsmen returned, Tristan raised his torch. "Let's go." He led them up the hill to the mouth of the bridge. As they neared, shouts echoed through the mountains as Faramos's shadowy army advanced.

"Are there any of our men on the bridge?" Tristan called to a nearby archer.

"Yes, sir."

Tristan turned to those in his command. "This is the plan. We need to retrieve our men first. You two carry the oil behind us. As we pull out, dump the oil on the bridge. When we reach the edge, Sam and I will ignite the fire. Understood?"

They nodded.

Tristan and Sam stepped onto the bridge and made their way further into the mountain pass. An occasional archer turned their way from the mountainside, but when the archers realized who they were, they returned to their positions.

As the moonlight waned, the darkness closed in. Torchlight danced across the dark stone, and shouts echoed off the walls, then faded. Tristan held up his hand. "Stay here," he mouthed to the other three.

Sam put both torches in one hand and placed the other on the hilt of his sword. Tristan shook his head. There would be no need for that. Their mission was simple. He edged toward the next bend of the bridge, then peeked around the stone.

Carrying large clubs, two trolls—smaller than usual but still larger than any of the soldiers—stormed the bridge. They swung at any soldier they encountered, knocking them over the railing, sending the screaming victims into the chasm below. The remaining temple soldiers staggered back in retreat.

Tristan turned to the group. "The soldiers are retreating. Have the torches at the ready. As soon as they fall back, we'll light the bridge. Start dumping the oil."

With difficulty, the swordsmen tipped the open barrel and then, with an awkward gait, headed back toward the temple.

The temple soldiers rounded the bend, terror in their eyes. They saw Tristan and the torches and pushed forward. Seven men rushed past them, and Tristan motioned for Sam to follow them. Five more soldiers ran by. Tristan brought up the rear, keeping his eye on what was behind him. Shouts preceded a heavy vibration from the solid wood of the bridge. They were being pursued.

Tristan emerged from the mountain pass to find the dozen men, plus a dozen more, waiting with swords and bows poised for battle. He nodded to Sam, and they put their torches to the posts at the end of the bridge.

The flames licked the wood and spread along the surface. Fire from Sam's torch swept into a fiery storm.

"Wait!"

The wail came from above them, and Tristan arched his neck. A griffin circled overhead, descending on top of them. Rashka? He pulled his torch from the bridge, but the monstrous fire devoured it. Shrieks echoed off the stone walls as the flames claimed their first victims.

"Sam." Tristan kept his eyes on the griffin as he pointed toward the sky. Sam's joyful shout echoed the excitement pumping through Tristan's veins.

Rashka landed in an awkward plop a few feet away. Karina dismounted and, with a flash of light, Rashka sagged to the ground. Karina knelt at her side and offered her shoulder as a crutch. Sam rushed to help.

With Rashka secured, Karina turned to Tristan. Her smile tugged at his heart. He wanted to pull her near and wrap her in his arms. But he resisted. Instead, he sauntered over. "You survived, I see."

Confusion knitted the creases of her brow, and his stomach twisted. Why couldn't he be honest with her?

She smoothed her wind-blown hair with one hand. "Yes, I did."

"Is the army coming?"

She nodded. "They just entered Shadowed Forest, so they are a day's march from here."

He let out a short growl. "That's still too long. The ships will be here tomorrow."

Karina looked to the fire behind them. "Why did you burn the bridge? The army will be unable to cross."

"We're protecting the temple. If we burn the bridge, the forces on the other side can't reach us either. We'll only have to contend with the soldiers on the ships."

She didn't look certain but yielded. "I need to let Lucian know I have returned."

She hurried toward the temple. His heart betrayed him. He didn't want to care for the dark-haired maiden whose faith made her stronger than anyone he had known, but he did. The Creator help him, he did.

"Dragons!" Someone shouted.

Tristan glanced up in time to see the beasts break over the mountaintop. He spun on his heels and took off before he knew what he was doing.

Karina was trotting toward the temple, unaware of the approaching dragons. Two of them circled the valley as if looking for something—or someone. A fog emanated from their heated mouths. Were those riders on the dragon's backs?

Tristan shouted Karina's name, but she didn't seem to hear him. He ran faster. If the dragons were looking for anyone, it was probably her.

Moments later, one of them dipped and headed straight for Karina. Tristan's stomach twisted in knots. He couldn't run any faster, but she was finally within earshot. "Karina!"

She paused, then turned. Her eyes widened when she saw him, and she stepped back.

He glanced upward. The dragon came at Karina from behind, its huge claws extended outward. Tristan pointed to the ground "Get down!"

"What?"

"Get down!"

The dragon let out a huge roar, and Karina spun around. Her ear-piercing scream rang out over the din.

Tristan prayed as he lunged to Karina's rescue. They collided with an oomph and toppled to the ground. Feeling the dragon's claws on his back, he closed his eyes, anticipating horrific pain—pain that never came. Instead, he became aware of a glowing light. When Karina gasped, he opened his eyes and rolled off her. The ring on his finger shone like a hundred torches, just like before.

The dragon was nowhere to be seen.

As the ring dimmed, Tristan could make out the heap of ashes before them. He sighed and let his head fall back against the ground. The Creator's ring had defeated the dragon. Karina clutched his arm, and he studied her pale face. At least she was in one piece.

When he stood to examine the dragon's remains, movement caught his eye. Off to the side, a hairless gray goblin leapt up and pulled its bow. So, the rider survived? How exactly did this ring work? Tristan pushed between the goblin and Karina.

The goblin drew an arrow from his quiver, and Tristan pulled his sword from his scabbard.

"You think your sword stands a chance against my arrows, bounty hunter?" The goblin cackled as he placed an arrow on his bow.

"I'm not a bounty hunter." Tristan gritted his teeth. Who was he kidding?

"Bounty hunter or not—these arrows are blessed by Faramos himself."

Tristan grinned. The goblin did not understand Who he was up against. It let the arrow fly.

Tristan dropped the tip of the sword and asked the Creator to show the goblin the reach of his power. The arrow stayed true, aimed right for Tristan's heart. He braced himself as he continued to pray.

A light flashed. The arrow disintegrated at Tristan's feet. *Thank you, Creator.*

The goblin pulled another arrow. Before he had a chance to shoot, a blade speared his gut from behind. Sam pulled the sword out as the goblin fell forward.

He scratched his head with his free hand. "That is one awesome ring."

Tristan grinned.

Karina slid her hand around his arm. "Apparently, the queen cannot walk safely around here on her own. Care to escort me to the temple?"

"My pleasure, Your Highness." Tristan gazed into her deep blue eyes— wells where he could easily become lost just as he had become lost in his former life as a bounty hunter. Only this kind of lost didn't come with regrets.

He led Karina and Sam, who assisted the weakened Rashka, to the temple. Once inside, Sam took Rashka to her room and went to find a healer, insisting Karina's attention was needed elsewhere.

Karina pressed her lips into a thin line but followed him to the sanctuary where Lucian still hovered over a table with Vyra and Paul. They looked up when Tristan and Karina walked in.

"Prophetess! You have returned." Lucian greeted her with the Blessing of Three Kisses.

Tristan chuckled. "I believe she is to be called Queen or Your Highness or something like that now."

Karina tossed Tristan an annoyed glance but then smiled at the older priest.

Lucian's eyes widened. "Oh, is that what took so long? Come, sit. You must be exhausted."

"Thank you, Lucian." She sat and folded her hands neatly in her lap. "It is true." She told him all that had happened at the royal house.

When she finished her report, Tristan whistled. "Well done, my Queen, well done."

She blushed, and he couldn't help but grin.

Lucian nodded. "I am sorry for your loss. Some people do not understand the plan the Creator has for them, and therefore allow what they perceive as a bad circumstance to fill their hearts with hate." He shook his head. "That is all in the past. You have the quest ahead of you."

"The army is on its way and should be here tomorrow evening. I gave instructions for them to rest only as much as necessary so that they will be ready to fight." Karina paced around the table. "I also had part of the fleet deployed as well. Hopefully, your soldiers can hold Faramos's ships off long enough for our ships to arrive. DeMarco said if the winds held out, they could be here the day after tomorrow."

"Captain DeMarco?" Tristan grabbed Karina's elbow and spun her around. "Please tell me you did not leave him in charge?"

Karina scowled. "He paid for his mistakes. He deserves a second chance like everyone else, does he not?"

Her piercing glare burrowed into his heart. Of course, by *everyone else* she was referring to him. "I suppose. My apologies."

"And to answer your question—no, I did not leave him in charge of the realm. And he has been demoted to the rank of lieutenant. Jace is my appointed steward. I promoted Henry Mason as the new Captain of the Guard."

Tristan was impressed, though not surprised at Karina's competency. He grinned and turned to Lucian. "When should Faramos's ships arrive?"

Lucian leaned against the table. "The scouts say they will be here tomorrow morning."

CHAPTER THIRTY

Sleep eluded Karina. So much had happened over the past few days that she had yet to fully process. Her family—all of them—were gone. She was now Queen of Aletheia. A great battle would be fought and either won or lost. And then there was still the matter of her quest. All these worries kept her awake.

Creator, please be with me tonight. These burdens are too much for me to bear on my own. I need your help. Please give me the strength and wisdom to get through the next few days. But most of all, at this moment, I need your peace, your assurance.

Warmth flowed through her body like a slow river. Her muscles relaxed, her mind quieted. She smiled. An unexpected joy filled her soul. Of course, the Creator had never left her. She only needed to be reminded of his presence.

Somewhere in the temple a trumpet sounded. The time for battle was upon them—Faramos's soldiers would be here soon.

Karina donned her oiled leather pants and a loose green shirt. She tied her hair in a fat braid and pulled on a heavy pair of boots. All the while, her mind was a complete blank. She could not allow herself to think, or she might panic.

A knock sounded at the door. She froze. Her heart pounded like a marching army.

"Karina, open up!"

Tristan, of course. She shook her head. How silly to be frightened by a knock. She hurried to let him in. Dressed in chainmail armor covered by a white tabard with a gold sun, Tristan was all seriousness. He paced around the room, stopping only to look out the window.

"Is something wrong?" Karina sat in one of the formal chairs.

He stared at her, his expression, unreadable. What was he contemplating? After a moment, he resumed pacing. Karina crossed her arms. Tristan's antics made her nervous. She blew out an impatient breath.

Finally, Tristan turned to face her. "You need to leave."

"What are you talking about?"

"I think you should leave. You are not a fighter—the Creator's belt does not change that. You still have a quest that needs completion. Rashka should take you on to Soter to find their temple. Sam and I can meet up with you after the battle."

Karina shook her head. "I am not going anywhere, Tristan. I may not be a fighter, but I am a healer, which means I will be needed."

"Stubborn woman," he muttered. "You are going to get yourself killed, and then what? Who will fulfill the Creator's quest then?"

Karina smiled. His worry touched her heart. "Tristan, I will be fine. If the Creator wishes me to see this quest through, then he will protect me. After all, he sent me you, did he not? And Rashka and Sam?"

Tristan did not return her smile. He half-growled, half-shouted, and then threw up his hands. "Fine." He stormed from the room, leaving the door open.

Karina shook her head. At least she knew he cared. She started to follow him but paused at the door. She hurried back to grab the Belt of Truth from the back of her chair. Who knew when the armor would be needed? With the belt in place, she left her bedchambers.

The main hall had been transformed into a triage center. Temple healers mulled about, setting out clean cloths and stocking more jars of ointments and pastes. Men brought in pails of water from the spring, filling massive tubs on both sides of the room.

Karina watched in awe for a moment. This was really happening.

Outside, commanders shouted orders for combat readiness. Karina wandered over to the open doors as the soldiers assembled.

Vyra, one of the Trium, appeared at her side. "The Creator's grace be with you this morning, Your Majesty."

Karina cringed at the title but forced herself to smile. "And to you, Lady Vyra." She inclined her head toward the triage area. "Should this not be in the dining hall?"

"What do you mean?"

"Well, I would imagine you intend to leave the doors open, do you not?"

Vyra nodded.

"If the triage remains here, you are putting the healers, as well as the wounded, at risk." Karina pointed at the doors. "With these open, arrows and even soldiers can rush in. If you put the triage center in the dining hall, then you put enough space between the doors and the wounded to avoid the rogue arrow."

"You make a good point, Your Majesty. You should instruct the healers and the laborers to the task." Vyra hastened back to the sanctuary.

Karina swallowed the lump in her throat. That was not exactly what she had intended when she made the suggestion. But Vyra probably had more important things to attend to. Karina turned to the crowd and surveyed what needed to be done. She took a deep breath and then stepped up on a nearby stool. "Excuse me."

Those people closest to her looked up but continued to go about their business.

"Excuse me!" she called a little louder.

Still, no real response.

"Attention!" she shouted.

Silence fell as everyone turned toward her.

She froze. What was she supposed to say to these people? She did not even know any of them, nor did they know her. But there was work that needed to be done. "For those of you who do not know me, I am Queen Karina. After a discussion with Lady Vyra, we have decided moving the triage area into the dining hall as a safety precaution would be best."

More stares.

Karina pursed her lips, praying the Creator would help her to appear brave, though her insides shook. She gestured to a few men near the fringe. "I need you to move tables in the dining hall. Leave four to be used for surgical care. Either remove the rest or push them to the outer walls. Go!"

The men hurried to the dining hall.

She gestured to the right half of the room. "The healers on this side— bring the cots and bed mats into the hall while the rest of you collect the clean cloths, jars, and other supplies. Hurry!"

Karina stepped down. There. She breathed deep and then grabbed the supplies from the small table next to her. For the next half an hour, she called orders, assisting where needed. Within the hour, the triage center had been successfully relocated. She procured two guards to stand at the dining hall entrance so that healers could focus on the patients without worry for their safety.

Sam sauntered in and waved at Karina.

She finished her instructions to an elven healer, then greeted Sam with a hug. "They listened to me."

"So I heard," he said with a teasing grin. "What were they thinking?"

She scoffed. "It is all so odd."

"Well, you are the queen now. People are going to start listening, and without question."

"But what if I am wrong?"

"I thought women were never wrong?"

She pinched his shoulder.

"Ow!" He rubbed the spot as he laughed. "Seriously, you are a good leader, Karina. You have a kind heart, not to mention the Creator's favor. Even if you make a mistake, the people will still trust you because of who you are."

Her cheeks heated, and she looked away.

He waited until she glanced back in his direction. "You are doing a fine job."

At least he thought so.

Several shouts came from across the main hall. Karina and Sam hurried to the massive doors leading outside. Lines of soldiers with bows and swords marched toward the inlet. Some wore chainmail armor while others were in everyday clothes.

Tristan broke from the side and rushed over. "We must hurry, Sam. The ships are maneuvering to the mouth of the inlet. They're too big to pass through, but they are sending their troops in on dinghies." He stopped for a quick breath. "Archers might be useful as the enemy approaches through the corridor."

"It's about time we saw some real action." Sam hooted, grinning when Karina rolled her eyes. He gently squeezed her arm, then scampered after the soldiers like a child at the New Year Parade in Calliope.

Karina chuckled. "I wonder if he will ever grow up." She turned to Tristan. "Be safe—and watch out for Sam."

"Take care of yourself as well." A small smile eased the corners of his mouth. He placed his hand on her shoulder, as if he were about to say something. Instead, he hurried after Sam.

Karina watched them go. Every fiber of her being prayed the Creator would protect them. That this would not be the end of their quest together.

A heavy silence settled over the courtyard, over the entire valley. Even the wind that usually whispered over the mountaintops had ceased, as if the world held a collective breath.

And then the screams began. Inhuman screams.

Karina shuddered. Mentally, she knew every battle had casualties. Still, her heart contracted at each shout, each pain-filled screech. Was there more of this in her future? What sort of pain was she going to bring upon the people in Soter, or even in Tzedek? Faramos may rule Tzedek, but that did not mean the people living there were evil.

A hand fell on her shoulder, and Karina startled. Vyra smoothed her cream-colored robe. "Battle is never an easy thing to witness, Your Majesty."

Karina turned her gaze back to where she had last seen Tristan and Sam. "No, it never is."

"In these circumstances, we can only pray the Creator will protect our friends."

True words.

"And now we must get back to the task at hand."

Karina continued to nod—and then stopped. Of course. She turned back to Vyra, humbled by her gentle chastisement, and followed her back to the dining hall.

In front of each fireplace were two tables, ready for the wounded. Rows of cots filled the rest of the room. Karina counted six deep and eight across—all tightly squeezed together but with enough room to maneuver as needed.

Clean cloths, jars of herbs, water and lanterns had been placed on the tables along the sides of the room. Amazingly, a brilliant light shown through the rafters—its source a mystery. No chandelier or candelabra.

"It's the Creator's light," Vyra whispered in Karina's ear. "It does not happen often, but when we have had the need and prayed, the Creator has always sent it to us."

"What kind of light is it?"

"We do not know. It has no source. Nor does it result from magic. We pray. The light appears."

Fascinating. Karina spun in a slow circle. The light, like a thousand fireflies, danced among the wooden beams. She could only thank the Creator for the beauty in this practical gift.

She turned her attention to the healers. "Gather around, everyone. Quickly." She arranged the group into a circle. "Let us join hands. Whatever happens today, we know the Creator is in control. This is his plan. Let us remember that as we tend to the wounded and be a blessing to them in any way we can."

All present bowed their heads as she prayed. "Blessed Creator, we thank you for your presence here with us today. You know the horrors we will see. Still, you go before us, and no enemy will conquer our spirit. Give us steady hands and clear minds. Bless us with your wisdom as we endeavor to protect our own. In the Creator's name."

"In the Creator's name," everyone repeated.

The door creaked open. "Got an injured one here," the guard shouted.

The healers looked at each other for a moment and then burst into action. Two men laid the wounded soldier on the table closest to the fireplace. An arrow protruded from just below his shoulder. Hopefully it hadn't struck his lung. The healers set about cutting away the soldier's leather jerkin and simple tunic. Blood oozed from the wound, but not as badly as it would when they removed the arrow.

His comrade stood to the side, shifting his weight as he tugged his beard, pain evidenced in his gaze.

Vyra whispered in Karina's ear. "Are you going to do something?"

Karina squelched a groan. She was not holding it together very well for a queen. Willing herself to action, she filled a mug from a nearby table and handed it to the older man.

"Take a seat over there and drink this." She instructed as she pointed to a line of chairs by the door. "Are you injured?"

He shook his head.

"Then, when you are ready, you may return to the battle."

"Will he—will he live?"

Karina's heart wrenched for the man. "I cannot say, because I do not know what damage the arrow has done. If it did not hit a lung, and he does not get an infection, he should recover with time."

The man dragged over to the chair.

There was no time to offer comfort to the worried friend. The injured man's needs must first be tended to. She went to the table where he lay. The healers had finished removing his shirt and were now turning him on his side.

"Do you need help?" Karina asked.

"Hold him still while I remove the arrow," an older elven woman snapped.

Karina held the soldier still with the help of the men who had laid him on the table. This was a good opportunity, not only to employ her skills as a healer, but to learn from other masters in a very hands-on manner. She supposed, in the Creator's wisdom, every tragedy brought a blessing in disguise.

The healer readied a paste she then placed around the wound on both sides of the man's body. "The arrow missed his lung—praise the Creator!" the woman whispered. She glanced in Karina's direction. "I need you to break off the feathered end on your side."

"Me?" Karina's eyes widened.

"Yes, you."

Karina bit her lip. There was not enough room to grab the arrow with both hands—she would need to avoid jostling the soldier too much. With her left hand, she grabbed the arrow as close to his body as possible, then slid her right hand under her left, not certain if she had enough strength to break the shaft at this angle. She applied slow force to the arrow. Nothing happened. She pushed harder. Nothing.

"Your Majesty, is something wrong?" the elven woman asked.

"I'm—I'm sorry." She applied a quick jolt of pressure, and the feathered end snapped off. With a sigh of relief, she handed the piece to one of the servants.

"Very good." The woman smiled. "Now I am going to pull the rest of the arrow through the body." She looked down at the man. "It is going to hurt."

Karina patted the man's shoulder. "On the count of three. One … two …"

The woman yanked the arrow out.

CHAPTER THIRTY-ONE

Karina wiped a shaky hand across her brow, probably smearing blood and grime across her forehead. She sank into a wooden chair and wiped her hands on her protective apron.

"You look as bad as the rest of them." Kona, the snow tiger shapeshifter, sat down next to her and handed Karina a mug. She did not look any better than Karina felt, but a sparkle of life still lit her eyes.

Karina stared at the floor. "I have never worked as a healer during a battle."

"You are doing a good job, Your Majesty."

"No, I am not. I am nothing like you."

Kona chuckled. "You may have started out a little on the queasy side, but you have held your own as good as any of these more experienced healers."

Karina's cheeks heated with the compliment as she scanned the room. Several of the cots held injured men and women—both elves and humans. All the major injuries had been tended to, and right now the other healers were administering herbs for pain and feeding those who could eat. The stench of blood and sweat hung heavy in the air.

"Does it ever get any easier?" Karina took a sip of water.

Kona shook her head. "I do not believe it does. However, we learn to momentarily push aside our emotions, get the work done."

"This one's bleeding again," a healer shouted.

"It never ends." Kona gestured for Karina to stay seated. "No, you rest."

A loud rumble shook the temple.

"Fire!" someone hollered from the entry hall.

"What's going on?" Karina stood.

Another jolt vibrated through the stone walls. A soldier ran into the dining hall. "Dragons, Your Majesty. They're hurling fireballs at the Temple!"

"This man is bleeding profusely," the healer called again, reaching for more cloths.

"Kona, tend to the wounded." Karina followed the soldier. "How do we stop the dragons?"

He shrugged.

Karina hurried into the hall with the silver pillars where she found Lucian and Vyra talking in hushed tones. "What are we to do?"

Lucian sighed. "I do not know what we can do. We have no defenses for air attacks. Archer's arrows will not penetrate the dragons' scales."

"This is not good—not good at all." Vyra wrung her hands.

Another fire ball struck. Screams could be heard everywhere. Karina could be of no help here. "Where is Tristan? Maybe he will have an idea."

Lucian shook his head. "He led a few temple soldiers to the inlet. We would have to send someone to find him."

"Then do it." She despised this helpless feeling. If she had been trained as a queen, maybe she could have been of more use. No, she would not let herself worry about that now. "If you will excuse me, I will return to the triage center."

Karina entered the dining hall. The aroma of vegetable stew, mingled with the scent of blood and sweat, turned her stomach. Still, she should eat something. She would be of even less use if she fainted from hunger. She hurried toward the fireplace.

"Karina!"

She spun around as Rashka struggled to help Sam into the hall. "The Creator's might! What happened, Rashka?"

"A sword to the leg," Sam seethed through clenched teeth. "He snuck up behind me. If I had not heard his footsteps, his sword would have been in my gut instead of mine in his." He chuckled. "At least I got the better of him."

Yet another fireball rocked the temple. The sound of crumbling stone terrified Karina. She forced a smile to hide her fear from Sam. "Good for you."

Rashka helped Sam onto one of the tables. He leaned back on his elbows.

Karina cut off the pant leg an inch above the wound—an ugly gash, about two hands' width long. After some prodding, she concluded the gash would need several stitches. "The wound is shallow, which means much of the muscle has not been torn. You will be sore for a while, but your leg will heal nicely, in time. You are definitely finished as far as this battle is concerned."

Rashka patted Sam's good foot. "I need to return to the battle. Farewell, Sam. Take care of him, Karina."

Karina followed her to the door and placed her hand on Rashka's shoulder.

Rashka turned.

"Can you not heal him? Like you healed me in the forest."

She shook her head. "Healing drains me. During battles, it is not wise to lose my strength unless absolutely necessary."

"So why choose to be a warrior instead of a healer?"

"The Creator is the one who choses my path. The ability to heal is a blessing he gives me in emergency situations." Rashka held up her hand. "Now, I must go. Take care of Sam."

Rashka left, and Karina returned to the table. She gave Sam a cup of doctored ale to ease his pain. Then, cutting a long piece of string, she doubled it over and threaded it through a needle. She then applied a mixture of paste to ward off infection. When she cleansed the wound, the bleeding resumed. Sam's gaze, etched in pain, followed her every move.

"Why do you keep looking at me?" She placed the bloodied cloth in the water basin.

"It is hard to believe you are the same girl who used to hang out in the back of the court. You seemed so timid. Now, here you are, giving orders like a seasoned queen and healing like a master."

Tears pricked the corners of her eyes. She wished she was that quiet girl from back then—did she not? Far away and so long ago. A person she hardly recognized anymore. "People change," she said, her voice hoarse.

"You misunderstand." Sam said. "I'm proud of you, Karina."

The room shook, and dust fell from the rafters. She and Sam exchanged glances. "Well, Sam, we shall see how you feel after I stick you with this needle."

He cringed. "Now you'll see what a baby I am."

She giggled. "Hold still or this will hurt worse." When she finished mending Sam's leg, she settled him into a cot near the fireplace. After he had consumed a bowl of stew, she gave him herbs to help him rest and a blanket to keep him warm.

The walls shuddered, and more dust fell from the rafters as the room went dark. The Creator's light had disappeared. "I think it's time to go."

"What?" Sam winced as he pushed himself up and swung his legs to the side.

"The temple is no longer safe."

Lucian and Vyra rushed in with Paul behind them. "We must evacuate," Lucian shouted. "The other side of the temple has been demolished. We need to get these people to safety."

In a flourish of movement, some of the healers and the able bodied began moving the wounded. Others stuffed clean cloths and jars into large bags.

The walls trembled, then cracked.

"We have to go, Sam." Karina pulled his arm over her shoulders.

"Here." Kona handed Sam a sturdy crutch and then resumed stuffing cloths into a bag.

Karina and Sam made their way out of the temple. Progress was slow but steady. Already beads of sweat dripped down his cheeks—his face pale, his breath hurried.

"Do you need to rest?" Karina asked.

Sam shook his head, so they trudged on.

The carnage outside the temple took Karina's breath away. Bodies were strewn all along the river bank. Smoke and fire encased most of the temple. Overhead, three dragons circled the valley, hurling balls of fire that exploded on impact.

Lucian came up behind them with another wounded soldier, and Karina glanced in his direction. "Where do we take them, Lucian?"

"To the edge of the valley, closest to the mountains."

"That's too far!"

"It is the safest place outside the temple. There's a cave that will provide shelter."

They maneuvered across the natural bridge that linked the temple to the mainland and then walked around the edge of the valley, dodging flying debris as they tried to hide from a dragon circling overhead. Karina gazed in the direction of the battle, hoping to spot Tristan. Where was he now?

At last, they arrived at the cave where many of the healers were already setting up the new triage center. Karina found an empty spot for Sam to lie down. Someone handed her a blanket, and she spread it out for him.

"By the way, how was Tristan faring last you saw him?"

Sam looked away.

She grabbed his hand. "What? Did something happen? Why was he not brought in?"

He shook his head. "As far as I know, he was not injured. He was, however, putting himself into a situation that will likely get him killed."

"What do you mean?"

"He was about to lead a small squad along the inlet to the main ship—to take it over."

"Why would they do that?"

"To cut off the enemy's resources, as well as their means of escape."

A pain seared Karina's heart. Something was not right.

Another arrow whizzed by Tristan's head, clattering harmlessly against the stone cliff to his left. A second dinghy drifted by—one with an archer. He signaled their own archer. The man paused, drew his bow, and sent an arrow flying into the enemy's chest.

He held up his hand to halt the squad—a dozen men at his disposal against Faramos's thirteen. "The next boat is the last. That is the one we'll hijack to get to the main ship."

As the dinghy floated to the inlet's mouth, the three archers took their aim, sending arrow after arrow into the boat of helpless men. Several fell out into the water, others merely slumped forward. At last, the entire crew was laid to waste.

"Now!" Tristan shouted, plunging into the water. His legs quivered from the freezing temperatures. He hissed through clenched teeth, finding strength to ignore the cold, grateful when they reached the dinghy.

They tumbled in one after the other and then tossed out the dead men. Four men grabbed the oars and reversed direction toward the flagship. "Remember the plan. The soldier force will be depleted. We'll take the deck, and then five of you will remain there. The rest of us will flush out whoever may be hiding in the hull. Understood?"

Everyone nodded. They shifted restlessly in the boat, ready for action. Paul had assured Tristan these men were their best fighters. Still, he wished they were trained soldiers from the royal guard.

The dinghy came alongside Faramos's flag ship. With no rope ladders, Tristan's men would have to board two at a time, using hand and footholds. He led the way, climbing hand over hand up the side. This was likely the largest ship he had ever seen, even bigger than Swiftwind, his father's flagship in an era long past. His hands tightened on the wooden grip.

He signaled for the other men to slow as he peered over the edge of the rail. From his vantage point, he could see two sailors on the main deck, three more on the captain's deck. Who knew how many below.

He swung over the rail without making a sound. However, the man behind Tristan grunted and alerted the two sailors swabbing the deck. The heavier one shouted to the captain's deck before Tristan's sword slid across his neck. The sailor crumbled to the ground while his partner struggled to pull his sword from its sheath.

Tristan plunged his sword into the man's side. As he pulled it out, his gaze froze on the blood-covered blade. A disgusting mess. Why did he care? He'd never cared before. Then again, he had not cared about anyone's life except his own until now. Had he really changed so much?

Shouts from his men broke Tristan's trance. He rushed to the captain's deck. Five of his men had already cornered the sailors at the helm, their backs to one another. "I take it you surrender?"

The sailors nodded.

"How many are down below?"

The tallest one wore Faramos's stripes, a symbol only officers wore. He spat. "Five men in the infirmary, another ten or so milling about—oh, and three cabin boys."

"What about the other ships?"

"Skeleton crews."

Tristan did a quick count. "Tie these cowards to the center mast." Tristan prayed they would not have to kill any more men. But many more men fell before the last man was secured in the cages in the ship's bowels. He sighed as he wiped his blade, and then ordered his men above.

Before they reached the deck, one of Tristan's soldiers stumbled down the steps. "Sorry, sir, but there's a problem."

"What's that?"

"The other half of the enemy's army, sir. They found a way over one of the mountains."

Tristan vaulted up the stairs. A line of lupens and soldiers crested the mountain closest to the water.

Karina.

CHAPTER THIRTY-TWO

Karina eyed the man who slept on the ground. His wounded shoulder had been placed in a sling. Beside him, against the wall of the dank cave, lay his armor—a heavy leather jerkin, a helmet, and a shield. She extended her arm over his body, trying not to wake him, grabbed the jerkin, and then scurried away.

Outside the cave, she pulled on the chest piece and strapped the sides below her arms. Her breath came in shallow gasps.

Something was wrong.

"What do you think you are doing?" Kona shuffled through the maze of wounded men, wiping her hands on her bloodied apron.

"Something is wrong, Kona. I do not know what it is, but there is something I must face."

"What do you mean?"

What did she mean? She had no idea why she was rushing off to help Tristan. She was certainly not a fighter, what good would she be? Still, a force from within pushed her. The Creator wanted her to step up, even more than she had so far. She subdued the rising fear. *Creator, please protect me.*

Kona pursed her lips as if she wanted to speak. Instead, she turned away and shook her head.

"I will be fine, Kona." Karina smiled. "The Creator is with us today. Have no worry."

"You do not fool me, Your Majesty."

Karina's lips tightened. Kona might not understand, but this was where the Creator was leading her. She grabbed Sam's sword and headed back toward the battle. The sword was heavier than she had thought—she would not be able to wield it with any precision. She handed the weapon off to a passing guard and reached for the dagger nestled in her boot.

Shouts sounded through the encampment. A group of soldiers scurried toward the mountains. What were they doing?

A young, human solider carrying a pike rushed past her.

"You, there," she shouted.

The young man turned. "Yes, Your Majesty? Do you need assistance?"

"Is something amiss?" She stumbled to his side. "What is all the commotion about?"

The man's gaze flicked to the mountains and back. "Pardon me, Your Majesty, but you should go back to the cave."

She crossed her arms. "Why?"

He cleared his throat. "My apologies, Your Majesty. The enemy has found a way over the mountains."

"What? How?"

"I'm not sure. They must have forged a path along the ocean side."

"It will be night soon. Why would they not wait until morning?"

The soldier shifted in place.

She shook her head. "I apologize. Please, be on your way."

"Thank you, Your Majesty." He gave a quick bow, then sped off.

This was not good news. Reinforcements would not be arriving until the following morning. She stood there a moment longer, not certain of what to do next. Maybe she should leave as Tristan had suggested. Maybe her quest was more important than this one battle.

The screech of metal clanking against metal continued by the river. Karina hurried across the natural bridge and moved to the side of the temple where she could view the ongoing battle. Men and elves fought the hordes who had floated in on small boats. A second regiment of elves and humans rushed to meet the oncoming lupens and soldiers on the mountainside.

They did not have enough fighting men. *Creator, what do we do?*

At that moment, she spotted Rashka in the middle of the action by the water. She pulled the bow string back and loosed an arrow into a goblin's throat, then plunged the bow into the eye of another goblin. Yanking it back, she shouted a warning to someone, as she poised her bow once again.

Rashka …

She could send warning to the reinforcements. But would that get them here any faster? Karina hurried toward Rashka, stopping as close to the fighting as she dared. "Rashka!"

At first, Rashka did not respond. Karina was not sure she was even heard. She shouted again.

Rashka acknowledged her with a nod and fought her way to the edge. She dodged a sword as she broke from the craziness, grabbed Karina's hand, and then pulled her from the fray. "What are you doing out here? Are you trying to get yourself killed?"

Karina shook her head. The fighting, the death—she shivered despite the layers of clothing.

She stared into Rashka's golden eyes as she grasped Karina's shoulders. "Easy there, Your Majesty."

"Please, do not call me that, Rashka. We are friends."

"Very well. I will not call you Your Majesty, and you will not fall apart on me. Agreed?"

Karina managed a weak smile. "Agreed. I need your help."

Rashka raised an eyebrow.

"I need you to fly out to the reinforcements and inform them of our situation."

"To what end?"

Karina furrowed her brow. "So they can hurry their march—through the night if necessary."

"But they would be too tired to fight." Rashka crossed her arms. "That is a good way to earn them their deaths." She tilted her head. "But ..."

"But what?" Karina leaned in.

Rashka tapped her chin. "I have an idea."

"Wha—"

Rashka dragged Karina back across the natural bridge to a small grove of trees and then knelt, nodding for Karina to do the same.

What? Were they going to pray? Although Karina knew prayer had its place—she had been praying all day—what did Rashka think she would accomplish here? She mimicked Rashka's position anyway and closed her eyes.

"Creator of all things, we beseech you. Your servants are in need. Only your blessing will ensure our delivery. Send help."

Karina peeked. Nothing happened.

"Karina, you must believe."

She opened both eyes and crossed her arms. "Believe what? I know the Creator is with us."

"But do you believe he will send help? That he will save us?"

Did she? *Creator, I want to believe. In my heart, I know it is possible, but my spirit is not aligned with that knowledge. Help me believe.* "Creator, please help us," Karina whispered.

A loud, crunching sound came from behind. She spun around. There was nothing there.

More snaps and crunches.

"Who's there?" Karina shouted.

Rashka laughed. "The Creator is answering our prayers."

All Karina saw were the trees, their branches waving wildly.

But there was no wind.

As if coming to life, a large root lifted out of the dirt and plopped to the ground. Then another, just as the first. Soon all the trees in the grove uprooted and moved toward the throng. Their limbs whipped around like ropes, snagging the enemy and throwing them around. Trees came down from the mountain sides, hurling rocks and branches.

Large birds—scavengers and eagles—swarmed the sky, diving to attack with their beaks and clawed feet. Other animals that haunted the mountains charged the soldiers, biting and clawing, tackling and maiming.

The whole of creation responded in a bound.

Rashka whistled at a horse that ran by. It paused long enough for her to swing up on its back. "The Creator still works miracles!"

Karina smiled. "He certainly does."

"I would advise you to return to the triage cave."

"I cannot yet. I have to find Tristan."

"Be careful." Rashka urged the horse onward, and they galloped toward the fight.

Karina pulled the dagger out again and followed behind them. Where was Tristan? Had he already gone out to the ship? Would he stay there, or return to the fight? Karina stayed on the perimeter, managing to avoid stray battles. No one seemed to notice her.

"What are you doing?"

Karina spun on her heels to face the masculine voice.

Tristan grabbed her elbows. "I asked you what you thought you were doing?"

"Looking for you. Sam said you were going to get yourself killed with some hare-brained scheme."

"I am fine. See?" He stepped back and held out his arms. "Not a scratch."

A goblin screeched as it flung himself at Tristan, sword extended.

Tristan managed to strike first, and the goblin lay dead at his feet. He returned his attention to Karina. "We need to get you somewhere safe."

"No, do not worry about me. I can return to the triage cave."

"I'm going with you."

Before she could protest, an elf, wearing Faramos's colors, aimed an arrow at her.

Tristan pulled her to the ground … the arrow missed its mark. "This way," he hissed, leading her across the natural bridge toward the back of the temple.

"But the triage cave is the other way."

"We'll take the long way." He pulled her along at a fast pace, even as she stumbled.

Where was he taking her?

The temple was engulfed in flames. Not even the back of the building, where the dining hall had been, remained intact. What a blessing to have gotten everyone out in time!

Again, an unsettled feeling soured her stomach.

She yanked her hand away from Tristan. "Why are you not on the ship?"

"Your Highness, why would I be on a ship? The fight is here."

Karina's eyes widened. *Creator, help me out here. What is going on?*

Her eyes blurred, and the world before her fell into shadow. Standing before her was Brusho, the dark elf. Impossible! Yet, that was what they had thought when he turned up in Shadowed Forest.

When the vision passed, she recognized Tristan's imposter. *Shapeshifter.* She took a step back. "Really, Tristan. Y-you should return to the fight. I will be fine from here."

"Nonsense." He reached for her again, but she stepped back even further. "What's wrong, Your Highness?"

She shook her head. How could she not have recognized Brusho before? She put her hand to her belt, grateful for the warning. "N-nothing. Let's go."

She moved to hurry past him, but he held up his hand. "Something troubles you."

She continued to shake her head, even as her eyes widened.

"Could it be this?" A light flashed. Brusho, in recognizable form, stood before her with a frightening grin. "What gave me away?"

"Tristan does not call me Your Highness. He knows how much I dislike the title."

"Young people these days have no respect for authority." Brusho gave a pretentious bow. "It is a pleasure to see you again. How do you like my party?"

"Y-your what?" Karina heart beat so fast she feared it would burst at any moment. "You-you think this is a party?"

He grinned. "Thrown in your honor."

She shook her head.

Brusho leaned in. "One word, and I can make this all stop."

"What do you mean?"

He held out his hand. "Come with me. Say yes, and I will call off my army."

Did she dare believe his words? *Creator, clear my vision.* Karina studied Brusho's dark eyes.

> The world fell away in a cloud of dust. Images of Brusho's life flashed before her. A young elf playing with other children. Courting Rashka a few years later—and all the feelings that went along with their romance. More years passed as greed took up residence in his heart. He lost his family, his position as guardian … Rashka.

More importantly, Karina saw his intentions. He would not stop the army if she went with him. He would take her to Faramos, but not before she watched every one of the priests and soldiers, every one of her friends die. Her stomach wrenched.

"What is wrong with you?" Brusho grabbed her arm.

"You are full of lies, Brusho. You have no intention of stopping this battle." She yanked free of his grasp. "I will not go with you."

His grin revealed shiny white teeth. "Very well." He chuckled. "Faramos prefers I bring you in alive, but given the trouble you've been, he also gave me permission to kill you if necessary." His gaze bored into hers. "I think it's necessary."

Karina shrieked as she stumbled backward. She tripped over a rock and landed on her back. A sharp pain pierced her left side. She gasped. *Creator, what do I do?* There was no warmth this time. No sense of peace. Maybe this was the end of her quest. Tears stung her eyes. Why? What had she done wrong? *Creator, please do not leave me!*

Brusho laughed. "Would you rather die at the hands of an elf or a lupen?"

Karina pushed herself up on her knees, but Brusho knocked her back down with a swift kick. She groaned as the world spun.

What could she do? All she had was a stupid belt that could see into a person's past, sense their intentions. What good was that in combat? She moaned as she received another swift kick to the stomach and a wave of pain washed over her. Unless … she reflected Brusho's past into his mind. Show him the pain he had hidden inside. She was not sure doing so would help very much, but it might buy her a few seconds to escape.

She managed to stand once more. She swayed and then steadied herself. Her head throbbed so hard she could barely see. What if she could not do this? She was drained and weak. Her spirit groaned. She must not allow fear to deter her from the truth of the Creator's word—nor let Faramos be victorious. Not while she still had breath.

She straightened her shoulders and raised her chin. "Brusho, you have no real power here. I am a prophetess of the Most High. You serve a man— an evil one who will not outlive the Creator."

Brusho smirked. "Big words for such a little girl."

Creator, use me for your glory. Karina met his gaze with newfound determination. When she again saw Brusho's memories, she deflected them back to him.

He dropped his bow and clawed his eyes. "No!" he moaned, jerking one way and then another.

Karina turned toward the cave.

Brusho growled from behind. "Oh, no, you don't." He let out a shrill whistle, and a lupen appeared at his side—the largest Karina had ever seen.

She gasped and covered her mouth with her hand.

Brusho mounted the lupen. "I gave you a chance. Time to die, Your Highness."

Maybe she could find a spot to hide amid the flames. Karina fled toward the temple, stumbling over rocks. The pain in her side slowed her down—she could not outrun the monster.

Brusho's evil laugh roared above the lupen's howls.

"Get her," Brusho shouted.

Karina yelled for help. Maybe one of the soldiers would hear her.

Something like a half-heave and a half-growl came from behind. Karina dared to peek over her shoulder—and tripped. She cried out as her knees hit the ground. A large body slammed into her, knocking her onto her back. The lupen bent over her, his hot, foul breath like rotting meat.

"Any last words, Your Highness?"

Creator, may my death be quick.

"Hey, lupen fodder, over here!"

CHAPTER THIRTY-THREE

Brusho and the lupen were after Karina. Tristan froze—for just a moment. If his heart could stop, it would have as well. He shook his head. This was a time for action, not fear. *Creator, help me to protect your chosen one.*

The ring on his hand glowed. A supernatural confidence filled him with renewed strength. He ran up the knoll to find Brusho hunched over Karina.

"Hey, lupen fodder, over here," he shouted as loud as he could.

Brusho turned to him with a lopsided grin. "Well, if it isn't the dark knight, traitor to Faramos." He patted the lupen's head. "Looks like we get to kill both of our targets today. First the traitor."

The lupen backed away from Karina, pawing the ground with anxious energy.

Brusho dismounted.

"You and me." Tristan said, raising his sword, "Let's end this."

Brusho shook his head. "I'd like to teach you a proper lesson, but alas, time is running out." He tilted his head toward Tristan as he shouted to the lupen. "Kill him."

The lupen lunged.

Tristan didn't flinch. *I'm ready, Creator.* The monster growled, and Tristan shoved his ring fist toward its jaws. A flash of fire. As the lupen soared over Tristan, it disintegrated into nothing. The wind scattered its ashes behind Tristan.

Brusho's grin disappeared. "Nice trick, bounty hunter." He retrieved his bow and pulled an arrow from his quiver.

Tristan stayed his ground.

"Be careful, Tristan," Karina shouted.

Brusho glanced back at her. "Don't worry, Your Highness. You'll have your turn. After I teach this boy what betraying Faramos buys you."

Tristan crossed his arms. "Take your best shot."

Brusho released the arrow. It whistled through the air, hit an invisible barrier, and incinerated. The small pile of ashes fell to the ground, just like the lupen.

Tristan laughed, his taunts like a weapon. "Seems it doesn't matter what you throw at me."

Brusho snarled as he ripped one arrow after another. Each one fizzled. His quiver nearly empty, Brusho's movements became frantic. He grabbed a dagger from his belt, then pounced on Karina, who stood only a few feet away. He pinned her arms to her side as he held the weapon to her throat.

Tristan swore.

Brusho sneered. "You may be invincible right now, but I have a feeling the courtesy does not extend to her." He jerked Karina's body closer to him.

Tristan's mouth had gone dry. He took a slow step forward. "You do not know that."

Brusho's eyes reddened with hate. "Why don't we find out?"

Karina remained calm, her peaceful strength in the face of death a weapon of its own.

Tristan inched a little closer.

"One step closer, and I'll slit her throat." Brusho pushed the dagger against Karina's throat, and a drop of blood slid down her neck.

Tristan hissed at the sight. Fury threatened his sanity. How could he protect Karina against Brusho's madness?

Karina whimpered as Brusho slid the knife lightly across her throat.

Tristan raised his hand. "No!" *Creator, protect her.*

The ring glowed brighter than before. A pink beam wrapped around Karina like a cloak.

"What the—"

Brusho howled, as if in excruciating pain. He released Karina and turned to run. Beams, like pin pricks, shot out of his body, glowing brighter until he became a pillar of light that shot into the sky. A moment later, the light disappeared.

Karina fell to her knees and buried her face in her hands. Her shoulders shook.

"Hey, hey." Tristan knelt before her. "What's wrong, Karina?"

She wiped her tears as she met his gaze. "I—I was so terrified. I thought it was surely the end. You—you saved me."

He pulled her into his arms. "Appears I did." He glanced at the red ring on his hand. "This little thing certainly comes in handy."

Karina grimaced as she peered over his shoulder. "Look."

He turned to where the battle raged behind them. Enemy soldiers swarmed over the mountainside like scavengers to a rotting corpse. Temple soldiers banded together, but they were outnumbered. Trees hunched over with burning limbs, and the animals cowered near their soldiers. Though seemingly hopeless, the war was not over.

Tristan helped Karina to her feet. "We need to get you to safety, then I will find Rashka."

Karina sighed as she leaned into him. "Look at all the carnage ... so much death."

He pulled her closer to him. "Such is the nature of war."

A chorus of horns echoed through the valley. Tristan looked toward the top of the mountain. The sun, setting behind him, glinted off a line of men in black armor.

Karina clapped her hands. "Reinforcements have arrived."

"Indeed." Tristan breathed a sigh of relief.

"What now?"

A reluctant smile erupted as he gazed into Karina's eyes. "I believe we have a quest to complete."

Karina tapped her foot as she waited for Rashka's griffin form to crest the mountaintop with Tristan on her back. The dark of night obscured her vision, adding to her frustration. She hated to leave while the battle was still happening, but the Trium had insisted.

Though her army finally made their way through the mountain pass, the enemy had forged onward, and the temple had been destroyed. Karina had given Captain Mason specific instructions to shelter the priests and the Trium in the royal house at Calliope until her quest was completed.

"You need to eat something," Sam said as he leaned back against a tree, munching on a bag of berries the priests had sent with them. Three horses were tied to the tree, made ready for her escape.

"I cannot leave." She wrung her hands. "Not until I'm certain Rashka and Tristan are safe. What do you think is taking so long?"

Sam waved his hand. "I'm sure it's nothing."

Karina fixed her gaze toward the mountain tops. "Rashka said if they did not return within a half-hour's time, to go ahead without them. I do not know if I can do that."

Sam hobbled over to the horses, placing the berry bag in one of the pouches. "And it has been over half an hour. We should go."

She shook her head. "We cannot leave them behind."

"We have to." Sam cupped her elbow. "As many have said before, your mission is more important than any one of us."

Karina's heart was torn. Sam was right, they needed to depart before the enemy realized they had escaped and tore the woods apart searching for them.

Sam pulled her to the horses. "Rashka knows to meet us in River Branch. We will need to gather supplies there."

Karina's eyes welled with newfound tears. She rebuked her weakness and then mounted Dom, who had returned with the army. They would follow the path Rashka had shown them … to the river and along the waterway until they reached River Branch.

They traveled in silence, Karina lost in thought. What would Soter have in store for them? The temple in her own country had been destroyed by Faramos's forces. What dangers lay in the wetlands?

They reached the river as the sun peeked over the mountainous horizon on Aletheia's eastern shore. The rays of light glittered on the calm waters, all the way out to where the mouth emptied into the vast ocean.

"Hey, you two. Wait for us."

Karina gasped as a griffin landed in front of her. Tristan hopped off its back, a lopsided grin on his face. "We couldn't let you two have all the fun."

Karina dismounted and ran into his open arms. "I was so worried."

"No need to worry." He surveyed the banks on the opposite side of the river. "Except for maybe what awaits us over there."

A blinding flash, then Rashka appeared, pulling her raven hair over one shoulder. "Soter is a beautiful country, with diverse cultures. My childhood friend is Guardian of the Wetlands. I look forward to seeing her—it has been too long."

Sam joined them, leading his horse by the reins. "Where is Soter's temple?"

"We do not know." Karina stepped toward the river, hands on her hips. "We must travel to Soter's capital city and seek an audience with the king."

Tristan gracefully mounted the extra horse. "Well, what are we waiting for?"

To Be Continued—

ABOUT THE AUTHOR

Whether she's wielding a fantasy writer's pen, a social media wand, or a freelance editor's sword, Ralene Burke always has her head in some dreamer's world. And her goal is to help everyone embrace their calling and #SHINEBeyond! She has worked for a variety of groups, including Realm Makers, The Christian PEN, Kentucky Christian Writers Conference, and for several freelance clients. Her fantasy novels are available on Amazon.

When her head's not in the publishing world, she is wife to a veteran and homeschooling mama to their three kids. Her Pinterest board would have you believe she is a master chef, excellent seamstress, and all-around crafty diva. If she only had the time …

You can also find her on Facebook, Instagram, Twitter, or at her website.